Countess di Brazzà

Old and new lace in Italy

Exhibited at Chicago in 1893

Countess di Brazzà

Old and new lace in Italy
Exhibited at Chicago in 1893

ISBN/EAN: 9783742833228

Manufactured in Europe, USA, Canada, Australia, Japa

Cover: Foto ©Andreas Hilbeck / pixelio.de

Manufactured and distributed by brebook publishing software
(www.brebook.com)

Countess di Brazzà

Old and new lace in Italy

OLD AND NEW LACE IN ITALY

Exhibited at Chicago in 1893.

DEDICATED TO

HER MAJESTY QUEEN MARGHERITA,

BY

Cora Slocomb di Brazzà.

EDITION DE LUXE

Old and New Lace in Italy

Exhibited at Chicago in 1893.

DEDICATED TO

HER MAJESTY QUEEN MARGHERITA.

BY

Cora Slocomb di Brazzà.

✦✦

VENEZIA

FERD. ONGANIA, EDIT.

1893

MAJESTY QUEEN MARGHERITA.

Your Majesty,

Many words were in my heart and were floating uncrystalized across my mind — with which to dedicate the work of our *Lace Committee* and this little guide book to Your Majesty — when my eyes rested upon the following lines, by Aurelio Passerotti, at the beginning of his *Pattern book for noble lace makers*, the only known copy of which belongs to *Count Nerio Malvezzi of Bologna.* — In them are mirrored all my thoughts, gracefully clothed in that old time phraseology which is as intricately and delicately wrought as the subtile fabric to whose treasury it serves as key, and whose gracious mistress it so respectfully lauds.

I therefore pray Your Majesty to accept this tribute made in a past epoch, to another *Royal Margherita* who, in that portion of the land over which she reigned, loved to protect and to encourage the arts of peace, as does Your Majesty throughout United Italy:

LIBRO DI LAVORIERI.

Alla Serenissima Sig.ra MARGARITA GONZAGA da ESTE

DVCHESSA DI FERRARA,

Patrona Colendissima.

* * *

* * *

M. D. XCI.

IN BOLOGNA.
Appresso Fausto Bonardi,
Con licenza de' Superiori.

SERENISSIMA SIGNORA.

AVENDO io racolti quefti varij diffegni di lauori in più volte, parte per compiacere ad alcuna di quefte Signore Bolognefi, & parte per proprio trattenimento in quell'hore che mi auanzano dalle occupationi mie ordinarie. Et effendomi rifoluto di darli in luce à fodisfattione delle virtuofe Donne, cofi perfuafo da alcuni amici; Non mi è ftato di meftiere l'andare molto penfando del nome di quale di effe particolarmente douefi ornarli la fronte, acciò più lietamente foffe dall'vniuerfale di tutte riceuuto; peroche in vn folo girar d'occhi mi fi è prefentata inanzi l'Altezza V. Ser.ma nò tãto per la eminenza del loco doue ella fiede in Italia, quanto per la inclinatione che tiene à tutte le nobili arti, che à grã Don na fi cõuengono, & à quefta in particolare; Onde auiene che cotefta Corte la quale à tutte l'altre d'Italia è ftata fempre effempio di coftumi, & di virtù, hora più che mai fiorifca, & rifplẽda fotto i benignifsimi influfsi, & chia ri raggi di lei, non effendoci hormai dubbio, che hoggi in Ferrara, fi come nell'altre nobili arti, cofi in quefta fi fono tanto auanzare le induftriofe mani delle virtuofe Donne, che poffono i lauori, che da quelle efcono, pareggiarfi non folo, ma anco giuftamẽte anteporfi à quelli, che di Spugna, & Fiãdra portano tanto grido per tutto il Mondo. Quefte cofe mi hãno perfuafo facilmẽte, che ella tia per riceuere cofi picciol dono con la folita fua benignità (al che fare humilifs. " la fupplico,) & tanto più quanto fpero che meno le habbia da effere di bri ga in difẽderlo da gli altrui morfi, non perche lo ftimi fenza imperfettione, mã per nõ douere egli effer fotto pofto ragioneuolmente alla cenfura di feuere perfone, anzi folamente di virtuofe, & gentilifsime Donne, che con fincerità lo giudicheranno. Viua la Ser.ma AltezzaV. felicifsima per molti Anni, che io in tanto humilifsi mamente con ogni riuerenza le bacio le mani.

Di Bologna il di 17. Agofto. 1591.

Di V. A. Sereuifsima.

Humilifs. & deuotifs. Seruitore.

A. P.

Cora Slocomb di Brazzà.

PREFACE.

his is not only a guide-book descriptive of the unique collection of antique laces from all parts of the world exhibited in the Italian section of the **Woman's Building at the** World's Columbian Exposition, held in **Chicago** during the summer of 1893, and kindly lent by **Our Most Gracious** Queen Margherita, and the ladies of **Italy, whose** names follow on the list of Directresses and Patronesses:

It opens with a description of every kind of lace-like fabric, *and forms a complete and succinct history of lace from its origin to the present day*; it contains a biographical sketch of those artists who have entrusted to us their finest productions — all of which are for sale — that there might be a worthy framing to the rarer laces.

It also has appended — compiled by the editor — a list of the books exhibited, which form a small and interesting library, with a complete collection of antique designs for lace-makers and embroiderers, placed, for reference and study, at the disposal of those visitors whom they may interest.

Finally and above all, it contains descriptive notices of all the Lace Schools and Lace Manufactures in Italy, founded or directed by women, with which the Committee has been able to communicate in the short time between its organization and the shipping of the exhibit to Chicago; these notices are illustrated by photographs and very complete albums of samples, as well as by large quantities of the laces Italian women produce, all of which are for sale with immediate delivery. For any information, or for the purchase of books or laces, visitors are requested to address themselves to the lady attendant, remembering that every piece of lace sold — however insignificant it may seem — means at least one hearty meal for some poor and industrious woman, some fatherless, dumb, or crippled child in Italy.

Part I.

Introduction.

A descriptive Enumeration of the most Celebrated Laces of the Past.

For a clear understanding of any chapter of the second part or history of lace making, without reading the one preceding it, it is necessary to thoroughly comprehend and impress upon the mind the following terms and their meanings, remembering that the older and kindred arts from which lace-making sprang are very nearly allied to it, and often produce such similar effects that it is impossible for the uninitiated to distinguish between them.

I. — **Passamano** or **Passamenterie.**

(**Gimp** and **Knotted Fringes** or **Trimmings**).

Their Manufacture.

These trimmings or adornments are now made by means of a long, narrow, bolster-shaped cushion screwed to a table; on this cushion the fringed-out stuff, or a foundation cord, is held in place by large-headed pins round which the threads that are to form the fringe or edging are knotted in various patterns; in the coarser work the fingers alone suffice to tie the the knots, but for finer effects the use of the crochet needle is necessary. To prepare a textile for its conversion into an ornamental knotted border, the woof threads are drawn out, leaving a portion of the warp of the width required for the fringe, the selvage is cut away and the threads are knotted as desired. Extra tassels are sometimes added for a finish.

Different Varieties.

Macramè is a modification of the ordinary passamenterie. Different kinds of macramè are known as:

Punto a Groppo, — knotted point.

2

Punto Moresco, — or Moorish point.

Punto a Groppo incordonato, — or corded, knotted point. The above are all terms used by the Venetians for this class of work.

II. — RETE *(Net)* and Maglia *(Knitting)*.

Manufacture of Knitting.

The italians have one generic term for the single stitches of both, viz., "**Maglia** „ Knitting. — (*Punto a Maglia*) is made with two long, blunt needles of wood, steel or bone, held one in each hand: over them a thread is knotted in and out continuously, until a flexible, elastic material is formed which is more or less ornate according to the object for which it is destined, and to the fancy of the knitter.

Manufacture of Net.

Rete (Net) — is made by means of a wooden, brass or bone needle, biforcated at either end, around which the thread or cord is wound; a little stick is also used, the width of which must be half the depth of the stitches or meshes required. The end of the netting cord or thread, is knotted in a loop to a solid peg; holding the stick in the left hand, the needle charged with the cord is passed around the stick through the loop and in and out again through the first twist made, which is held in place by the stick and thus forms a knot. The stick is then removed and another mesh is begun.

Different Varieties.

Frivolité — *tatting*. For this, the little stick is replaced by the fingers of the left hand and more complicated knots of different varieties are made.

Modano — a very ancient net lace that is made without any embroidery and is quite artistic in effect. The meshes of Modano may be large or small, round, square or shell-shaped, according to the size and form of the stick which is held in the left hand, and the number of meshes taken or skipped in knotting into the row above. This netting can be varied indefinitely; it is often very pretty, and to the untrained eye, it greatly resembles some of the varieties of pillow lace.

Manufacture of Lacis.

Merletto a Maglia or **Maglietta**, LACIS. — (*Net Laces*);

Merletto a Maglia Quadrata (*Square Net Lace*);

Merletto a Retino ricamate (*Embroidered Net Lace*);

These are all terms used for the embroidered nets that were so much the fashion in the middle ages. — After making the meshes of the desired size and to the desired number, the fabric is firmly sewn to a metal frame covered with tape to keep it perfectly stretched, as the beauty and regularity of the work depend greatly on this; it is then embroidered with a needle and thread in different stitches, such as darning, wheel, and button-hole stitch.

III. — **Punto Tirato** or **Punto Disfatto** — (*Drawn Work*).

Punto Tagliato (*Cut Work*).

These titles comprise all the earliest needle laces; the most elaborate varieties might really be treated as Point Laces if judged simply by their appearance; these laces are worked in linen on lawn.

Manufacture of Burato.

Burato is an embroidery in which drawn work, outlining and cross-stitch are combined. It is made on finely spun though coarsely woven fabrics; and was used for underwear and household linen.

Punto in Stuora — (*Sheeting or Curtain Stitch*), TRAPUNTO.

This is made with silk or thread forming what people commonly call *Sicilian embroidery or Lace;* the ground of this lace, instead of being drawn and embroidered in the textile, is often made with bobbins the threads of which form a kind of very coarse, twisted gauze or fine net, on which the designs are afterwards embroidered.

Punto Tagliato or *Cut Work.* — The design for this work was first traced on a piece of linen which was then drawn very smoothly over a leaf of parchment attached to a hard cushion called a " *balon* „, and firmly basted down. Then a coarse thread was served over the carefully traced outline and a *Punto a Festone*, or button-hole stitch, was worked over this round the entire design. Then very carefully cutting away the intervening material that none of the threads composing the stitching might be frayed, double parallel threads were drawn from angle to angle in the empty spaces; these threads were intercrossed and button-holed to enrich the design, or they were caught around pins at the border, forming an edging of purled loops called *Cecchetti* and *Smerli*.

Different varieties.

Punto Calabrese (*Calabrian Work*) very closely resembles the last, but is adorned with high reliefs.

IV. — **Punto a Reticella** or **Radixeli** — (*Net Point*).

Manufacture of Reticella.

This is a combination of drawn and cut work; no design is traced, but the threads of the linen are counted and drawn out in such a manner as to form alternate squares from which the warp is then cut away and the remaining threads are used as a foundation which is button-holed over, the spaces being filled as in *punto tagliato* with fancy stitches.

Punto Surana was a kind of *Reticella* with oriental designs.

Punto Greco and **Punto di Zante** were names given *Reticella* coming from Greece and the Archipelago.

Punto Reale or *Royal point*, was the contrary of *Reticella*, although executed in the same manner, for in it the linen ground was left and the design was made by cutting, and then filling in the open spaces with fancy stitches.

Punto di Cartella or **Cordella** — (*Card Work*) is a lace having a similar effect to that of *Reticella*, but instead of having the ground made by drawn work in linen, the button-holeing is done entirely on a foundation made by sewing coarse threads and bits of parchment basted upon a most carefully drawn design, and then covering these with button-hole stitch.

Reticella edgings.

Punto d'Arcato — (*Arched Point*). When the loops or *smerli* of the edge became deep and more ornate they received this distinctive appellation.

Punti Fiamenghi (*Flemish Points*). These were rectangular and therefore rather broad and shallow. They were often alternated in two sizes and always retained the same form.

Punto Spagnuolo — (*Spanish Point*) was like the preceding, save that the points were all of the same size and much longer narrower and more pointed, and surrounded by elaborate small *smerli*.

Punto Gaetano was a combination of Spanish and Flemish Points attached together by *smerli* at one third or half their depth; they were filled in with the usual stitches, thus producing a varied effect which resembled a double row of *smerlatura* or *turretting*. There were many other fancy stitches generally known in Italy at the beginning of the sixteenth century which continued in use after the introduction of the *real points* or needle laces without foundation of textiles, as for example:

Punto Damaschino or *Damascus Point*.

Punto a Filo or **Punto a Festone** a variety of *button-hole stitch*.

Punto Rilevato *Raised stitch* or *stitch in relief*.

Punto Sopra Punto a *loop stitch in relief*.

Punto Ingarseato (*gauze stitch*) used as filling.

Punto Ciprioto, with an effect resembling the open work ground in Greek and Turkish embroidery.

Punto Pugliese, which resembled Russian and Roumanian embroidery.

In fact wherever lace was made there were local terms used, as is the case in every other industry.

V. — **Point Laces.**

Manufacture of Point Lace.

This variety of lace is made entirely with the needle, and is as susceptible to the surrounding influences of climate, peoples and national characteristics as are the architecture, sculpture and painting of different countries. This delicate art is indeed so sensitive to change that, strange as it may seem, the same patterns wrought by lace-makers of neighbouring towns and villages produce entirely dissimilar effects. Some general rules are however necessary; the design must first be very carefully drawn upon a piece of parchment which has been so tinted as to form a dark back-ground, and a large thread, or several fine threads, twisted together, must be sewn with great exactness round the edges of all the flowers, scrolls and other figures of the design as a foundation, using as few stitches in this sewing as possible, all the figures of the design are then filled in between the outlining threads, with close and varied stitches; the ground is made of meshes, (tulle stitch) like *Burano Point*, or of purled gui-pure like Venetian Point and lastly the foundation threads which follow the edges of the design are more or less elaboratly button-holed over to form the reliefs. The lace is detached carefully from the parchment foundation by cutting the fastening threads, and the different pieces composing the desired length are sewed together, the finishing touches being added by an especially skilled worker. In the making of point lace the needle women are usually divided into six sections to each of which a different portion of the work is allotted such a grounding, tulling, etc., thus affording not only greater rapidity, but also more skilled and practised workmanship.

Punto di Venezia or *Venetian Point*, also called *Parchment Lace*.

This is a comprehensive term under which the following varieties of nee-dle laces with open grounds are known; the *Punto di Venezia* differs from the *Punto in Aria* in having the scrolls farther apart, is more insignificant in design and is surrounded by button-hole stitch.

Varieties of Venetian Point.

Punto in Aria (Lace woven in air). In this lace the flowers, scrolls and designs of animals were wrought with very fine thread in varied open work with very small stitches, the threads forming the foundation were but-ton-holed over before the filling of the designs, and the whole was held in place, where the design did not connect the parts, with button-holed purled loops or guipure bars.

Punto ad Avorio (*Ivory Point*) was a variety of the above with designs copied from the beautiful flowered scrolls of the *intarsia* (inlaid) work of the sixteenth century; it was made with very close stitches and low relief which producing a solid effect caused it to look as if carved in ivory.

Punto dei Nobili or *Carnival Lace* was especially manufactured for marriages, births and grand family or civic festivals. Its designs pictured warriors on foot or on horseback, hunts, castles, towns, animals, cardinals' hats and princely crowns, gods, goddesses and mermaids; in fact nearly every kind of object real or imaginary. In case of a treaty or a marriage the arms of the contracting parties were liberally introduced into the design.

Punto tagliato a Fogliame (*Flowered Lace*).

This is a lace composed of scrolls and flowers that seem literally *carved* in flax; it is the richest Point lace ever invented and formerly was made in silk, gold and silver as well as thread. Using the *Punto in Aria* as a foundation, stitches are made upon stitches and row is superadded upon row of button-holeing. The flowers were formely packed with horse-hair instead of with thread that they might stand out in fuller, richer reliefs, detaching themselves more perfectly from the ground-work or foundation. Thousands upon thousands of microscopic loops — sometimes five or six rows deep — more resembling the perfect flowers and fairy landscapes created by hoar frost than the work of even the daintiest human fingers, were then, — with infinite patience — made all round the edges of those wonderful flowers and scrolls, and upon the insides and pinnacles of every relief. Modifications of this celebrated lace, sung by poets, described by historians and a source of commercial rivalry between powerful potentates, were known as:

Punto di Spagna, point made in Spain.

Grand point de France also called, **Point Colbert** from the prime minister of Louis XIV who introduced it into his country from Venice.

Punto Neve (*Snow Point*), which was very beautiful with its ground of starred threads that resembled flakes of snow.

Punto di Rosa (*Rose Point*). The bars of this lace were placed close and firm, forming a regular sexagonal net-work, with innumerable raised flowers and tiny scrolls.

Punto a Fogliame (*Leaf Point*), with graceful tendrils predominating in the design and many loops upon their edges.

Punto a Gioie (*Jewelled Point*), which is frequenly mentioned by old writers though no example of it is left for the instruction of the industrial artists of to day. It was into this lace that pearls and other gems and even the Venetian beads, that so closely resembled gems, were introduced with most gorgeous effect; these laces were also varied by using silk, gold and silver instead of linen thread.

Burano Point and the Laces to which it gave origin.

Punto di Burano is so called from the place of its manufacture, Burano, an island of the lagoon east of Venice. This flowered point lace with a gauze ground was very highly prized; and the following celebrated laces were all copied from it.

Argentella. A fine needle point lace resembling the Burano Point but with a curious kind of spider-web ground introduced. Mrs. Bury says it was invented in Genoa, but I am inclined to believe that it is the Italian term for early Argentan Lace, for there are no proofs of point lace making having flourished in that city.

Point d'Alençon and Point d'Argentan.

The manufacture of these laces was introduced into France under Louis XIV, through the importation — at great expense — of Italian lace-makers to teach their art to the lace makers of France, who of course modified it. These laces, copied from antique designs, are now produced in as great perfection in the cooperative lace schools of Burano as they were a hundred years ago at the time of their greatest glory in France.

Point d'Alençon has the same squarish mesh ground as Burano Point, but it is not quite so fine as is that of the early Buranese specimens; the foundation contours of the reliefs were frequently formed with horse-hair covered by the usual button-hole stitch and purled.

Point d'Argentan. The ground meshes of this lace are larger than those of the *Point d'Alençon*, their hexagonal form is perfect, and is frequently composed entirely of microscopic button-holeing; the flower designs have a much closer filling and the open work spaces are larger and more varied in their stitches than those of Point d'Alençon.

Vieux Point de Bruxelles — (*Old Brussels Point*) exactly resembles the earliest Burano Point, the only real difference is that its ground stitch is slightly rounder than in Burano Point.

Mixed Points.

Point de Bruxelles (*Modern Brussels Lace*) is composed of flowers, scrolls and ribbons of needle point sewed upon a fine, machine-made tulle which is cut out beneath the flowers, and the whole is so perfectly darned together that the lace appears as if made in one piece.

Point Plat *in Brussels Lace* is so called when the flowers and scrolls transferred to the net are, like Honiton Lace, made entirely with bobbins.

Duchesse Lace or **Point d' Application** resembles the Brussels Point Plat, the only difference being that in the *Duchesse Lace* the tulle foundation is not cut away. The tulle or meshes in **old Brussels bobbin lace** are hexagonal in form; four of the sides of the mesh are composed of two threads twisted together twice, and two of the sides are composed of four threads plaited together four times.

Honiton or **English Point** is like the *Duchesse Lace*; or else if the work-woman is to make an all-over design of flowers, she executes the parts separately, and they are afterwards connected by purled bars.

English Needle Lace has never been manufactured in large quantities; it was always copied from Italian, French or Belgian Lace and therefore has no distinctive terminology.

In the last twenty years a lace composed of narrow, machine or hand-made braid and point lace stitches has become fashionable in England as fancy work; some of the designs are very good and the stitches are pleasantly varied. This lace is really a revival of *Punto di Ragusa*, but is much less artistic and has a meagre appearance. It is generally known as *Point* without any other definition, and sometimes is called *Braided Lace*; in Italy it is known as *Guipure a Spighetta Inglese* or *English Braided Guipure*.

Venetian Guipure, was a *Mixed Point Lace*. The scroll work and flowers were outlined in pillow lace; then the designs were filled in and reliefs were made with the needle, the ground being connected by purled bars; this lace was sometimes made in silk.

Turkish Point, a fine needle lace made on the edge of stuffs, is artistic and very original. It is composed entirely of the stitch of the *Punto in Aria* without button-holing, or ground, or connecting loops. It is made in imitation of flowers and fruits in their natural colours, or all of white silk with gold and silver threads. At other times it forms a narrow edging composed of simple, geometric designs.

Irish Point, is made on fine lawn by stitching a coarse thread all round the design and then cutting out the ground work, filling in the open spaces sometimes with connecting loops and knots and at other times with *Punto in Aria*.

Broiderie des Indes, — when Indian muslin scarfs — with their exquisite open work lace stitches, were introduced into Europe, — all laces

3

made on a muslin ground, received this name; even though produced prior to the origin of this fashion; some specimens of this embroidery, made in the seventeenth and eighteenth century, look exactly like Venetian or Burano point lace.

Irish Guipure, is made with a crochet needle and fine linen thread; its designs are copied from the best old patterns, and it is frequently very artistic.

VI. — **Merletto a Fuselli. (Bobbin Lace).**

How Manufactured.

Merletto a Tombola. (*Pillow Lace*), or **Merletto a Piombini.** — This lace derives its name, from the word " Piombare „ which signifies to hang vertically. It can be made of cotton, flax, fibre, or gold and silver thread. In its fabrication a quantity of threads are interwoven in various stitches ; the meshes and openings or " a giorni „ in the design are made by introducing pins into it and twisting threads about them in diverse ways; as in Point lace, the effects produced are varied, but the system employed is always the same; round a roller-shaped cushion, which is stuffed with chopped hay, saw-dust, or wool, and is covered with some dark woollen stuff, is carefully stretched the design which has first been drawn upon stiff paper and then pricked out along the outline. — Then the cushion is placed upon a little rest, shaped to fit it on the one side, and to fit the laces on the other, or it is placed upon a stand in front of the work woman, or grasped between the knees. From right to left, the thread is wound rapidly upon the bobbins and tied at the top in a loop that permits it to gradually slip off the bobbin when it is pulled — as occurs continuously, in working. The bobbins themselves are all cylinders of wood with a knob at the top. All the threads are then attached to hat pins which have been stuck firmly into the cushion to give a good purchase hold, and the lace maker is ready to go to work.

She begins by interlacing the bobbins, which are used in pairs, and by placing small pins in all the perforations, crossing the bobbins after the insertion of each pin. The bobbins not in use are kept from becoming entangled, by large hat-pins that hold them back on either side of the design. Sometimes a coarse thread follows the entire outline to make it more effective and marked.

The throwing back of certain bobbins so as to leave them out in the middle of a flower or scroll, and the taking them back into the design, after an interval, produces the raised work that is called *Punto riportato sopra.* As the manufacture of the lace proceeds — being worked from left to right and right to left -- alternately -- the furthermost pins are removed to be re-used in the holes as required; and the lace becoming detached from the cushion may be cut off at any length desired. A coarse thread is sometimes run round the design, with a needle; it is afterwards finished and entirely removed from the cushion.

Guipure from Guip.

Guipure. — *Guiper* is a very old verb meaning to roll a thread round a card. In the early part of the sixteenth century lace always contained a guip that formed the pattern which, together with the term has been preserved although card or parchment has long fallen into disuse; the name of Guipure, in modern parlance, is applied to any lace with Geometrical designs, conventionalized flowers, or arabesques held together by a grounding of purled loops or bars, in contradistinction to other laces that are made with an all over net ground.

Varieties of Guipure.

Bobbin laces are easily and rapidly executed; — they are therefore made all over the civilized world, with perpetual reduplication and yet with almost endless variety in design. Some of the most celebrated among these Guipures are:

Maltese Point, or *Punto di Malta*, from which the famous *Genoese Guipure* was copied; its designs were always highly ornamental, and its edge was composed of very deep indentations — much resembling the decorations of the Alhambra; it will be remembered that flowers and animals were never pictured in early Arabian work, they are therefore absent from all lace inspired by designs by Mahometan artists.

Guipure di Genoa, is, as has been indicated, the counterpart of *Punto di Malta.*

Punto di Genoa — also sometimes called *Guipure de Milano*, so greatly resembles Milanese and Neapolitan Points that it is easily confounded with them, — the chief difference being that the scroll work of the design in the *Genoese* as in the *Spanish Flat Guipure*, consists of a broader, more varied ribbon. A very fine variety of this is called **fugio** (meaning *I flee*) from its running scrolls and airy quality. In all these laces, a crochet needle is used to join the bars and design; one thread is drawn through a pin-hole in the lace, thus forming a loop, and then the knot is closed by passing the free bobbin of the pair through this loop and tightening.

Guipure Fiamengo, (or *Flemish Guipure*) cannot be distinguised, save by experts from, *Spanish flat lace.* Varieties of this lace were made all over Europe and were introduced into the Colonies of Italy, Spain and Portugal, by the Jews.

Russian Lace and **Hungarian Lace** — are varieties of the Flemish Guipure but follow the same principles in their manufacture.

Punto di Ragusa, was made like the *Genoese and Milanese laces*, save that its ribbon of bobbin lace was edged on one or both sides with a thick cord sometimes increased in size — as in the Venetian Point — by winding thread around, or by button-holing over the edge of the braid after basting a cord upon it. *Venetian* and *Ragusa Guipures* are often considered identical, but they are very different in execution, — the *Punto di Ragusa* having a decidedly Byzantine effect.

Merletto Greco, o *Greek Guipure* has also one or two cords following the curves of the braid, but its effect is much less rich and heavy than that of the *Punto di Ragusa.*

Cartisane is one of the earliest and rarest of lace Guipures; it was made of a coarse net consisting of four twists and then four plaits made with the bobbin. Through this were worked simple and artistic Arabesque designs consisting of or more strips of thick paper or vellum each wound with fine silk to resemble a ribbon. The edge of the lace were straight and unornamented; as this lace did not wash well, it was soon abandoned.

Punto di Rapallo, or **Liguria,** is formed by a ribbon or braid of close lace following the outline of the design, with fancy gauze stitches made by knotting with a crochet needle and forming quaint geometrical reliefs. The special characteristic of this lace, is that the braid is constantly thrown over what has gone before, thus forming large loops in the scrolls. The parts of the design are held together by purled Guipure " brides „ or bars.

Punto a Vermicelli, is a modification of the *Punto di Rapallo* — in which the braid is made very fine and narrow, the turnings are extremely complicated, there are no fancy stitches between.

Merletto Polichrome or *Parti-coloured lace* was invented and perfected by the Jews, and was made in silk of different colours representing fruits and flowers; This industry has been revived in Venice and carried to great perfection.

VII. — **Pillow Laces With Net and Mixed Grounds.**

The most celebrated of these laces are all known under the general name of *Flanders Point*, and many of them are as fine as the subtlest webs.

Varieties.

Point d'Angleterre is a superb and especially fine variety of Brussels Pillow lace with mixed ground. It is characterized by a raised rib of plaited threads worked at the same time as the edge of the lace; this rib outlines all the veinings and other salient points of the design, rendering it beautifully artistic. It generally represents garlands and other floral designs, and sometimes birds, figures and architectural details are introduced. It owes its name to having been originaly made to be smuggled into England and sold there as English lace, and was of a type entirely different from the original old Brussels Pillow lace. It was widely known and especially appreciated in France and Italy, always retaining however its distinctive appellation. The mesh of which its ground is composed is hexagonal, with four of the sides of two threads twisted twice, and two of the sides consisting of four threads plaited four times.

Mechlin or **Malines,** is so named from the Flemish town where it is manufactured. It has a very fine mesh, sexagonal in form, with four of its sides made by twisting two threads together twice, and four threads all plaited together three times to form the other two sides. The ground is generally strewed with tiny spots, flowers or leaves, surrounded by a coarse thread. Flowers or leaves, or both alternated, form the pattern along the heading, and the edge is more or less undulated according to the design of the flower border. — The old designs were sometimes rendered more elaborate by introducing vases, flowers, hearts and other details, with open work centres, but even these always retained the detached and self repeating composition characteristic of this lace after the middle of the seventeenth century.

Old Flemish Point — properly so called — was made with a very loose ground resembling squarish cob-webs with round pin holes between the close parts to outline the design. It had a running design of conventionalized fruit and flowers frequently interlaced with a ribbon design which contained open work and added lightness to the whole effect. Its edge was straight, with tiny purls.

Trolle Kant, — resembles the *Old Flemish Point,* but its ground is clearer, with rounder reliefs, and the designs are surrounded by a coarse thread or by a number of threads worked on one bobbin. The pattern is always so managed as to combine with the edge of the lace and to form shallow undulations, or is scallop finished — like all Flemish laces — with purls.

Antique Brussels Pillow Lace. -- Its designs resembled those of *Trolle Kant* on a net ground of round or hexagonal mesh, or a combination of both.

Antwerp Lace, was especially celebrated for trimming caps. In Antwerp, all the laces made in Brussels were imitations, but it also had an especial lace of its own called **Potten Kant**, in which the design – a vase — was worked like antique Brussels — except that the net of which the ground was formed consisted of triangles with hexagonal meshes or openings.

English Prolly Lace, was formerlly made in Hampshire and was copied from *Potten Kant,* just as the **Baby Lace** made in Bedford, Buckingham, and Northampton, was a modification of the **Lille Lace** which was sometimes called *English Point de Lille.*

Binche is a most exquisite, cobwebby, pillow lace from the Province of Hainault, in Flanders. It contains designs of flowers, fruits and figures wrought of the finest, most fairylike thread, connected by tiny rounds or discs of close weaving, with meshes of insertioned threads holding the whole together as through the designer had tried to picture a Dutch flower-garden in a snow storm. This beautiful lace has a straight edge, and the finer qualities, being no longer made, have become priceless.

Closter Spitze (*or Convent Lace*). The manufacture of this lace was originally confined — as the name indicates — to convents, especially to those in the North of Europe. The present centre of its fabrication is Bohemia.

Its treatment and is grounding are identical with those of Binche Point, but, unlike this lace it is coarse though sheer. Modified by the vicinity of Milan, Closter Spitze was also made in Southern Tyrol.

Point de Bruges was the name given to a lace made in and about that historic old town.

It much resembles Malines lace, but the Arabesques of its designs were out lined with several fine threads, instead of one coarse one; flowers, filled in with open work, were introduced with pleasing variety.

This lace, which was very fine and sheer, was also made in silk; its usual width did not exceed three to five inches. Like Antwerp Lace it was used chiefly for cap trimmings.

Point de Paris. This it the name by which the exquisite pillow lace made in the vicinity of Paris was known during the 18th Century.

It is an extremely fine and dainty lace with beautiful garlands trailing over the tulle and edging the flounces. This tulle is called " *champ double* „ , (double field) its mesh is round and strong, though very fine, and is produced by doubling the quantity of threads, (using eight instead of four); Point de Paris is as fine in quality as old Brussels, but it more resembles the richest laces of Bruges.

Valenciennes Lace is known in all the world wherever lace is used on linen. It is made with a solid square or diamond shaped mesh, platted with four threads on each side. It has a somewhat stiff flower or arabesque border made in close stitch along the edge, which is finished off with purls. The antique Point de *Valenciennes*, made at the French town of that name, was the most perfect pillow lace ever manufactured and was of fabulous price. It is composed of the finest thread ever spun in Europe and is almost indestructible. Some of the present machine-made laces are copied from its most graceful designs, which much resemble those of Point de Paris; but the manufacture of this lace in Valenciennes has entirely ceased. The fabrics now sold under that name are manufactured in Belgium, especially in the neighbourhood of Ypres; they are also produced in large quantities in Normandy and other Provinces of France, in England, in Ireland, and in Naples.

Point de Lille; -- so called from a town in northern France — is a fine lace with a resemblance to *Malines*, and also to certain varieties of Point d' Esprit. The old English Lace called Newport-Pagnel strongly resembles it.

Chantilly is a silk or thread pillow lace made with either a coarse or a fine tulle ground, produced without plaiting by simply twisting the threads together, and is strewn with close and varied flower designs or conventional patterns surrounded by a coarse thread; the English lace of Lyme Regis somewhat resembles it though it is more ordinary. Since the revival in the manufacture on a large scale of lace in France, — every kind of silk or thread lace is made, or its production abandoned, as fashion dictates in the different lace centres, such as Normandy, Surillac, Auvergne, Lorraine and la Touraine. To these productions, modified by the prevailing fashion, the manufacturers give fancy names so as to attract the attention of the general public which is known to prefer novelty to a strictly beautiful although old fashioned object. For example, *Cluny*, which is so often quoted, has never existed as a distinctive lace; it has never been manufactured within the memory of man inside the walls which bear that name, for *Cluny is an old Castle* in the heart of Paris, turned into a Museum of Industrial Art; and some clever manufacturer, inspired by specimens of the rare old *Genoese Point* existing in the Museum's rich collection, having invented a fresh and effective combination in Guipure, gave this name to his production, so as to attract the shopping public by means of that charm which clings to the name Cluny, knowing that the word would conjure up the historical walls of the quaint castellated Museum, and the memories of mediæval Paris.

Passements, All narrow edgings were called by this name which, originating in Italy, passed into France where it was used until the 17th Century as a general designation for what we call lace and gimp, though after that period it became confined to trimmings. The most celebrated of the ancient Passements were of *gold* and *silver* and *clinquant*, (plated copper), and were made in France and Italy. The great centres however, from which metal laces were sent all over Europe were Genoa, Milan and Florence. Some, of these were most sumptuous in appearance, and, considering the costliness of the raw material, of surprising widths. Coloured silk was frequently mixed with the other threads to diminish the cost without destroying the general effect.

La Bisette — was a coarse, narrow, heavy, unbleached lace, without any distinguishing characteristics, used by the middle classes in France and Belgium during the 17th Century.

La Gueuse (Beggar lace) was a great favourite in 1700; it was also unbleached, was sheer and narrow, with a coarse net ground and graceful pattern.

La Campane was a very fine narrow, white or unbleached pillow lace, used for the edging of caps or broad strips of lace. The derivation of its name is to be found in the Italian word *Campane* (bells) because it formed a bell shaped edge to all it trimmed.

La Mignonette — is from " Mignon „ meaning small and graceful. It was sometimes also called " *Thread Blonde* „, it was a fine thread edging with light transparent meshes.

Blonde was originally a narrow lace which took its name from the pale yellow or blond tint of the unbleached silk of which it was made. The simplicity of this lace soon disappeared owing to the introduction of rich designs in bleached and dyed silks, frequently varied by gold and silver threads. — *Modern blonde* is more largely manufactured in France and Genoa than in Spain where it originated. It is a wide, round meshed, sheer silk lace, with designs composed of large, flat surfaces made in a close stitch, surrounded by a coarse silk thread. In the more ordinary qualities, the design is embroidered by hand upon machine-made tulle and linen filled in by darning; it is also very easily imitated entirely by machinery. At one time Blonde was extensively made made in Venice, but this branch of industry has died out there since the revival in the production of thread lace and guipures at Palestrina. Genoa and Cantu are the actual centres of its manufacture in Italy, and our exhibit contains some beautiful modern specimens from the provinces of Liguria and Lombardy.

Point d'Esprit, Brittany Lace, or **Embroidered** or **Tambourtulle Lace,** was made in large quantities in Devonshire (England) in Brittany, and around Genoa where its production continues. The bands of embroidered tulle which still trim the caps of the good wives in the little town of Tulle, in France, are made entirely by bobbins and have given their name to the round mesh ground of every variety of lace. Many very clever lace makers formerly spent their lives in doing nothing else but produce these patternless bands ready for other hands to embroider, but after the introduction of an inferior price of machine-made tulle, it no longer furnished a means of livelihood and the poor workers were forced to seek fresh occupations. On the band of tulle, known to commerce as " footing „ there are embroidered, (in fine darning stitch), charming flowers with open-work heart, or small detached, conventionalized designs; the ground is also frequently strewn with little embroidered dots, to which the lace owes the name of " *Point d'Esprit* „ or " *Spirit Point* „. A coarse thread is drawn round the embroidery forming an outline to the flower stems and leaves. The edges of the antique laces are left without ornamentation. The common, machine made, embroidered cotton-tulle that drugs the market is copied from it and is very pretty for window curtains and furniture, although its use on clothes is decidedly unartistic.

Punto di Milano - Punto di Napoli. — Milanese Point and Neapolitan Point, are different names for a lace with round mesh ground, so named from the Italian cities of Milan and Naples which were the two great centres of its fabrication. This lace has always been a favourite, as it washes well and is exceedingly strong, and its manufacture has spread to all the countries of Europe. It resembles Genoese pillow lace in having the same scrolls and flowers formed by a ribbon in close stitch, with a mesh or tulle ground, whereas the Genoese Lace is held together by bars. The Neapolitan point has a much rounder mesh than the Milanese, and the character of the design also plainly indicates in what part of Italy the lace was made; this same rule applies to all Europe, for although in the coarser qualities the technicalities constituting a lace named after a special town were adopted as a standard for the same kind of lace produced in other places, transplanting even to the nearest village gradually altered the quality of the lace in the finer varieties.

Torchon-Lace — Torchon is the French generic term by which the following, ordinary Pillow-laces used on personal and household linen are commercialy known: " **Wirthschafts-Spitze** „ or household lace — is the name applied to it in Germany.

" **Merletto di Cantù, di Palestrina, degli Abruzzi, etc.** is the name by which it is called in Italy, after the great centres of its production. It is an ordinary pillow-lace with a net ground, and is universally used on underwear and on household and church linen; it is worked straight along like

4

weaving without the assistance of a crochet needle, as in Milanese point and Guipures — so that it is in reality the simplest and purest of bobbin laces. Its special qualifications for general use are great strength, endless variety of patterns in geometrical combinations, and low price.

Machine-made imitation of Torchon costs two thirds the price of real Torchon and is very easily torn, whilst the real Torchon outlasts the garments on which it is placed and is therefore the cheapest pretty edging that is manufactured. Owing to the facility of communication and the exigences of fashion the same designs that are made all over Italy are adopted in France, Belgium, Bohemia, Portugal, Ireland, England, India. Colombo, Saxony, Germany and many other countries. — A few of the most distinctive varieties which may interest the reader are here named, those which coincide in design being placed together.

Varieties.

Dalecarlie, is a Swedish bobbin lace resembling that of " *Offida* „, a variety of Italian lace made in the Province of the Marche, as well as the common, "**Abruzzi-lace** „. These laces are all worked without any drawing, the rude design being made by skipping the pin holes on a geometrically perforated card. The pattern thus produced is surrounded by a heavy thread, and composed of a close stitch worked between the meshes of the coarse net-ground.

Sometimes the heavy thread is left out this work in the last remaining tradition of a most exquisitely fine pillow lace which was made a century ago in these provinces; latterly in Sweden the manufacture of lace has been protected, and the workwomen have been directed with loving care and the happiest results, whereas the workers in the Marche and Abruzzi are entirely neglected, although with a small capital in ready money, and a little patience this industry could be revived with great profit to the capitalist and enormous benefit to the surrounding country which is excessively miserable and poor — the women are ready and willing to work, but requiring instruction and direction.

Mediæval household lace, was made in most of the Spanish, Dutch, Danish, German and Italian Provinces. It always ended in a straight edge finished off with purls, and the design was often so thick with interlaced patches of close work that the net-ground was almost or wholly suppressed, so that it appears like drawn work executed in a fancy pattern upon house linen. The open work is left by twirling two or four threads several times together, and by the holes in which the pins following the contours of the drawing have been prinked.

Reticella a fuselli. Is a mediæval pillow lace which is an exact copy of the celebrated *punto greco*, *punto tagliato* and *reticella*. In certain museums I have seen the finer examples placed and classified with the needle laces which bear the above names, no one having observed under the microscope the difference in its execution. It was used extensively in household linen with most happy effect to replace those more expensive and tedious points.

Madeira lace, has a close stitch without a regular set ground, being instead formed of varied webs and open spaces, and has oriental wheel like designs which are very artistic and pleasing.

Ceylon-laces, as also those from the Mediterranean Islands have a mediæval and charming effect, sometimes resembling the above, at others seeming counterparts of certain Maltese-Laces.

Sicilian torchon, has no design drawn upon the parchment. The peasant lace-maker follows the dictates of her fancy, forming capricious combinations of webs and nets by introducing the pin, or skipping the holes which are pricked at regular intervals all over the strip of parchment which is firmily sewed upon the cushion or " *ballon* „. Sicily was formerly celebrated, for its gold and metal laces, but its production has nearly died out, and some philanthropic souls are now trying to organize and procure a revival of this industry so as to give a means of support to the women of Palermo and other populous centres. — At Messina many varieties of lace are produced with great exactness.

At present every variety of fancy-work receives its own distinctive appellation, and all the old stitches that enter into its composition are decked out with new and attractive names, and in the past, in the same way, the laces made in every town, hamlet, castle or cottage, by young and old, rich and poor, alike received special designations applied to the designs and, stitches at the dictation of the head workwoman's imagination, and which were afterwards adopted by her companions.

Brief as is this introduction, it has described one hundred and twenty two of the principal kinds of lace, and although the reader's patience and memory have already been severely taxed, yet not a quarter of the appellations by which these laces and their varieties are known in different countries have been mentioned. Multiplying one hundred and twenty two by four and the product by twenty, the average of nine thousand seven hundred and sixty is produced, a sum representing the names of individual stitches which, for brevity and to avoid tedium have been omitted.

Many laces, however have forty or fifty different terms applied to their component parts, each given because of the introduction of some different stitch or combination, and the stitches composing even the narrowest torchons are six or seven in number, so that the general average given above is very low; — were I to add the terms applied in different places to the materials and implements employed in the manufacture of lace, the description would become very long and wearisome, and the enumeration of the terms would form a good sized vocabulary. I have therefore drawn attention to these figures simply that they may serve as a refutation to a general and erroneous impression, common to many highly cultured people, that *Lace-making* is only worthy to be classed among the secondary industries, instead of standing high among the textile and decorative arts which adorn our homes.

If this preparatory study has appeared long, it has assumed its present form in order that the " *History of Lace* „, which follows, and which also serves as a Catalogue to our Exhibit at the Columbian Exposition, may not be full of wearying technicalities and voluminous notes.

I trust that the following chapters will justify the course adopted. If not, the fault lies in the inexperience of the narrator, and not in the lack of interest and variety to be found in tracing through the Ages the developement of this graceful, refined and ornamental branch of **Industrial Art.**

Part II.

The Birth of the Textile Arts and the Origin of Lace.

Man loves ornament; had he existed when the earth was without form and void, it might have been different, for first impressions are indelible; but, when his mind opened to look about him and observe, ornament attracted his attention on every side. Cradled in the lap of a young world, he saw fair nature robed in a many hued garment, covered with reliefs of shrubs and trees, chequered by cunning traceries of branches and leaves and their shadow dancing in the sunshine. — Her mantle was trimmed with open-work borders of meadow-land, fretted with great patches of parti-colored flowers, while dainty fringes of interlaced ferns and grasses nodded on the edges of the silvery water courses. When winter came Nature prepared to sleep, and then changed these robes for a beauteous white sheet of dazzling snow, diversified with wondrous interlaced patterns, worked by the magic touch of frost in ice and rime. Then for the first time man saw, mirrored in God's handy work, the exquisite designs which in future ages his descendants were destined to copy in producing lace.

The mind of primitive humanity was however as undeveloped as that of a young child, and could neither analyze the impressions received nor even realize their existence; and yet in making for itself rude coverings of skins and plaited grasses, or utensils of bone, it sought to copy surrounding objects, groping darkly for that with which to adorn the person and property.

When we look back into the misty vistas through which prehistoric man wandered, we find his traces on the rocky paths of the Stone Age, marked with curious carvings of zigzags, curves and animal designs.

Nature, well pleased at the compliment paid her in these early efforts, covered them over with earth, hiding them away until the time should come when mankind would be so developed as to appreciate the value of these records of his past; just as a fond mother, after long years, draws from some private recess a carefully treasured object, rudely executed, and shows it to her grown-up son, to prove to him how clever he already was at the time he thinks he must have been only a stupid, useless burden to her.

At the earliest moment of his existence, man must have felt the necessity for some means by which to snare birds and beasts and fish for food; and observing how they were sometimes caught in the tangled weeds and thickets, he invented the twisting of grasses and fibres into ropes, which when knotted rudely together formed primitive nets.

Naturally the first ornaments for the person and attire were the trophies of prowess, such as pierced teeth, tusks etc. worn strung together as necklaces, bracelets, etc.; and on the garments they consisted in fringes formed by the long hair of furs. These all served as the models from which the first trimmings on rude textiles were copied.

The Lake Dwellers.

In Europe, the earliest race of which we know anything definite is that of the **Lake dwellers,** whose industries are most interestingly illustrated by the fragments of their utensils found in the great bogs and lakes of Switzerland. They existed from the time of the Troglodytes through the Stone and far into the Bronze Age, some say into the Age of Iron, although they had become extinct before the invasion of their country by the Romans.

In *Asia* we find the earliest artistic, ornate textiles among the Assyrians and the Indians,and in *Africa*, among the Egyptians; but, as the foundation of Art (as we understand the term) — and the unbroken chain of evidence with regard to its history, is to be found in their monuments and sepulchres, we will first examine the Stone-Age in Europe as illustrated by the **Lake Dwellers**, and then, turning to Assyria and Egypt for instruction, we will only leave them when their arts have accomplished the civilization of the Peninsulas of Europe and of the northern coast of the Mediterranean.

One can understand that in the dry atmosphere and sand of Egypt, delicate objects like textiles would resist the wear and tear of Centuries, although marvellous it must ever seem to touch objects produced by human skill thousands of years ago, — but it is nothing short of a miracle, that beneath peat and mud and slush, frozen and thawed alternatively for ages beyond the memory of man, such perishable things as cords and stuffs, made of a curious flax developed from the wild variety which is a native of the west coast of the Mediterranean, prepared and spun as it would be by a peasant of today, should have remained to give us proofs — meagre though they must perforce be — of this early race of Europeans. Besides the baskets that were most artistically woven of bark, fibre or sedges, and the fishing nets made of coarse linen or fibre twine knotted into as regular meshes as if produced to day, especially interesting for our branch of study, are the remnants of stuffs and the bone, horn, and bronze needles and crochet hooks used for making nets and knotting fringes into the edge of the textiles.

Samples of all these objects are exhibited on the *Revolving screen*, which serves to illustrate through them the origin and history of lace — whilst the voluminous objects are placed round the walls in the glass cases nearest to the Screen.

Rothenhausen and Ugenhausen,

N.º 1.a. and 1.b. Screen.

N, 1 A and 1 B are illustrations of Textiles found at Rothenhausen by Herr K, Forrer, and Herr H. Messikommer, and are taken by kind permission of the Authors from an interesting pamphlet on the subject of Lake Dwellings published by them and entitled: *Prehistorische raria* as dem *Antiqua*, special — Gatschrift für Vorgeschichte — Zurig 1889.

67 represents a twisted hank of flax

74 a skein of twine

63 a tassel made of twine

70 a piece of rope

68, 69, 73 and 75 basket work of woven sedges, **straw and woody fibre**

59, 60. 61, different qualities of net

62, 71 textiles with and without sedge

72, 73 embroidered textiles

94, 65. Textiles edged with fringes; though not reproduced here, these **fringes** were frequently twisted together and knotted at the ends.

70 A. Textile with Passementerie fringe.

N. 1 C is a real piece of the coarse basket plating found in Rothenhausen.

N. 1 D contains **two** bits **of** loomwoven textiles from Rothenhausen.

When Herr Messikomer's father found the first fringed stuff at Rothenhausen in 1857, he showed it to an expert who said it was modern Parisian Passementerie work, **but** soon other pieces were found in the same excavations and in the midst of surroundings which furnished positive proofs of their authenticity as work of the ancient Lake Dwellers.

Simple but practical weaver's frames, thread and twine from the size which serves now for sewing sails, up to the dimensions of large cords, have been found in skeins or already worked into stuffs, nets, tassels or fringes. Also a peculiar, very strong material, plaited instead of woven out of strong twine, has been found, and which might have served as a kind of sail cloth.

At Ugenhausen, in 1882, the embroideries illustrated on the screen were found, the designs of which may have served as models for the perfected ornaments of the Bronze Age. The rarity of these objects is explained by their being found only among the remains of dwellings destroyed by fire in windless weather, combined with circumstances which would cause inflammable stuffs to drop into the water uncharred, when the floors beneath them were reduced to the fine, close packed ashes suited to preserve textiles from destruction by insects or by the waves. To form a better idea of the men and women among the Lake Dwellers we must look for the race which at present best illustrates the savage life of the past, and, allowing for the influences of climate and of contact with the Arabs and the Europeans, **it appears that** Central Africa can furnish the information we desire.

Card II, A, B, C, D. Screen.

Card II shows four sketches of savage dwellings.

II A. represent a Lake-Dwellers settlement — reconstructed according to the opinion of one of the most eminent professors of archæology.

II B. represents a *grainery* of the Babusessé tribe as illustrated in Henry Stanley's latest work on Africa.

II C. represents part of a Bougos Village in Africa.

II D. represents Aboriginal Lake-Dwellings in New Guinea.

The Africans use boats hollowed out of trees as did the Lake-Dwellers, their pottery has the same ornamentation and is baked in the sun as was that of the Lake-dwellers: they live in settlements instead of following a nomadic life and have many other customs in common, therefore in studying their rude arts and divisions of labour, we may hope to ascertain much about the daily life of the Lake Dwellers at the time of their greatest developement.

All through the interior of Africa and in the basins of the Upper and the Lower Ogowé and the Congo the woman does all the hand-work, while the man reserves to himself what may be called the *amusing occupations*. He goes to the two big fishing reunions that are held every year at the time when the water in the great rivers is at its lowest; he snares birds and animals for food and clothing, he goes out to the hunts and battles, to war and to plunder and thoroughly enjoys the excitement of this life, whilst the woman remains at home and busies herself in a modest daily round that is startling in its fatiguing variety. Besides the care of the domestic animals, she does all the field and farm work, cultivates the cereals, cuts the wood, and fishes along the smaller streams. She gathers up and carries on her back all the produce of her labour, and the fruits from the plantations that are often at great distances from the village; arrived at her home, she helps to tidy up the village and then, instead of resting, she grinds the flour, cooks the meals, and still finds time to weave artistic palm mats and sheetings, and to model and to bake the simple pottery that is needed for domestic use.

The smiths and the weavers of fine " *Rafia* „ cloths are men especially apprenticed to the trade, and remain always faithful to their tools.

The industries in which savage man *indulges*, when at home, for he never *works*, are the making of fishing and hunting nets, the sewing together with great neatness of the squares of rafia produced by the professional weavers, the making of " *Puka* „ (or bags) in fine needle work, ornamental carving and the shaping and polishing of the wooden parts of weapons; when necessary he also attends to the construction of " pirogues „ and huts, the only two of all these occupations that are really hard work.

Card III. 1. and 2. Screen.

Card III contains two pen and ink sketches that were made on the back of an English Cotton-goods label by my late brother-in-law, Giacomo di Brazzà, who spent several years in Africa —together with Cavaliere Pecile — on an exploring expedition which was commanded by his brother, the celebrated African Explorer **Pierre de Brazzà**, actually Governor of the French Congo.

III. 1. Is a sketch of a wig or hat worn by a Batcké chief; it is composed of fringes and cords in pine apple fibre, dyed black, and knotted like the above mentioned "*Parisian Passement*„ of the lake dwellers,

Card III. 2.

III. 2. represents a fringed square of woven Rafia (of the natural color of raw silk) such as is worn by the Batcké as a kind of cap or head handkerchief.

N.º IV. Cases.

Number IV is a piece of Rafia with knotted fringe, which has been placed in the glass-cases with the following voluminous pieces of African-lace kindly lent by Cavaliere Pecile.

N.º V. and VI. Cases.

Number V is a "Puka„ (bag or pocket) made with the needle, in a curious, complicated lace stitch. These pockets are everywhere used in the Upper and lower Ogowé and in many parts of the Congo-Country; the band is slipped over the Arm and shoulder-blade, with the bag hanging underneath the arm-pit; and they serve as pockets as well as travelling bags in that land where clothing is too scant to furnish a fold in which to place one; they are more or less ornate according to the fancy of the artificer, and no self-respecting Ogowéan would be without one unless he could neither make, borrow or steal it.

Our particular "Puka„ is the work of a member of the Abomba tribe, which is also distinguished for its tonsorial artists. These black Truefits produce marvellous effects on the pates of their fellow tribesmen, whose woolly hair they plait and clip and shave into most complicated and ornate headdresses, adorned with gew-gaws, and bisected with little shaved lines and spots which meander among the knobs of wool and cause these heads to resemble relief maps of their dark native continent:

But to return to this Puka, which is very commodious, elastic and decidedly stylish, with is adornment of elephant bristles, and the large iron bell

5

that has charmed the tedium of many a long journey with its clatter. These pockets are made of fine twine manufactured from the leaves of the pineapple plant. The workman cuts the leaves into strips about half an inch in width and passes these between his index finger and a sharp knife-blade, thus most daintily removing all the leaf part that covers the fibres, then he rolls the latter into a fine double twine, a couple of yards in length, by rubbing it carefully with the palm of his hand on his leg above the knee until it becomes perfectly smooth and even; this twine he threads into a needle and, beginning the bag at the small end, he works spirally, widening when necessary, first with a double button-hole stitch and afterwards with one much more complicated until the whole is completed with one continuous thread; to avoid knots, every time the worker's allowance of twine is nearly exhansted, he unthreads the needle and splices the end of the twine with fresh fibre, rolling it into a fine twine as before upon the flat of his knee; and continues repeating the same operation every time fresh thread is required until the bag is finished.

One may imagine that these articles are not completed in a day, Cav. Pecile told me that on an exploring expedition he observed a denizen of a certain village on the Upper Ogowé working industriously on one of these bags; — returning to the same place six months later he found the same villager sitting at the same spot, and working on the same bag, which was still far from being completed. An African in his native wilds is never over-industrious; therefore the friends and advocates of limited labour and fresh air for the working classes need have no fear that this man did not enjoy sufficient exercise and recreation during the time which elapsed between Cav. Pecile's two visits.

VI. Cases.

Number VI is a gem in more ways than one, for it is not only considered locally very valuable, and is worn by chiefs on the shores of the Loanga as a badge of office, — but it is *real lace made with a needle*, and its stitches are the counter-part of those in the beautiful *Punto in aria* of Venice. It is a cap shaped like a Phrygian or a Neapolitan fisherman's cap.

Especial attention should be given to its shape, as much will be said in the following pages about this particular kind of head gear which is gradually becoming obsolete. The fabrication of this African cap begins at the centre of the crown with a tiny but perfect wheel which is increased by alternate open and close stitches of exceeding fineness, made with perfect regularity of spacing and depth; at intervals diamonds are formed of close work alternating with a ground of open stitch, and the completed cap is finished off with a band at the edge produced in quite a different kind of stitch. The thread used is fine, strong and pliable, resembling unbleached flax or hemp, but is seen to be not of the same construction as these when examined under the microscope. Might not this be the fibre used by the Lake Dwellers which scientists have failed to classify, and which has successfully resisted the wear of centuries?

Leaving the Savage races in order to search among those of known civilization we may go back for centuries without finding the origin of textiles. The ancient monuments of Babylonia and Assyria furnish the names of kings who reigned three thousand five hundred years before Christ, living to the great age of the early patriarchs, and some of these princes must have existed near the time af the flood, as frequent allusions are made in these inscriptions to that awful calamity.

In studying the history of the world as depicted on the monuments of Egypt, the Exodus of the Jews appears a trivial bit of Modern history; and Abraham's visit to that country, during which his pretty young wife, Sarah, attracted great attention at Court by her beauty, grace of manner and accomplishments, seems a romantic episode in the life of an ancestor. The Egyptian hieroglyphics which represent long lines and dynasties of kings, majestically arrayed, go back so very far that we lose our awe for the age of the Book Manin, the Ramayana and the Mahabharata which describe the civilization of India; the Illiad and the Penteteuch seem works of nation history and we look upon the Book of Job, written two thousand five hundred years before Christ as a comparatively modern classic. Whether the Egyptian and Assyrian races were twin sisters, or which was the first created we cannot tell, but both bear marks of the same Semitic parentage in lineaments and character. In any case the stock was prolific, and a branch of it pushed into India in the vanguard of the Arian race, which, when the ground had been well cultivated by its industrious forerunners, in its turn emigrated, and commingling is richer, more fiery blood with that of its predecessors gave a fresh incentive to all the arts of peace and war.

These old nations were full of intuitive knowledge which it has been the fate of our modern civilization to rediscover and classify, for they even realized the existence of microbes although ignorant of the means for destroying them, and so the pantheistic religion of the Romans included special exorcisms, and prayers addressed to their personification as a god.

We will take Job as an example of these ancients, for, in his exquisite poem, we receive the story of his life and experiences from his own lips, while Homer but repeats and idealizes what he had heard from others. — Job was a rich Aryan chief or king; he possessed a palatial residence constructed of baked bricks, having a portico adorned with columns. This dwelling was furnished with couches and beds, and with tables on which his meals were served on gold plate. At night the apartments were illuminated by means of lamps and candles. Utensils of copper, iron, and earthenware, as also bottles made of skins, and sack-cloth bags served for the baser domestic uses.

Job lived in or near a city, for he speaks of the princes covering their mouths in token of respect when he passed them in the gate, and of the nobles and old men rising to do him homage and waiting to be spoken to, with the same courtesy that is now shown towards rulers. He wore a diadem or crown of gold, gold ear-rings and a flowing robe edged about the neck with a collar; this was girded with a leather or embroidered belt and over it he wore a rich mantle hanging from his shoulders; he had also a mirror in which to admire his toilet when completed.

The garments he describes were carefully fashioned and sewn, and the cloth which composed them was dyed of various hues and woven of thread spun from flax, wool, camel's hair, and perhaps even silk; but this is not certain, for, although a legend ascribes to him a knowledge of the use of silk, it cannot be proved.

In summer, the woollen stuffs were packed away in chests with strong-smelling woods and spices to save them from destructive insects, as so well described by Homer centuries later.

The Treasury contained fine gold of Ophir, gold dust, jewels of fine gold, gold coins, alloyed silver, sapphires, rubies, crystals — by which term perhaps diamonds are meant — pearls, onyxes, coral and Ethiopian topazes. The city in or near which he lived had gates and walls, and was surrounded by a moat. His fields were laid out with land-marks, fences, hedges and ditches; he rented additional fields from his neighbours, and employed a thousand yoke of oxen to till his land. He had one wife, who lived with him, while his three daughters and seven sons had each a separate home; his own household consisted of hired servants and slaves, since prisoners taken in war were also in his time compelled to do the hardest work, including the building of great monuments which princes caused to be erected during their lifetime to serve as mausoleums, and which were adorned with laudatory inscriptions carved in stone or traced on terra-cotta tablets. Books were written with iron pens and may have been composed of tablets, or of rolls of palm or papyrus, and possibly of leather, since there were boots, bridles, slings and water-bottles all made of tanned, skins. Job speaks of swift ships, of the phenomena of the sea, the forces of nature, the condensation of rain and the purifying effect of frost: he is also well acquainted with astronomy and natural history, for he speaks of the North Star and of the Pleiades, and minutely describes the whale, the camel, the ox, the ass and the horse, as also sheep, goats, fowls, ostriches and innumerable wild birds and animals. He occupied himself with commercial as well as agricultural pursuits, and had scales for weighing merchandise. He sent out couriers and tax-gatherers and was so frequently visited by travellers and merchants from different countries that he kept interpreters in order to be able to converse wih them; he also was himself a traveller, and when on a journey or on a hunting expedition made use of tents.

In his time there were judges and physicians, and horse and foot soldiers organized in troops and armies, furnished with iron and steel shields and breastplates, and armed with swords, pikes, lances and bows: flint heads for the arrows, and sharp stones for the slings — remnants of the usages of the Stone Age — were still used. In hunting and fishing he possessed — in addition to the above named weapons — traps, snares, nets made of cord, hooks and harpoons. He and his children were very hospitable, and gave frequent feasts which sometimes lasted late into the night, and to which they invited not only their neighbours but also guests living at great distances; the food was cooked and seasoned with salt, olive-oil, butter and milk; it consisted of meat, fowl, eggs and vegetables, and cakes made of corn, wheat or barley ground betwen two stones into flour by the women: nuts, fruit, honey, and cheese came in as delicacies. The usual beverage at these banquets was wine made from grapes.

Job's religion was monotheistic; and though the sun and moon were worshipped in his neighbourhood, idols of wood or stone had not yet become a part of the religion known to him — All these details have been mentioned to prove how little certain oriental races have altered in their customs since the oldest historic epoch, although in the last fifty years the penetration of European customs into the East has produced innovations.

No poet, singing the heroic deeds of his nation, would interrupt the flow of stately verse to introduce trivialities which would mar the completeness of his ode, or retard its climax, but sometimes when describing fair women and their attractions, the ancient authors linger lovingly over their charms and even add a description of the personal adornments which enhanced their loveliness, and these brief word-pictures coincide with the cartoons on Egyptian and Asssyrian monuments, and Etruscan vases and tombs; whilst in the secluded homes of Indian princes this type of woman-hood is still preserved. Graceful female forms are there still veiled with gauzy materials and robed in richly spangled tissues, or draped in cunningly wrought mantles embroidered along the hems with divers colors, and trimmed with rich and complicated fringes; about their pretty feet, bangles and bells tinkle as they move about busied in their household duties, or raise the curtains that veil the door ways of their apartment to catch a glimpse of the great world outside. These curtains are made of rich carpets or heavy materials adorned with cunning designs wrought in needle-work by themselves or by the maidens under their skilled direction.

But if we wish to touch and examine the textiles mentioned by Homer and his contemporaries, we must turn to the tombs in Egypt. The Egyptians believed in the bodily resurrection of the dead, and therefore caused the bodies of the departed to be carefully embalmed with spices and bitumen. This, combined with the dry atmosphere and many wrappings and mummy cases, has preserved the rich garments in which the remains were clothed so that their beloved might not blush for his mean attire on appearing before Osiris and the shades in the other world. Besides this, the Egyptians adorned the walls of the tomb with drawings, absolutely truthful in every detail — illustrative of the occupations and past life of the deceased, however simple and uneventful it may have been — and of the number and employments of his servants.

The following illustrations of some of these cartouches which, together with the information regarding them, we owe to the kindly interest taken in our work by Prof. Schiaparelli of the Egyptian Museum in Florence, while the collection of textiles, without which this exhibition would be incomplete, is due to the well-known antiquarian author and critic, Herr. R. Forrer, of Strasbourg. I therefore gladly avail myself of this opportunity for heartily thanking them both in the name of the committee and in my own for the valuable information they have contributed to this book, and for the benevolence and patience with which they replied to our frequent importunings.

XIV. A. Screen.

Nets were made in Egypt in great abundance and from the remotest times; the process of their manufacture is pictured — N. XIV. A. — on the tomb of the feudal prince *Nekira*, near Beni-Hassan in Upper Egypt, and which was decorated under the Twelfth Dynasty about 2500 B. C.; the same design is, with slight variations which prove it to be original, repeated one thousand years later in a tomb of the XVII Dynasty near Thebes.

XIV. B. Screen, XIV. C.

Shews two ways of snaring birds with nets, and is from the same tomb, as also is XIV. c. which indicates that the Egyptians, like many savage nations, and like the American and Asiatic Indians, used nets for carrying heavy weights. This cartoon represents a water-carrier with two jars borne in nets.

It will be observed that, instead of using a biforcated needle in the manufacture of these nets, two workmen employ balls of twine, and that the net is stretched on a flat frame and worked at both ends at once. These large nets were made of flax or cotton twine, and were used alike for bird-catching and for fishing, as well as for curtains in the doorways and windows of houses to exclude flies and other insects.

XV. Screen.

Is a much older illustration of the use of nets than the preceding cartouche, and is taken from a bas relief in the tomb af the dignitary *Iebehmi* near the great pyramid, constructed under the rule of the fifth Dynasty 3300 Years before Christ. — It represents a man carrying a pole on which are hung several bird cages — just as on any autumn morning one may see an Italian bird snarer carrying his decoys to the trimmed thickets where his nets are spread. — There are many monuments, older than the above, which also illustrate the use of nets in Egypt.

XVI. Screen.

Is a drawing which represents a fine net in the Egyptian Museum at Florence. It is of twine rubbed with bitumen and is also evidently made for catching brds or small fish, as it is composed entirely of little, close-set bags of net in which the game — once entered — must remain suspended without power to move, thus resembling in its effect the fine net left loose between two coarser ones at present used for bird-catching in Italy. In the Florentine Museum there is another net made entirely of leather, in which material slits are regularly cut close together on the same principle and with like effect as our Christmas Tree nets for sweets, clipped out of silver paper. — These leather, net-like curtains must have served in the doorways and windows of the wealthy, or perhaps to save animals from being tormented by flies and gnats, in the same way as nets are now thrown over horses in summer, in warm climates, with the same object in riew.

XVII. Screen,

N. XVII represents a little, double knotted bag which was made to hold a porhyry balsam bottle.

It is more artistically worked in Macramé stitch, and resembles, in its effect, the meshes of the celebrated *rescau double*, or double ground of old Burano lace. We find the reproduction of nets in endless variety on Greek and Etruscan vases, but, notwithstanding their universal use for domestic purposes, we have no proof that they were adopted as embroidery for clothing, although many of the elaborately knotted fringes of the Assyrians and Jews produce the effect of nets.

Fillets were in general use among the Greeks and Etruscans for binding up the hair, and were worn with diadems and with and without veils; they are often represented as ornamented with designs, but we cannot tell whether these represent gold buttons, or embroidered or filagree work, for in the decorations on the vases the treatment is somewhat conventional. In VIII. A. are shewn Greek costumes photographed from the famous Sysiphoz vase in the Munich Museum.

XVIII. B. and B, Screen., XVIII. C. Screen.

The earliest Egyptian *Mummy-cloths* are, like those of the Peruvian Mummies, almost prehistoric, and have the same weaving and texture as the stuffs of the Lake-dwellers. We have no illustrations of these, but XVIII. A. will serve our purpose though it is of a later period from Achmim Panopolis. — In it the warp threads are left as a fringe, and XVIII. B. shews how, after working an inch or two of texture, the woof was omitted or drawn out so as to form a transparent border. This was varied by spaces

of open-work, as in XVIII. C., in which the weft is shot across behind
the warp at regular distances for a certain number of threads, and then
the ordinary weaving continues, thus forming alternate squares; these woof-
threads are then cut away if desired; at a later period these open spaces were
filled in with coloured embroidery.

IX. Screen.

N.º IX. represents a skirt embroidered round the belt and furnished
with braces to support it from the shoulders. This design dates from an inscription belonging to the XII. Dynasty, 2500 B. C. and preserved in the Florence Museum.

The early Egyptians also made fringes which were either knotted into
the material they were destined to adorn, or sewed on afterwards. We frequently find examples of garments trimmed with them, especially sashes and
the edge of skirts. Deep fringes were also worn round the neck; when this
is the case the women are represented as engaged in menial service or manual labour, thus indicating the lower classes, who may have adopted the
fashion in imitation of the rich necklaces of their betters, or to satisfy their
love of colour and ornament at small cost. — These neck fringes remind us
of the artistically plaited grass necklaces made and worn by the wild tribe
of Matheran in Northern India, the work in which is identical with that which
served as a model for the beautiful Oriental gold necklaces found in Etruscan tombs, and which are still made from the same designs by workmen
in India who, despite the innovations of the British dominion and the XIX.
century, still cling with loving faithfulness to the traditions of their ancestors.

The bas-reliefs executed in honour of the princes belonging to the XIX.
and XX. Dynasties in the Royal Tombs in the Valley of the Kings, near
Thebes, furnish us with many illustrations of elaborate fringes,

X. Screen.

N.º X. represents Queen Tachat, mother of the Pharaoh-Amonmensis on
whose tomb she is portrayed, and who reigned in the XIII. century B. C.

XI Screen.

N.º XI. represents Queen Isit, wife of Rameses VI. as she is depicted
on her own tomb; she belonged to the XX. Dynasty, XII. century B. C.

XII., XIII. Screen.

N.º XII. represents Rameses VII. and N.º XIII. his wife, both copied
from his tomb of the XX. Dynasty, 1200 B. C.

1300 BC a 1200BC

The wife of Ramses VII from his Tomb near Thebes. Egypt.

XXXVI. A., B., C. Screen.

A. B. and C., **N.°** XXXVI, **are** illustrations also taken from the Royal **Tombs** at Thebes. A. represents an Arab **chief** of the Abshà tribe which **migrated into** Egypt during the XII. Dynasty, about 1600 B. C. B. represents **Arabs of the** same tribe.

C. represents the Phœnician prince Refa bringing gifts to a Pharaoh of the XVIII. Dynasty, about 1900 B. C. — The garments of this prince are beautifully worked and trimmed with fringes, cords and tassels.

A correct idea of the princely and priestly clothing used **in** Egypt at the time Moses wrote his laws and the history of the ancestors of his Race — about 1500 B. C. — may be obtained by reading the instructions given in Exodus XXXVIII. and following chapters for the fashioning of the Jewish priestly garments, which were copied, with modifications, from those of the Royal Princes who, at that period in Egypt were considered as also belonging to the hierarchy of religion, and so had a double hold **on** the superstitious populace; and it was in this capacity **that** Moses acquired much of his erudition, and of his knowledge of sanitary laws

The **costume of the** Jewish High Priest, according to the prescriptions **laid down by Moses,** consisted of an under robe, long and full in the skirt, **and with sleeves to the** wrists; under this robe was to be worn a pair of breeches, both garments being made of white linen. Over the robe was worn the Ephod, or tunic of *fine twined linen*, an expression which modern criticism considers here incorrectly translated, as the same Hebrew term is elsewhere used for *silk*; the ephod was therefore probably made of spun silk dyed blue; it was scant in the skirt, and reached only to the knees, had short sleeves, and was bound about the neck with a piece of the same material that it might not be torn in putting it on and off; **this** binding **was** adorned with a border embroidered in gold, purple and scarlet, in buttonhole stitch round the edges **and round** the openings through which the gold chains supporting the breast-plate **were** to pass: an onyx stone engraved with the names of the tribes of Israel **was** set in rich embroidery upon each shoulder; the hem was adorned with a rich border, repeating the designs of the shoulders and **neck** and edged with gold bells that tinkled as the wearer moved, **alternated with** pomegranates made in needle-work of purple **and** scarlet, forming **a kind** of passementerie resembling the needle lace on the edge of Turkish **veils.** — The Ephod was belted in at the waist by a richly embroidered girdle **to** which, **by** means of rings in its lower edge and of a *blue lace* passing through them, the glorious, sacred breast plate, composed of a mass of gems and sparkling embroidery, was attached. The High Priest wore upon his head a mitre of fine linen, a kind of veil with fringed edges held in place by a gold diadem about two fingers deep, and reaching from **ear to** ear; this was sewed **to** another piece **of** *blue lace* which bound it **about** the head and was **tied** in a bow with embroidered and fringed ends falling behind, over the mitre. Tradition explains this *blue lace* as fringed and worked in silk of various colours; in that case it must have been a kind of passementerie, or needle lace.

A large and ample cloak or coat, made of fine embroidered linen, was thrown over the shoulders to complete this regal costume. From this description it is to be inferred that two kinds of work, not embroidered in the stuff, were executed on the garment, one being the pomegranates in coloured silks that hung between the bells round the edge of the Ephod, and which would coincide in design and treatment with Turkish needle-lace of the XV. century of our era, and the " blue lace „ made of silk and thread that was knotted together like a passementerie or macramé bobbin lace. Cotton was never highly esteemed for textiles in the West during classic times; it is first mentioned in the Book of Esther, though it must have been in use in the East for centuries before.

The occupations of the Jewish women, the trust placed by the men in their advice, the selection made from among them of rulers and judges, their erudition and literary accomplishements, the direction of the house, the management of the slaves and of home-industries, their simple amusements and their intelligent devotion to the rearing of their children, all resemble these characteristics as portrayed in the lives of the most chaste class of Greek and Etruscan matrons who, by their education and retired mode of life, became most intelligent, serious and philosophic, and were thus prepared to become the first brave disciples of Christianity, so that the costume they wore preserved one type for centuries, and, slightly modified by climate and nationality, is that of the women of the early Church. On the other hand, the style of garment suited to the more enervated life and looser morals of India, Syria and Egypt was adopted by the gay-hearted dancing girls and the less sedate women of the Roman Court.

A Matron's costume consisted of a flowing under tunic or *stola* with long or short sleeves, composed of heavy or light material as fancy or the season might dictate: over this stola a shorter tunic was worn made full at the neck, or of one straight piece clasped on either shoulder and draped across the chest. The waist was girt by a belt of metal, leather, or passementerie, or else the draperies were held in restraint by a simple ribbon.

The feet were protected by shoes, slippers, or sandals, to which stockings — biforcated at the toes to admit the sandal strap — were added in winter. When walking abroad, and also at home in chilly weather, the matron wore a full toga edged with embroidery, or fringed or scalloped round the borders. A long veil made of transparent material, more or less richly fringed or embroidered according to her wealth and the position the occupied in the social scale was artistically draped over her hair and made to hang down upon her shoulders. — The draping of this veil and the combing of the hair beneath it was considered of great importance, and a diadem with any quantity of pins, ribbons, fillets and jewels were used to adorn her locks, which were braided, waved, curled or frizzed quite in modern fashion. Blind Homer in wandering from palace to palace, must have heard this branch of the feminine toilet freely discussed, since he accurately describes it precisely as we see it represented on Greek vases adorned with representations of Andromache's grief:

> " Her hair's fair ornaments, the *braids* that bound,
> „ The net that held them, and the wreaths that crown'd:
> „ The veil and diadem threw far away „ etc.

Besides the gold wreaths that encircled her Greek knot, and the jewelled hair-pins that held her veil in place, the rich patrician had numberless brooches, rings and bracelets, clasps and ear-rings, as well as chatelaines composed of innumerable tiny chains by which were suspended all the objects that could possibly be of use to her in her toilet, either when from home or during her household occupations. -- The gleaming fillet or net that contained her hair was often composed of precious metals cunningly and exquisitely wrought, like the *golden net of Hephæstus:*

> " Whose texture e'en the search of gods deceives,
> Fine as the filmy webs the spider weaves. „

The young girls often allowed their hair to flow loose under their veils, or they plaited it in long tresses, binding a simple ribbon or net round the brows. — They wore shorter and less ample tunics than the married women, and no jewelry, or only a brooch of the simplest pattern to clasp or to pin together a garment when necessary.

The Jewish men, who were neither athletic nor equestrian, wore clothes very like those of the women, supplemented by a coat with arm-holes instead of the toga; this coat was generally dyed a dark colour and was freely adorned with fringes.

The men of Etruria, Greece, and Rome had flowing robes for certain festivals or offices, just as they had suits of armour for war: but their daily costume consisted in the short full tunic, with or without sleeves, belted in at the waist and covered by a toga that either hung majesticallly from their shoulders, or was wrapped about them in folds so full of grace that they are still called *classic.*

Sometimes, for riding and travelling, and in cold weather, the men adopted short breeches that were hidden beneath the tunic, — a custom deriving, perhaps, from contact with the East — as also a sort of cloth stocking or legging strapped with leather thongs proceeding from the sandal or or leather shoe, a fashion that is still followed by the mountaineers about Rome. They also had regular leather boots, gauntlets and wallets. They wore helmets in time of war, and on parade, but when following peaceful occupations they made use of caps and fillets.

XIX., XIX. 1., XIX. 2. Screen.

N.º XIX. illustrates certain of these garments: XIX. 1. represents a tunic embroidered with a *clavem* or stripes. XIX. 2, is a tunic embroidered with squares -- like those described in the Ephod — on either shoulder; both these drawings also illustrate the embroideries on other parts of this garment.

XIX. 3. Screen.

XIX. 3. represents a *toga* with *fringed edge*: the *toga* and *pallium* are succeeded in these modern times by shawls, and by the blanket of the Red Indian.

XIX. 4. Screen.

XIX. 4. is a drawing of a knitted woollen sock of mitten shape, thus made to allow the sandal-straps to pass inside the great toe.

XIX. 5. Screen.

XIX. 5. represents a leather slipper.

XIX. 6. Screen.

XIX. 6. is a shoe of the hygienic heel pattern; such as we might wear to-day.

XIX. 7. Screen.

XIX. 7. is a leather boot. The embroidered bands worn on the tunic and the toga in the time of the early Roman Empire, as well as the borders and fringes worn by the Jews, denoted by their size, form and colour the rank and occupation of the wearer, and were etablished by Imperial decrees. Roman citizens alone were allowed to use the various shades of purple; the Senator's distinctive was a broad band or *clavem* which, passing over the shoulder of the tunic, descended before and behind, often reaching below the waist. Equestrian rank was denoted by two narrow strips; the embroidered design on the shirts -- the tradition of which still exists in those worn by the Italian *ciociari* -- were often round or oblong instead of square, in which case the pieces in the four lower corners of the tunic were shaped and designed to correspond with them; at other times the neck-opening was widened and made to descend, like a deep collar, several inches over the back and chest. A band of embroidery or a stripe, either woven in the material or sewn on afterwards, ran round the bottom of the richer tunics which were woven in one piece with an opening through which to pass the head, and were sewn together on each side from the arm-pit to the hem. The toga for a full-grown man was about a yard and a half wide by two yards and a quarter long; it was often fringed or embroidered, or was woven with stripes at the ends or sides; rounds or squares of embroidery to match those on the tunic with which it was worn were also introduced at its corners. The women of the period wore, instead of the toga, an exaggerated veil gracefully draped over the entire figure; this veil was called a *pallium*, and was made of thin delicate material embroidered or woven with fringes or borders, or scattered over with regularly recurring designs of flowers, leaves, or birds, and usually finished with a fringe at the ends.

The garments above described are illustrated in the Italian Lace Exhibit by pieces of embroidery and textiles manufactured and worn by men and women in the first centuries of the Christian Era in the manner above described, rare examples, obtained from Herr. R. Forrer's unique collection of the textiles he found in graves in Achmin — a city on the right bank of the Nile in Upper Egypt, now containing a population of only about 30,000, — of which number 1000 are Coptic Christians — but in classic times it was large, prosperous, and celebrated under the name of Panapolis, and enjoyed special reputation during the Roman Empire as a manufacturing centre of costly stuffs and finely woven linens. — The oldest graves lie about five feet below the level of the ground, and often there are several superimposed, which shews the great antiquity of this burial place; in fact it must have been used at least from the III. century of our Era till the time when Mahometanism had become predominant throughout Egypt. — The graves consist of holes, dug in the sand, in which the body was laid between boards, and they contain every imaginable article of the toilet as well as the implements of various trades.

The stuffs found there consist in gauzes, silks, damasks and satins, made of pure silk or mixed with flax, woollens, linens and gobelin tapestries — and are striped, rainbowed, flowered etc. by means of weaving, embroidery, or stamping. — The embroidery is executed on a ground formed in close textiles by leaving or drawing out the weft for a certain width, and in gauzes and muslins by pushing it apart. — The design was embroidered upon the threads of the warp with a coarse white thread.

XX. Screen.

N.º XX. is a water-colour drawing from the Egyptian Museum in Florence shewing part of a border worked in this way, and which had been sewn on a linen tunic of which a piece still remains as foundation.

XXII. A. Screen.

XXII. A. shews a piece of the same work inserted in the material on the bias. Here we appear to be face to face with *Punto Tirato* or Retcella, but alas, we soon discover that this resemblance is illusory, caused by the gnawing fangs of Time which have eaten away the woollen *filling* made in real Gobelin stitch to form the ground, the white threads having only served to outline the design and to constitute a framework for dividing the colours.

XXI., XXII. B. Screen.

XXII. B. represents XXII. A. filled in with Gobelin stitch:

XXI. shews us the wrong as well as the right side of a piece of finished embroidery.

XXIV. Screen.

XXIV. represents a piece of later embroidery or gobelins of a period at which the white outlining had ceased to be used; the figures in this are roughly shaded, precisely as in the tapestry or the Middle Ages. The above articles date from the fourth to the seventh century of our Era.

We will now examine the real pieces of stuff.

XXV. A. Screen.

XXV. A. is a medallion of embroidery which has lost nearly all its woollen filling, and therefore excellently serves to illustrate the process followed in making trimmings. In order to accelerate the production of the latter, the weaver made strips of belting of the desired width, — notice the selvage on the sides and the raw edge at the ends — and wove a bleached woof into an unbleached twine warp, counting the stitches and so leaving out a perfect oval of twine grounding of the required size and shape on which the embroideress could begin to work without wasting time in drawing out the threads of the material. — One corner is turned over to shew the wrong side of the work, the outlining being executed in a kind of back-stitch.

XXV. B. Screen.

XXV. B. is the piece of linen on which the above embroidery, A. was sewed; the coarse threads are left in it, shewing that, to keep the medallion from slipping while attaching it to the material destined to receive it, it was basted across the middle in both directions, after which it was whipped neatly round the edge, the raw ends being turned in.

XXV. C. Screen.

XXV. C. is part of a medallion of the same design but in better preservation. The ground is filled in with red wool, and the white scrolls and circles with various colours. — In the center of this piece of work is the conventional little bust of Christ with a glory, surrounded by a black border

which is patterned in small crosses of red, green and yellow; this, as is indicated by the scrolls in the design, is early Byzantine work and is graceful
despite the presence of the inartistic little bust.

XXVI. Screen.

XXVI. is the same ornament, introduced in very fine linen in a space
left in the weaving; as in the unembroidered piece of XVIII.B, it is more
antique and artistic in design than XXV.C., being work of the best Roman
period when embroideries were always made with a ground of solid colour,
generally either black, or one of the numerous shades of purple, with white
outlining. The piece is probably a remnant of a woman's tunic manufactured
about 300 A. B.

XXVII. Screen.

XXVII. is of the same period as XXVI. but is of coarser material and
execution, and may have formed the widened shoulder embroidery of a cla-
vem-trimmed tunic; its purple colour denotes the Roman citizenship of the
wearer:

XXVIII. Screen.

XXVIII. is part of a square of stuff woven at the same period, but
the ground is left of warp alone, the weaver having stopped the woof on
each side when he reached the space to be embroidered, thus forming a
selvage. Judging from the wrong side, which is too untidy — owing to the
long threads hanging from it — for that of a toga, this piece of stuff seems
to have formed part of a tunic; the outlining in the embroidery was executed *after* the space had been filled in with the woollen ground; the stitches
resemble those used in outlining Sicilian drawn lace.

XXIX. Screen.

XXIX. is of the same period; it is a black border worked — with equal
neatness on both sides — in a strip of warp left in the weaving of a fine
linen toga. The design represents a grape vine with the white thread worked
in before introducing the coloured wool.

XXX. Screen.

XXX. is a piece of border of more recent execution; it is artistically
drawn, and represents a purple dog, with red tongue and leading strings,
playing in a circle formed by two interlaced scrolls; the angles are filled

48

with red or green leaves. This border probably trimmed the toga of some child, since the effect is very youthful in comparison with all the other pieces in our collection.

XXXI. Screen.

XXXI. and the two following numbers date back at least to the V. century. XXXI is coarsely executed in narrow stripes of dark *ecru* running, at regular intervals, along the length of the white étamine-like material; between these stripes a basket of flowers is worked in parti-coloured wools and without any white outlining. The basket is purple, with yellow and white designs; the flowers are indicated by vermilion and white spots on a dark red ground, surrounded by green leaves. This embroidery must have decorated a woman's toga **or** pallium, and have been repeated **at regular intervals** along the border.

XXXII. A., B., C. Screen.

XXXII. A., B. C. are ends of scarfs, shewing their entire width, belonging to the seventh or eighth century of our era. XXXII. A. ends in a fringe **above which** narrow stripes of red wool are introduced after an inch of **plain** weaving in linen thread; then follow six inches of plain weaving **and** a space of four inches of warp left for the embroidered Gobelin border. This border has a red ground, framed on either side by a black stripe edged with yellow, and dotted with little yellow squares at regular intervals. — Three shields, which may have been coats of arms, divided by rows of a kind of herring-bone stitch in white and yellow are embroidered on the red band; recurring between these are allegorical designs representing the Tree of Life. The middle shield is charged with a green parrot with yellow legs, outlined in black and white, the other two with white lions are outlined in black; everything is upside down, shewing that the embroidery must have been done before the material was **removed from** the loom.

XXXII. B. Screen.

XXXII. B. is a scarf end of coarse muslin, such as is to-day in use in the East. The design is embroidered in the same back-stitch as in the ordinary kind of Oriental reversible needle-work. Its discovery is a treasure trove for our branch of textile art, for it has a border about the edge, overcasting and ornamenting the hem, which very much resembes modern Turkish work, and is the first example we possess of stitches similar to those used in oriental embroidery of which a small, three-cornered piece has been placed beside it.

XXX. C. Screen.

XXXII. C. is woven in the same way as XXXII, A.; the embroidery is however, worked in Gobelin stitch, and imitates the jewelled borders we see on the Byzantine mosaics of this period.

XXXIII. A., B., C. Screen.

XXXIII. A. is a paralellogram of pure Gobelin tapestry sewed on a piece of fine linen, and so cunningly worked with the needle in divers colours that when new it must have been resplendent. Each upper corner of the design contains a duck standing on its tail, with its feet turned to the right and its beak to the left. In the middle of the design is a saint with a sword in his right hand, seated on a throne: along the lower border we discover what, with the aid of a lively imagination, we may suppose to be yellow dogs or lions seated on their haunches. Two oblong bias strips placed at right angles to the saint's neck, and having narrow black borders spotted with yellow, are adorned with four ducks each, all in a row and standing on their tails, with carefully embroidered feet and toes in mid-air to the right of their breasts. — The visitor to the Italian section may not discover all these details for himself, but it is well to know that they exist, as it shews the ludicrous combinations which the debasement of drawing, and its subservience to the frenzy for colour was capable of producing at the epoch of Byzantine supremacy.

XXXIII B. is a piece of belting; both the warp and the woof in it are of a fine indigo colour, embroidered with white thread in a conventional pattern by darning, which produces a pretty effect resembling " Alt Deutsch " work.

XXXIII. C. is a red stripe darned into a coarse muslin and evidently forming the border of a woman's garment. The effect obtained in the treatment of the design also has its counterpart in work of the XV. century in Europe; its particular interest with regard to the subject we are treating lies in the fact that between the rows of darned work the threads of the textile have been removed, and the remaining threads caught together by hemstitching. The corners of the two samples are turned over to shew the work on the wrong side.

XXXIV. Screen.

XXXIV. is interesting, first because stripes of quadruple woof are introduced at regular intervals: secondly because the open warp, which has been made to take the forms of birds and tiny squares, was not picked out but was made to assume these shapes in the weaving: and thirdly because the fringe is hemstitched just as it would be on an article manufactured to-day.

XXXV. Screen.

In XXXV. we have the sheer material we call gauze, so often depicted on vases and monuments as forming the garments of the goddesses
and women of Greece, Etruria and Rome, two of which are reproduced in
XXV. and XXXVII. Homer frequently mentions this gauze: thus in Canto V.
of the Iliad:

> " Pallas disrobes; her radiant veil untied
> With flowers adorned, with art diversified. „

And in Canto VI. id.:

> " The Phrygian Queen to her rich wardrobe went,
> „ Where treasured odours breathed a costly scent:
> „ There lay the vestures of no vulgar art;
> „ Sidonian maids embroidered every part,
> „ Whom from soft Sidon youthful Paris bore
> „ With Helen, touching on the Tyrian shore;
> „ Here as the Queen revolved with careful eyes
> „ The various textures and the various dyes,
> „ She chose a *veil* that shone superior far,
> „ And *glowed refulgent as the morning star.* „

And in the Odyssey he describes it as forming part of the costume
of Ulysses:

> " Fine as a *filmy web* beneath it shone
> „ A vest that dazzled like a cloudless sun. „

Lucian, in recounting the feast offered to Cæsar by Cleopatra, says
that the queen's costume consisted of *wondrous web of thin, transparent
lawn*; this doubtless means a gauze embroidered in silk, like XXXV., which
is unique, and represents two crested birds executed in embroidery such as
is produced to-day in large quantities at Delhi and in other parts of India.
This material may have been imported from that country. Pliny records the
tradition of this kind of garment into Europe, and describes its manfacture
in silk.

XXXVI. Screen.

N.º XXXVI, is a gauze veil made in dark blue wool; it has a fringe
made of the warp twisted and knotted: a white silk and red wool stripe
forms the edge above this fringe, and several other stripes are woven in the
material at regular intervals some of which are embroidered with darned
work in white silk, in letters and geometrical designs, so that what forms

the relief on the right side constitutes the ground on the reverse, as in the netting described at XXXIV. C.

We have now reached the limit of close embroidery, or embroidery without real open work in the design.

XXXVII. A., B., C. Cases.

A Turkish scarf, XXXVII. B., belonging to Herr von Ugon, will be found in the glass cases near the African work. It is of about the same width as the scarfs XXII. A. B. C., and is embroidered with gold and silver and shaded silks on a cotton-muslin ground with the same stitches as are found in Byzantine work; the silver thread draws the light ground together in the hearts of the flowers with the effect of Sicilian point; a scallop in gold thread button-hole stitch runs round the edge and forms a regular needle lace.

XXXVII. A. is a broader scarf belonging to the same exhibitor; it is of the same period but is much more complicated in execution. Hungarian and Roumanian embroidery of the present day have preserved and developed the traditions of this work. The lace about the edge is of a curious pattern, being a kind of Macramé made with the needle.

XXXVII, also belongs to Herr von Ugon's collection; it is the knee-covering of a pair of breeches from the island of Rhodes. The coloured embroidery has the geometrical designs of XXXIV. C. made in the early Sicilian stich, but without the second, smaller one which, used alternately, draws the ground together and forms the open work or small chequers from which the laces with tulle grounds have been evolved. A veritable Reticella in white silk runs between the coloured bands: its stitch is woven upon the threads left by drawing out the woof and is identical with that used in embroidered lacis and in Gobelins embroidery, so that the varied openings and simple stitches of this narrow insertion may serve to bridge the the chasm that lies between the coarse close Gobelin ornaments in dyed wool, and the airy fabrics of Venetian points and guipures.

XXXIX. Screen.

XXXIX. is a veil of antique embroidered muslin such as Turkish ladies are in the habit of keeping within easy reach to throw quickly over their heads on the entrance of a visitor. This veil is a modification of the classic and more voluminous Palia which was evolved from the women's head covering of the time of Moses. The design is thoroughly Jewish or Assyrian in character, with its stiff trees and regular flower-pots disposed in conventional niches with a minaret over each, all done in fine needle-work on a ground of Sicilian point. Pots of lovely silk flowers and baby-trees, worked in exquisite needle Point without any foundation hang all along the edges of this veil, recalling to mind the purple and scarlet pomegranates that hung between the bells at the bottom of Aaron's Ephod. They are made on a narrow, black silk heading and are afterwards sewed onto the veil; the stitch in which they are worked is the same as that used in the Ogowé cap: they are essentially *Punto in Aria*, and in consequence real lace.

XL. Cases.

This work is complicated in design and difficult of execution; it is still made in Turkey and always imitates flowers, leaves, and bell-shaped birds or fruits. The Turkish Ambassador in Rome — who with kindly interest obtained for us the seven pretty examples we exhibit in N. XL. — informed us that the Turkish word used to designate this lace is the same that is used for fuchsias, hare bells and other pendent flowers, as well as for pendent ornaments and earrings.

XLI. A. and B. Cases.

XLI. A. and B. are other pieces of Turkish lace which belong to Lady Layard; the material is white silk, and they were made according to the old Turkish system in the embroidery schools founded under her Ladyship's auspices in Constantinople. In these laces the garlands and sprays of flowers are made to interlace, while preserving the bell-like characteristic of the antique from which their designs are adopted.

Modern Turkish ladies dress like their European sisters, and the real and imitation lace they wear is all sent with their toilettes from Paris; but these veils and scarfs, which have resisted the innovations of modern fashion, are, on arriving, still trimmed with narrow Turkish edgings. — The Constantinople school of embroidery has revived many old stitches and designs, and tends to keep up the artistic traditions of Turkish needle-work, and its influence is greatly appreciated by English visitors and tradesmen.

It seems to me that, on emerging from the barbarous state attendant on the decline and fall of the Western Empire, the peoples of Europe began to realize the attraction of riches obtained by peaceful barter and sale instead of being snatched with rude violence from weaker neighbours, to be shortly again lost by the same lawless means; and the desire of artistically adorning their churches — no longer threatened with perpetually recurring pillage and destruction — returned with the realization of stable fortune.

Hidden away from the din and clatter of arms raised by the boisterous race which had poured out from the North and over-run fair Italy, the sister arts of embroidery and lace-making practised by the cunning daughters of the needle were still to be found in the dwellings of the Jewish and Oriental merchants who had settled on every part of the Mediterranean Coast. Rich and rare mediæval silk laces, unequalled even by the most celebrated specimens preserved in the Christian churches and cathedrals, are still to be found in the old Italian synagogues. — The energy that predominates in the European character belonged alike to Jewish teachers and to Christian pupils, and caused them to exercise their vivid imagination in the development of these arts into products of rare beauty, whereas the embroiderers of Oriental races have ever been governed by a conservatism which has caused them to remain unaltered for centuries, thus preserving for us the type of needle-work that was used on Aaron's Ephod three thousand years ago.

All the silk passementerie, the gold, silver and polychrome lace of the early Renaissance were made by the Jews, who were also the chief producers of other varieties of lace in Spain where this people exhibited much greater luxury in the appointments of their places of worship, as well as in their homes, than did the Christians.

When they were reduced to penury by perpetual persecution and confiscation, and when they were finally expelled from Spain, they made use of their arts to maintain themselves in their places of refuge, and as there was a constantly increasing demand for trimmings and laces all over Southern Europe, they employed apprentices — who soon became skilled workwomen — to help them to execute the numerous orders they received. These pupils became teachers in their turn and spread the knowledge of and taste for these fabrics, and when another wave of persecution came, this time turned against the protestants, a great many of them, — who for the same reason as the Spanish Jews had become diligent lace makers — emigrated to England, to protestant Germany and to Sweden, carryng with them the tradition of the art ever further a field.

Perhaps, like many ceremonies in the Christian Church, the custom of using fringes and laces on the vestments and church linen may have been imitated from the Jewish ritual, though, when intolerance and cruelty towards the Hebrew Race prevailed in the Middle Ages, the Christian women developed new varieties of lace, their piety being intensified by horror at the thought of decking the altar consecrated to the Holy Trinity with the work of unbelievers. — The art, once developed, became a source of amusement and rivalry in the narrow lives of cloistered women, and they dedicated all those energies which were deprived of natural outlets to the invention of new stitches and more wonderful traceries, until the superb Venetian point laces and needle paintings sprang into existence. But whence came Bobbin or Pillow Lace? When was it invented? A blue lace bound the diadem on the brow of the Jewish High Priest: this lace must have been not a simple cord — but a flat fabric — for tradition says it was *wrought in colour*, and fringed at the ends, hence it was probably worked with bobbins.

Writers about laces have filled pages with speculations, quoted from Moses and the Prophets, and ended with the assertion that the first positive evidence of the existence of Bobbin lace is an Italian document of the XV century — of which we shall later on reproduce a part, — and a Dutch wood-cut of the XVI century; and this while the sands of Egypt and the rich soil of Italy were reserving their evidence.

Like the Tartars of to-day, the Phrygians, Assyrians, Persians and other peoples of South-Western Asia all wore conical caps, and introduced their use into the countries to which they emigrated, or with which they traded. The Phrygians, who very early over-ran Northern Greece, introduced into that country the use of woollen caps during the winter, and of flax nets or conical fillets in summer. Caps became the fashion in Egypt with the introduction of the religion of Mythras by the Persians.

This form of head covering was considered a sign of freedom, and no slaves were allowed to wear it. The ceremony of freeing a slave consisted precisely in placing a red cap on his head and acclaiming him as an equal. This cap was sometimes truncated like the *fez*, and in this form it must have given origin to that Mahometan head covering, just as in the original pointed shape it became the model of the Doge's *Corno*, as also of the Liberty caps placed on the heads of Britannia and her fair daugther Columbia.

In the days of the French craze for classicism the Republicans re-dyed this emblem in the blood of aristocrats, and waving it aloft as their standard, acclaimed it with its original name of " Phrygian „. — Caps of this shape must have become the fashion at the time when the Persian religion of Mythras gained ascendency among civilized nations just before he Christian era, when its communistic tenets resisted the Christian religion in Rome even after the general conversion of the Latins, and had so strongly impressed the popular mind that some of its forms have survived in the present rules of Free-Masonry.

XLII. Screen.

N.º XLII. is a drawing taken from a bas-relief in the Louvre, and represents these caps as worn by the priests of Mythras. We may iudge from the numbers of fragments found in the graves in Panapolis that they were very much in fashion.

XLV. Screen.

N.º XLV. is a section of a truncated cap; the little sketches A. B. C. D. shew the way in which they were worn, and that their shape must have greatly resembled the knitted and crocheted ones worn by our own young people. — The winter caps were made of red wool, or were striped in colours, while a cord ran round the edge to tighten them if necessary.

XLVI. A. Screen and XLVII. A., B,. C. idem.

XLVI. and XLVII. A, are also parts of these caps, while XLVI. and XLVII. B. are new pieces that were copied from them by the young lace-makers in the school at Brazzà. XLVII. C. is a photograph of some fragments numbered 12, 15, 16 of the same kind of work. These caps are neither knitted nor crocheted, for the meshes do not consist of loops; neither are they embroidered, for the threads are continuous and we find no knots. All the learned professors who have seen them unite in saying they were interlaced by fingers, but *how* they cannot tell, as they have found no lace-bobbins in connection with them: still they were made with bobbins, since, without a reel at the end of the threads to shorten them to the desired length for working, — by winding them round something heavy — it would be quite impossible to avoid most hopeless tangles and interminable series of Gordian knots. Allowing for the difference in wool, and for the regularity produced by constantly working at the same design, the copies made by the inexperienced Italian children in the lace school are not bad; the girls worked by interlacing two bobbins instead of the four that are at present used in the manufacture of lace, and they had to twirl the bobbins from left to right, which is the contrary of the twist now given and very aggravating to modern workers.

XLVII. B., C., D. Screen.

XLVII. B. C. D. shew the manner of wearing these caps and the summer thread linen nets in ancient times, as also a Neapolitan fisherman with one of these same caps which are still worn by men of his class along the coasts of Italy, Spain and France.

XLVIII. Screen.

XLVIII. is a perfectly preserved quarter of one of these thread nets bound with red wool.

XLIX. Screen.

XLIX. is a quarter of a lace net executed in a different design.

L. Screen.

L. is a well preserved and fresh looking half net of more elaborate lace, executed with remarkable precision.

LI. Cases.

LI. is unique of its kind, being a complete lace net or bonnet made of soft thread with red binding: it has been placed on a barber's poll to shew how these nets were worn.

LII. Cases.

LII. gives an idea of a classic lace cushion with the same kind of lace mounted on it in process of execution by means of wooden bobbins copied from the bone ones of that epoch; for, *mirabile dictu*, last May (1892) while we in Rome were planning our Exhibit, Professor E. Brizio, Director of the Etruscan Museum in Bologna, was excavating among the ruins of the old Roman town of Claterna, ten miles from Bologna on the Emilian Way, and which S. Ambrose describes as already ruinous in A. D. 393. Here, at the bottom of a filled-up well, of Roman construction, the Professor found a quantity of small, solid, long, wasp-shaped cylinders, the use of which he could not understand, as they resembled none of the Roman implements with which he was acquainted; this was quite natural, considering that lace-making by no means formed part of his professional acquirements or teaching, and moreover that he lives in a part of the world where lace is not produced; the mystery was, however, soon cleared up for him; one day he happened to pass a bric-a-brac shop in the window of which was a completely equipped lace-maker's pillow which attracted his attention; he at once recognized that the bobbins hanging thereto were the exact counterparts of his curious bone cylinders, and therefore felt convinced that he beheld the solution of the mystery which surrounded not only them but also another similar instrument which had been for years in the Bologna Museum. Another proof which of course neither he, nor anyone who had not been accustomed to lace-making could have recognized lay in the fact that these ancient bobbins were found in couples, or in groups of couples, with the exception of one, which was reduced to fragments. The Professor kindly furnished me with fac-similia of these valuable documents in the history of lace making, and they are shewn under numbers

LIII. and LIV.

LIV. A. is a double-hooked crochet needle which has, for many years, formed part of the collection in the Bologna Museum; its origin is quite unknown, although supposed to be Greek. — Cavaliere Augusto Castellani's superb collection of Etruscan and Roman Antiquities contains many of these bobbins, but they were purchased by him, among numbers of other Roman relics, in the old-fasioned way, without enquiry as to the circumstances attending their discovery and they therefore attracted no particular attention; indeed, owing to their shape, they were thought to be a kind of *stylus*, for writing on a waxed surface, the round head being taken for a classic rubber for cancelling errors. Signor Castellani however became of another opinion when he observed that the knobs were often sharp or jagged, and that the end which should — if a stylus — have been pointed, was usually as blunt as the knob.

The pioneers of pillow lace in the XVII. century found the semibar-
barous peasant and fisherwomen in the Hartz mountains and on the coast of
the North Sea, making *elastic caps and nets* for the men by plaiting threads
together by means of rude bone bobbins, used by twos instead of by fours,
thus following the same process the Brazzà lace girls were obliged to adopt
in imitating the Panopolis lace nets. History adds that these women learned
the art of complicated lace making with surprising rapidity, and quickly
became proficient and artistic workwomen.

The Neapolitan fishermen and the Spanish muleteers of to-day both
" on and off the stage ", cover their locks with pointed nets made of red
silk or wool, and gallants and pages in the time of the Troubadours wore
them, as we see in portraits and historical paintings. — In England the old
lace makers in Devonshire call their bobbins *bones*, because they say that
formerly they were made of small pieces of sheep's bones, and owing to
this they call their bobbin lace *bone lace*. The early annals of England and
of other countries mention teaching new stitches and designs, and contain
notes on the importation of clever teachers from other parts to instruct the
natives in new stitches and fresh designs, but not with the object of founding a new industry. — We may thus consider pillow-lace to be a direct
inheritance from classic times ; an inheritance which, though possessed of rich
possibitities, long lay fallow, till in the XV. and XVI. centuries it was found
of easy cultivation and productive of most gorgeous blossoms. — Perhaps a
longer and closer study than is possible during the few months at our command, in which to prepare this exhibit, would bring to light more facts about
the origin of this art, reaching even still further into the remote Past.

After the long journeys we have made far afield in search of the earliest
proofs of the manufacture of lace, we will now enter the fair garden in which
the splendid flowers and luxuriant grasses of Nature have been transformed by
the magic of gentle fingers into beautiful, curious, and everlasting hybrids, that
European kingdom in which the ideal and the material are continually at war
and yet exert a happy reaction on each other, and once in Italy we need
not again leave that sunny land, for busy merchants will bring to its markets
the produce of other countries and will recount narratives of what they saw
there. But before crossing the threshold of the Middle Ages we must take
one more peep below the soil and see what remains of the Umbrians and
Etrurians, of the civilized inhabitants of Italy when the land was young.

LV. Wall.

LV. represents an Umbrian cinerary urn of the VIII. century B. C.
These urns were always covered with a veil or cloth, and the rude drawings that decorate them usually represent a net with dentated edges, trimmed
with tassels, and much resembling the nets used in the well-known Gitana
or Spanish Gipsy costume.

LVI. Screen.

LVI. is the design of an archaic Greek figure, with borders painted on the garments to represent coloured embroidery. Some writers on lace speak of such borders as evidencing the use of bobbin lace at that period, but it strikes me that this is a weak foundation on which to build such an argument.

LVII. Screen.

LVII. is a figure of Minerva, copied from the painting on one of the Parthenopean vases, of about the IV. century B. C.

XXXVIII. Screen.

XXXVIII. is a charmingly graceful figure of the same goddess, beautifully drawn, from an exquisite vase in the Etruscan Museum in Rome : it most decidedly appears to reproduce a kind of open work that adorns the edge of her lighter garments. Besides this figure, on the same card, is a bifurcated netting needle, natural size, [exactly like those which are found in great numbers in the Tiber, and which must have been used in making fine hair-nets.

LVIII. Screen,

LVIII. represents a gold bracelet or cuff of the VI. or VII. century B. C. The original of this bracelet was evidently copied from needle-work consisting of drawn work alternated with linen bands; it was found in the Vetulonian excavations in 1890, and is now in the Etruscan Museum in Florence. The Director of that Institution, the first of its kind in Italy, told me that ample proofs exist of the use of delicate embroidery, open work and nets for the adornment of apparel and the toilette by Greeks and Etruscans, but he is of the opinion that pillow lace, made with bobbins, was unknown to them. While talking with this Professor in his study, I observed there a Greek platter, of the end of the V. century, made of rare white patrina and adorned with the figure of *Arachne,* the rash nymph who dared to compete with Minerva in the arts of the loom and the needle, and who was, in consequence, transformed by the irate goddess into a spider and condemned for ever to weave those magic circles, those airy webs which are rivalled by the lace fabrics produced by human fingers.   *

This Greek legend may be based on some fact adorned by the romantic imagination of a bygone poet, or it may have originated in metaphor alone : in any case it inspired the charming odes of the Renaissance, in which the poets unanimously attribute the invention of embroidery to Minerva, while they ascribe that of the subtler and more delicate art of lace making

to Arachne. They entwine, in their lays, the ancient Greek fable with the
arts, and with the designations of lace stitches with quaint effect, even as
the fair fingers whose praises they sang so deftly interlaced the threads of
silk and gold.

Thus Agnolo Firenzuolo who, in about 1520, wrote his *Elegia sopra
un collaretto*, describes, with loving, lingering detail, a piece of lace that had
caught his fancy:

> *Questo collar scolpé da donna mia*
> This collar was sculptured by my lady
> *Di basso rilevar ch'Arachne mai*
> In bas reliefs such as Arachne
> *E chi la vinse non faria più bello.*
> And she who conquered her could ne'er excel.
> *Mira quel bel fogliame ch'un Acanto*
> Look on that lovely foliage, like an Acanthus,
> *Sembra che sopra un mur vada carponi.*
> Which o'er a wall its graceful branches trails.
> *Mira quel fior ch'un candido ne cade*
> Look on those lovely flowers of purest white
> *Vicino al seme ap'ar la bacia l'altro.*
> Which, near the pods that open, hang in harmony.
> *Quel cordiglin, ch'l legan d'ognitorno*
> That little cord that binds each one about
> *Come ci levan ben! mostrando ch'ella*
> How it projects! proving that she who wrought
> *E la vera maestra di quest'arte.*
> Is very mistress of this art.
> *Come son ben compartiti quei punti!*
> How well distributed are all those points!
> *Vè come son rigual quei bottoncelli.*
> See the equality of all those little buds
> *Come s'alzano in guisa d'un bel colle,*
> Which rise like many fair proportioned hills,
> *L'un come l'altro ....*
> One like the other ....
> *Questi merli di man, questi trafori*
> This hand made lace, this open work
> *Fece pur ella, e questa punta a spina*
> Is all produced by her, this herring bone
> *Che mette in mezzo questo cordonatto.*
> Which in the midst holds down a little cord.
> *Ella il fè pure: ella lo fece*
> Was also made by her; all wrought by her.

LXVII. Screen.

LXVII. and the following numbers are specimens of the various implements made use of in spinning, embroidery and lace making in all times.

LVII. Wall.

LVII is a distaff, used for spinning flax, and was made by a peasant
of Moruzzo, the township in the Province of Friuli in which the Castello di
Brazzà is situated. — This distaff ends in a coloured ball, and is most beautifully and artistically carved, the inspiration of the original designs having
come from the heart of the carver who made it as a gift for his future
wife; on it he has represented their persons, their homes and their hearts;
four-leaved clovers, horse-shoes, and an infinity of other emblems of love
and fortune; pendent from it is the spindle, and it is hung to the wall by
means of the wrought brass pins by which our peasant women support the
distaff, utilizing their belts as rests while spinning as a they walk, or when
following their sheep to pasture.

LXVI. Wall.

LXVI. was carved by the same man later in life as a present to his
daughter; the hearts are therefore represented as having flowered, truly a
very pretty and poetic conceit, while the point consists of the brass fork
used in spinning wool. — These two simple implements, rendered so beautiful by the hand of love, form a true illustration of the affectionate character and devotion to the beautiful that distinguishes the Italians; hence it
is that the graceful arts of lace making and straw plaiting come naturally to
every daughter of the people.

LVIII. Cases.

1. 2. 3. 4. 5. 7. 8. 9. are specimens of spindle whirls used in spinning
by hand in different parts of the world; they date from the Stone Age and
its Lake Dwellers down to the present day. The spinning-wheel was invented
and adopted in Europe at an early date, but the women in certain parts of
Italy still make use of the old-fasioned distaff, which enables them to spin
at odd times when it would be impossible to use a wheel.

LVIII. 6. Cases.

LVIII. 6. was found in Greece, and is a complete ivory spindle of classic
times; such specimens as this are extremely rare.

LVIII. 10. Cases.

LVIII. 10. is the only ancient wooden spindle with earthenware whirl attached to it as yet discovered; it was found at Achmim Panapolis and may have served to spin the flax of which some of our specimens are woven.

LX. Cases.

LX. 1. to 23. are Peruvian specimens, and are particularly interesting as they date from an epoch long anterior to the event we are now celebrating: the discovery of America by Columbus. They are also especially interesting in connection with our subject, as the mummies with which they were found were swathed with the same description of textiles as those discovered at Achmim, thus shewing that a kindred civilization existed in the *New* World at an early date, since the evidence afforded by the one necropolis corroborates and completes that of the other. Here we have spindles, knitting and other needles with the yarn still on them, and with small cases to protect their points; here is also an ordinary ball of blue cotton which might have come from the work-basket of any modern housewife.

LX. B. Cases.

LX. B. is a *fac-simile* of the already mentioned double hooked crochet needle preserved in the Etruscan Museum in Bologna.

LXI. A. B., C., D. Cases.

LI. is a sketch of prehistoric needles by Herr R. Forrer. It will be noticed that A. and B., — natural size — which were taken from the homes of the Cave Dwellers at Thaijngen, are more perfect in form than is D. a bone needle — also natural size — of the Stone Age from the Lake-dwellings at Banschanze on Lake Zurich. The Cave Dwellers were in many things more civilized than were the Lake Dwellers their successors, and must have embroidered on leather with quills and grasses as their prototypes the Esquimaux and the Alaskan Indians do to-day

LXI. D. Cases.

LXI. D is a drawing of a wooden hook preserved in the National Museum in Zurich. It has a disc as handle, evidently added to facilitate the boring of holes in skins or textiles, while the hook served to draw through the thread necessary to form a seam or fringe.

LXII. Cases.

LXII. consists of nine antique needles. N.ᵒˢ 1., 2., 3., 4. are specimens of the early borers called *prieme*, the use of which preceded that of needles as we now know them; and as 1 and 2 are made of rudely carved bone and date from the Lake-dwellings of the Stone Age, N.ᵒˢ 3. and 4. are of bronze, and are from the Lake dwellings of the Bronze Age. N.º 5. is a knobbed *prieme*, or eyeless needle of horn, from the Lake dwellings of the Stone Age; a hole having been bored, this implement served to draw through the thread tied to its knobbed head. N.º 6. is the same kind of instrument from the Lake-dwellings of the Bronze Age. N.º 7. is a coarse, round eyed needle of the Bronze Age, from Italy. N.º 8. is a fine, long-eyed needle of the Bronze Age from the Lake dwellings of *Grosserhafen* on Lake Zurich.

LXIII. Cases.

LXIII. is a drawing of a most elegant needle stuck through a coil of gold thread; it was found in a tomb at Visentium and is now in the Etruscan Museum in Florence.

LXV. Cases.

Under this head are exhibited six plaster fac-similes of the Roman bobbins found last May — 1893 — by Prof. Brizio at Claterna, which I have already mentioned and which are now in the Bologna Museum; the seventh and smallest is the one which previously existed there. Finally, there are four wooden bobbins, such as are used in the great centers of Italian Lace making, viz. Venice, Genoa, and Cantù near Milan, as also one of the covered kind used in Saxony which has been adopted in the schools at Brazzà because it keeps the thread cleaner.

In closing this division of our book, which treats exclusively of the production of woman's agile fingers when the art of needle making was in its infancy, we present a little child's sock of rare value though apparently worthless:

LVIII. Cases.

LVIII. is the earliest known specimen of knitting, an only sock found in Achmim Panopolis; it is ribbed and striped in red, purple and black with great neatness and loving care for the protection of the little foot in winter, and is so perfectly preserved that one might doubt its authenticity did not the divided toes and seamless heel — the instep being seamed instead — prove it to have been made to wear with a sandal, of which the strap must have worn the holes existing between the toes and the instep at least one thousand five hundred years ago.

As we look on this most ancient baby sock, this little relic so long preserved in the vast ocean of Egyptian sands to be at length cast up for our instruction, and to shew us that the world — in some things — has not so much changed after all, we realize that loving mothers span and knitted to keep their children warm, and that little ones ran and jumped and wore out clothes and patience then just as they do now. Meditating on this we cannot but feel a great sympathetic tenderness well up in our hearts for those long past generations; the dust takes shape, the dry bones are again clothed with life, and the little Christian lads of Panapolis, clattering through the great gates, or off to school with carefully sandalled feet plainly rise before the Mind's eye; their agile bodies are clothed in tunics and warm togas trimmed with pretty designs illustrative of thoughts pleasing to children, while their heads are covered with bright, snug woollen caps, and each boy, with strapped tablets slung across a shoulder, gives himself an air of importance and manliness though his young mind is much more intent on fun and frolic and tricks innumerable than on the difficult passages in his Commentaries of Julius Cæsar, on his Latin Grammar, or his Greek translation.

C.A.S.a. Hüffer 1898.

500 B.C. to 400 B.C.
Pallas Athene on a Greek vase.
in the
Etruscan Museum at Villa Giulio, Rome.

500. A. D.

The Empress Theodora, a fragment, from the mosaics
in the Basilica of St Vitale, Ravenna.

Part III.

The Renaissance.

The word *renaissance* (literally rebirth) is accepted as the definition of that awakening of the European mind to the beauties in nature, art and literature from the profound sleep and troubled dreams of superstition, interrupted by the long nightmares of barbarian and gothic invasion which followed upon the fearful orgies in which the Roman Empire expired.

The Christian Church preserved a tradition of the Past in its teaching and decorations, but the heavenly flame of art was so buried beneath the ashes of strife, controversy and narrow-mindedness that the feeble spark which perpetuated its eternal fire was unrecognizable.

In Byzantium alone it flickered up a little amid gorgeous costumes and decorations of church and court which warmed the imagination; and here as in Sicily — which, owing to its insular form and its Southern position suffered less severely from invasions — we find that the gentle art of lace-making continued.

When the Saracens conquered northern Africa, Sicily and Spain, they caused the inhabitants to instruct them, as well as assist them in producing and perfecting articles for which they were already celebrated.

LXX. Screen.

N.º LXX. from A. to J. inclusive, consist of a few precious rags from an Hyspano-Moresque tomb of the eleventh or twelfth century. They fill the void between the lace caps from Achmim-Panopolis and the first examples of Venetian work, and give us the earliest piece of point lace made entirely with a needle and thread without other material used as a foundation. These samples are in a much worse state of preservation and are much more fragile than those from Achmim, being apparently records of a more remote date, but this condition is produced by the difference of climate.

LXX. A. Screen.

LXX. A. is a piece of lace knotted as in *punto in aria*, and made entirely with the needle out of linen thread, waxed to stiffen it, and wound with gold foil; it forms a quarter of a head-dress.

LXX. B., C. Screen.

LXX. B. is a piece of red silk ribbon used to cover the seams of the above mentioned head-dress, and is braided in fine gold or silver thread spun with linen or cotton as is done in the East today. The design of the braiding is roughly sketched by the side of the ribbon, as is also that of the broader ribbon, LXX. C., used to edge the head-dress.

LXX. E. Screen.

LXX. E. is a piece of the finest gauze veiling woven of silk or flax; it was evidently used under the head-dress and allowed to float loose over the hair and shoulders so as to be drawn across the face when desired.

LXX. F. Screen.

LXX. F. is a piece of the border of such a veil, wrought in silver, with little groups of tiny silver tassels at regular intervals; this must have had a charming effect in the sunlight when all was new, white and dazzling.

LXX. H. Screen.

LXX. H. is a piece of thin material striped in silver and gold, such as we call *bayadère* stuff, and may have formed the skirt or shawl of this costume.

LXX. J. Screen.

LXX. J. is as a piece of the same kind of material bordered with a very fine fringe, and must have formed part of a scarf or sash.

LXX. I. Screen.

LXX. I. is a piece of fine, thin cloth of gold.

LXX. G. Screen.

LXX. G. is a piece of real bobbin lace composed of fibre such as was made everywhere in the islands and on the northern coast of the Mediterranean for centuries; it shews a great advance in workmanship from the lace of Achmim-panopolis, for here the bobbins are used in pairs instead of singly, just as every lace maker twirls them today.

LXX. D. Screen.

In the little stetch LXX. D. we have the whole head-dress reconstructed in its bright original colours, and the mind at once reverts to the Crusades and Richard Cœur de Lion, Saladin, and the fair women made so popular by Sir Walter Scott in his novel of Ivanhoe; and as we continue to gaze these heroes and heroines of a bygone age become materialised and move and breathe in actual reality, called into life by these old moorish rags which cause us to realize that with all the riches and barbaric splendour, movement and strife of that epoch, the gentle art of lace-making continued to develope.

Photographs of Ravenna, with Countess Pasolini's laces from the school of Coccolia. Cases.

Under the last of the Western Emperors, the Goths and the Byzantines, Rome was abandoned as the capital, and the seat of government in Italy was transferred to the more easily fortified sea-port of Ravenna. In the mosaics which adorn this city's unique Basilicas, which were constructed in the VI. century, are found the only remains of European Art of that period; and it will be seen from the photographs exhibited by Countess Pasolini with the laces from her school at Coccolia, that the Empress Theodora and the ladies who formed her court wore costumes composed of the same stuffs as the fragments from Achmim. One of the ladies in particular carries a worked and fringed veil over her arm, resembling those still in use in Turkey, which is interesting as illustrating our special branch of textile art.

LXXI. Screen.

LXXI. is a narrow piece of blue bobbin lace of which three examples only are known to exist in Italy. It was sent in the Eleventh Century from Constantinople to Spezia, then known as *Luni*. The blue square mesh ground is made entirely by bobbins, and is the same as that of all old Italian and Sicilian lace resembling net.

It is embroidered, with little white birds made in the same darning stitch that was used in the Gobelins style embroidery formed at Achmim. This kind of lace must have been the *Lacinia* of the Latins (from which the English term Lace is derived) and was in general use in the Twelfth and Thirteenth centuries. References in old books are constantlly found to blue " *borders* „ or " *friezes* „ embroidered in white birds and lions, which indicates this kind of work.

LXXII. Cases.

N.º LXXII. is an altar cloth trimmed with a variety of this blue lace embroidered in white, exibited, as well as many of the following examples, by M.rs Arthur Bronson of Venice; In it the design is of the Fifteenth Century and the bobbin ground (called *maglia quadra*) and the embroidery are much more roughly executed than N.º LXXI; it has pretty blue and white antique pillow lace " *campane* „ sewn on the edge. The mixing of two or more colors was very fasionable, as were all the *polychrome* or divers-coloured laces in the Fifteenth Century. The perfection of the edging and the negligence in the execution of the Byzantine lace in N.º LXXI. prove the change of style which had occurred before its manufacture, for in the Fifteenth century this lace, which could but produce a stiff effect, rapidly lost ground before the newer and more varied and graceful trimmings composed of embroidered net " *punto a groppo* „ now called Macramé and complicated bobbin lace.

The following are examples of Byzantine lace or " *Maglia quadra* „ and shew what rich effect could be produced in this simple kind of work with symmetrical designs and a happy blending of materials and colors.

D. Cases.

N.º D. is made with a blue silk ground embroidered in buff silk and white thread; it belongs to Signora Antonia Costa of Rome, as does

CCCCLXXXVIII. Cases.

N.º CCCCLXXXVIII. a piece made all in white linen thread, and which was sewed on to the end of a towel.

LXXXVI. Cases.

N.º LXXXVI. is the same kind of lace producing a very different effect, since the ground is made of aloe thread dyed brown and embroidered in " *punto a sacchetti* „ or square point, with an unconventional pattern executed in silks and exquisitely tinted in browns and heliotrope greens and yellows.

LXXVIII. Cases.

N.º LXXVIII. belongs to M.rs Bronson. The ground is made with remarkably soft écru thread and embroidered with " *punto a spina* „ or " herringbone stitch „ in delicate buffs yellows and peacock blues and greens; along the edge runs a most interesting antique and rare polychrome " *campane* „ lace of fine silk, this repeats the colours and the design of the wider lace and was evidently made on purpose to edge it.

CCCXXXIX. Screen.

N.º CCCXXXIX. is an interesting sample of the same, dating, to judge from the design, from the Twelfth or Thirteenth Century, and is embroidered in red and green silk.

CCCXLI. Screen.

N.º CCCXLI. is embroidered in cream and blue silk, and dates from the Fourteenth Century.

CCCXLVII. Screen.

N.º CCCXLVII. is embroidered in red silk and belongs to the same period.

CCCLV. and CCCLVII. Screen.

The design in N.ᵒˢ CCCLV. and CCCLII. indicates work of the early part of the Sixteenth Century. Byzantine lace was also made in a modified form entirely with bobbins and fine white thread, and was composed of narrow stiffly flowered bands with a close ground, ornamented by the simple designs left in open work.

XCV. Screen.

The sample, N.º XCV. and the frill in the pink and silver brocaded babycap, as well as the following

CXXX. Cases.

N.º CXXX. (of the Sixteenth Century) are of this lace; it was used throughout Europe to trim baby clothes, and is still to be found on baptismal garments — such as this brocaded cap — which have been religiously preserved in certain old families on the Continent and in England from generation to generation. M.ʳˢ Bury Palliser, in her celebrated book on lace, speaks of this as well as of " blue wedding lace „ made at Coventry, in England, during the Middle Ages and distributed to all the members of a bridal party. She quotes an account of Queen Elizabeth's visit to Kenilworth, in which the youths of the parish are described as walking in front of the procession, carrying branches of fresh broom and wearing " *blue bridal lace* „ as if they were grooms-men at a wedding. With the spread of puritanism and of the harsh decrees it inspired, this old custom, like many others, died out in England, as did also the manufacture of the celebrated blue thread in Coventry. No relics of this lace now remain, but it must have resembled the above examples.

In this case, as in many others, we find proofs of the much earlier Renaissance of the arts in Italy than in England, embroidery alone excepted; this is explained by the fact that a powerful, unbroken tradition remained in the English convents of the artistic needle-work learned from the Phrygians, so that the " *opus phrygianum* „ of the ancients was merged in the celebrated and beautiful " *opus anglicanum* „. The coldness of the climate tended to keep the women at home, and make them alive to the attractions of a sedentary occupation which they could follow beside the hearth, and it naturally caused them to prefer embroidery to lace; airy open-work and transparent fabrics were not suited to their cold, sunless, stonebuilt homes, either for household or personal linen, until time and fashion introduced luxury in the shape of collars, frills and cuffs as adornments to neck and sleeves; these becoming objects being purely accessories of the toilet, the volume and not the quality of which could affect physical comfort.

The first examples of lace and *punto tagliato* in England, such as the shroud of St. Cuthbert who was buried in Durham Cathedral in the Twelfth century, his vestments which are preserved in the library of the Chapter, and the open work represented on monuments, all belong to ecclesiastics and may have been brought from Italy as attributes of Church ritual in exchange for the English embroideries so much prized by the Popes and Cardinals in Rome.

We find however that in 1363, under Edward IV. gold and silk laces trimmed the garments of the laity, for an edict which that monarch then promulgated, forbade their use. They were all imported from Italy, and Richard III, at his coronation in 1438, wore a robe of crimson satin laced with two bands of gold and silk *passement* which had been made in Venice on purpose for that occasion.

The Queen of the Adriatic, owing to her commercial intercourse with Byzantium and the Orient was, throughout the Middle Ages, the most luxurious and refined city of Europe, and from a very early date in her existence minute descriptions of costumes, with the prices paid for their component parts were noted in documents carefully preserved in her State Archives. Thus in 1219, we learn from an old account-book that tailors charged twice as much for a border of needle work, called " *fregio* „ or " *frixatura* „ as they did for one of fine fur, which indicates that the work must have been elaborate.

Frequent allusions to various kinds of trimmings are found in the registers of the Venetian Customs offices of the Fourteenth Century, as well as in the account books and records of law suits and wills belonging to private families. In the earliest mosaics of the Basilica of St. Mark they are also rudely represented on the garments of grotesque saints and mortals; they are also reproduced, with minute faithfulness of detail in the gracefully executed miniatures which enrich the manuscripts of that period.

LXXXIX. Screen.

N.° LXXXIX. is taken from a manuscript of the Thirteenth Century containing the statutes and byelaws of the guild of Bolognese bakers; it represents an angel presenting St. Mary Magdalen, who is kneeling in her hermitage, with a scarf or toga edged with a blue lace border and fringe.

CXIII. Screen.

N.° CXIII. consists of four sketches taken from the illuminated headings, dating from 1439-1455, of the " Rotuli „ or rolls of the University which are preserved in the archives of Bologna. In them the bishop Petronius (her patron saint and martyr), is represented in full canonicals with his right hand raised in the act of blessing the University, whilst in his left he holds the walled city, recognizable in the exaggerated representations of the Towers of Garisenda and the Asinelli. His mantle is edged with fur, and the deep trimming on his glove and sleeve illustrates the lace of the period, Reticella, which must have just come into fashion and have deeply impressed the limner; for in the earlier and later Rotuli, though the execution of the painting is more artistic and the designs are more beautiful and floreate, we do not find the lace distinctly represented. These Rotuli are written on parchment, superbly illuminated, and form an almost complete series from 1438 to 1799, besides a few scattered numbers of the Fourteenth Century. They have never been published, although they constitute an exhaustive and unequalled illustration of miniature painting in Italy. These rolls contain the list of those persons, for celebrated women as well as men figure among the lecturers, who were called by the Rector, with the approbation of the civic authorities, to read on or teach various subjects which, with the hours allotted to each, are minutely detailed; two rolls were issued every year, one for the " Jurists " and one for the " Artists. „

In 1347 people still called gowns tunics, and several for women and children are described as " laboratum ad intavos, „ i. e. open or carved-work, from which punto tagliato originated.

Others are mentioned as trimmed with an exaggerated quantity of gold, silver, pearl or glass buttons and richly wrought button holes.

The sleeves were the most elaborate part of the costume and reached to an enormous size, vying with the fashion of today; they were loaded with buttons and loops innumerable, and profuselly trimmed with gold and beaded " Tressas „ or tressed work, which can have been no other than a kind of gimp or passement. One tunic in particular is described as having a " low-cut body „, the first, I find noted, and the usual rich sleeves; trains or trailing skirts are also mentioned as forming part of the women's costumes of this period.

Until the end of the Fourteenth Century these superfluous buttons, jewelled borders and fur linings continued to be the fashion despite the constant edicts published against their abuse, such as the one of 1299 limiting the price of borders to 5 *Lire di piccoli* per ell; and it must have been their costliness and uncomfortable weight, combined with the fear of prosecution that caused gold, silver and clinquant (plated metal) passements, lace and open work insertions to replace them.

The demand for every kind of trimming at this period was so great that their manufacturers became rich and powerful, so that in 1343 they separated from the association of weavers, of which until then they had formed part, and organizing themselves in a separate guild, produced gold, silver, linen and silk thread, cords, lacings, gimps, fringes, " doppioni " and all other articles used as — or in the production of — trimmings. They received the title of Masters " *Bordorum subtilum de filo subtili* " which denomination must have been considered appropriate to lace-makers, for even after their art became a great source of wealth and glory to Venice, this epithet, denominating the guild of which it formed part, remained unchanged.

The repeated edicts published by patriarchal and protectionist governments, forbidding the importation and limiting the width and value of trimmings forced mercers to invent some cheaper through effective edgings with which to supply their customers; and they naturally resorted to flax, aloes, and silk as first materials of comparatively small value with which to produce pretty designs in drawn work, embroidered net and bobbin lace, which being easy and rapid of execution coued be sold with profit fat a low price.

These edgings, " frizidor „, " smerli „ or " merli „ (so called from the Byzantine terms *mèrmis*, bobbin, and *mermiriso* to turn) were a novelty and pleasing to the eye; the customers, on their part, found that they furnished the desired trimming for garments with the added charms of cheapness and novelty, and so accepted them eagerly and they became the rage. But as usual, once the fashion established, rivalry in elegance developed and the original object was lost sight of; merchants and consumers alike ever incited the workwomen to fresh inventions, more perfect designs and minute details, until the beautiful thread points of the Golden Age of Lace became far more costly and valuable than the jewelled borders which wrought such havoc with the purses of the Fourteenth Century.

In the other provinces the same conditions existed; in 1341 the patriarch Bertrando of Aquileja, sovereign of the Patria (Friuli) forbade the use of gold embroidery, but permitted a trimming of cord or lace worth 40 francs per ell, a price not to be surpassed under pain of fines and excommunication. The will of the Countess Pierina della Torre, of Udine, dated 1396, mentions a silk kerchief ornamented with " Merli „ worked in gold leaves, These kerchiefs for head and neck furnished a field for the exhibition of fine embroidery and lace. In a Venetian account book we find carefully registered under various dates from 1437 to 1439, a great number of these ar-

ticles of feminine adornment which are perpetuated in the shawls, necker-
chiefs and *Zendade* or veils.

CCXXVIII. Cases.

(See N.° CCXXVIII. in tambour work of 1846) still worn by the
Venetian patrician ladies on solemn occasions, and by the women of the
people daily. — The kerchiefs were made of coarse *burato* linen, silk, muslin,
or the finest silk gauze brought from the Orient and unrivalled by the products of modern industry. Those of the Fifteenth Century are described as
straforatto (literally excessively pierced) with work in wheel shapes, such
as we see in

CCCCVII. Screen and CXXXIV. Cases.

N.° CCCCVII. and other samples on the screen in N.° CXXXIV., worked
in " Cartiglia „ which belong to Countess Valentinis of Friuli.

CXXVI. Cases.

N.ª CXXVI. is an heirloom in the historical Colleoni family. This
kerchief dates from about 1600, is made of the softest silk gauze, and is embroidered in the finest gold and silver thread with open work and relief round
the four sides; it was allotted the first prize assigned to this kind of work
at the historical Exhibition of Textile Arts held in Rome in the Spring
of 1887.

CLXXXVIII. Cases.

N." CLXXXVIII. is evidently a neckerchief of sheer gauze dating
from the same period, and very daintily and artistically embroidered round
two sides with gold thread and gold foil, interspersed with conventional
flowers and fruits exquisitely shaded in coloured silks; owing to the daily
use to which such objects were destined specimens of them are very rare.

The above mentioned Venetian account book also describes kerchiefs
worked with *chari* (openings) in coloured silks; this is a term used at that
period for a simple variety of *punto tagliato* or *trapunto* (drawn work).

LXXIII. Screen.

N.° LXXIII. is a fine specimen of this stitch, having a design consisting of chimerical animals left in the linen, whilst the reticulated open work
ground is executed in red silk and edged with a narrow fringe worked in
the material.

CCCXXXV. *Screen*

has gold introduced in the ground and fringe

CCCXXXVII. *Screen*

is finely executed and dates from the Thirteenth Century; it is a most interesting sample of that curious work in human figures animals and flowers left in linen, with an open-work ground, which was so much in vogue at the time of the troubadours.

CCCLI. *Screen.*

Is purely gothic in design, and is a sample of the open work which at that period was imported from the Island of Rhodes.

CCCLIII. *Screen.*

Is of the Fifteenth Century, and has a design of acorns and leaves worked in red silk.

LXXIV., LXXVI. *Cases.*

These numbers represent two beautiful pieces of trapunto worked in *chari* and equally finished on both sides; they belong to Mrs. Arthur Bronson. N.° LXXIV. forms the border for a bed-spread worked in a Byzantine design of mermaids, stags and dragons with little lions and small birds interspersed among the principal figures to fill in the empty spaces.

These creatures are left in the linen with the features worked by overcasting neatly in yellow silk, and the outlines are formed in the same way, whilst the ground is embroidered in tiny work squares with the same silk; the edge consists of a narrow silk fringe of the same colour wrought in the material which characterizes this kind of work.

LXXVI. *Cases.*

Is made in very fine linen, and must have served on a luxurious gown or apron. The design is of the Renaissance, gracefully composed of large interlaced conventional foliage and scrolls; around this runs a beautiful simple border; the overcast outline and shading are everywhere composed of yellow silk, whilst the fine recticulated ground is made in pale blue silk, the whole being edged with a narrow appropriate footing which was subsequently added.

CCCXXIV. Cases.

Is a pillow-case in fine white linen worked with thread in trapunto, with an all over Gothic design.

CCCCLXXXVI. Cases.

Is an altar cloth or dresser scarf of the same kind of work, belonging to Signora Costa, and contains birds, animals and letters forming initials, monograms and words which stand out from the *Cavato* ground owing to the superimposed embroidery and raised-work.

CCCCXCII. Cases

belongs to the same proprietor, and is rarely fine in material and work.

DCVIII. Cases.

N.° DCVIII. comes from Ravenna; it is a table cloth in white linen, worked in a Byzantine design and edged with very antique pointed pillow lace of the Fourteenth Century.

DCIV. Cases.

N.° DCIV. is a table-cover of the same material and work, but executed at a later date as is seen from the broad, beautiful Genoese pillow-lace, composed of great wheels in oriental design and artistically executed, which is sewed on either end and indicates the beginning of the Sixteenth Century.

In the Thirteenth and Fourteenth Centuries the coloured embroideries called *punto a crocetti* as well as trapunto, were very much appreciated, and in 1781, when the body of King Ferdinand the Second of Sicily was discovered in a perfect state of preservation in the Royal Sepulchres at Palermo, it was clothed in a shirt of the finest linen — which had been presented by the Saracens to king Otto IV in 1210 — worked upon the collar and sleeves in arabesques and cufic inscriptions.

At present this work is again the fashion, and as examples are rare they are eagerly sought after by merchants and collectors and command high princes. The " Crocetta „ embroidery is executed on fine linen with bright coloured silks in scachetti, square, back-chain, cross, and other stitches so neatly executed that the finish of the wrong side is equal to that of the right; the effect is generally enhanced by fringes wrought with the needle into the edge of the border with the same tinted silks that compose the design.

LXXVII., LXXIX., LXXXI. Screen.

N.° LXXVII. and LXXIX. are samples of this work, the latter is particularly fine in design and dates from the Fifteenth Century; its chief interest lies in the well drawn and well executed human figures and animals of which it is composed, recalling the embroideries of the most artistic period of the Roman Empire.

DCXXXII., DCXXXIV., DCXXXVI., DCXXXVIII. Cases.

These numbers, represent 21 superb examples of this kind of Italian embroidery, composing a rare collection brought together during years of research by, D.ʳ Silvestrini of Bologna who offers them for sale. Supplemented by the trapunto and by embroideries from Achmim-Panapolis exhibited on the screen, these numbers afford rare facilities for the study at their source of the changes which, in the fifteenth century, gradually stole over the art of designing for decorative work, and the successful struggle to regain the congruities of composition. This kind of embroidery continued the fashion until the Seventeenth Century, and was extensively used alike on men's and women's linen as is seen in portraits of this period, such as that of the historical Count Hippolito di Porto in the Museum at Vicenza, and as is recorded in the court inventories and chronicles of Queen Elizabeth and her contemporaries. Another Venetian document, dated 1439, is an inventory of the wardrobe belonging to Lorenzo Donà, whilom Governor of Friuli, and it repeats the same endless enumeration of fine cloth, silk, velvet and satin garments adorned with fur, gold lace, beads, metal, tinsel and silk gimps and borders under the names of *tarnato, frizo d'oro*, and *d'oro Vallenzane* (from Valencia in Spain) *chamossa* etc., whilst others mention, *oro di Cologna* (from the city on the Rhine) *limbus, grammata, fimbria, tressas* and endless other terms applied to the multitudinous trimmings of that day.

Other cities of Italy were not far behind Venice, for the constant intercourse with the great commercial centre required by the exigences of trade furnished them with an opportunity for studying the fashions. Count Gandini has spent years in forming the superb historical collection of textiles in the Museum of Modena which bears his name and which is unsurpassed by any other in Europe; he has also patiently studied the masses of inedited documents relative to the Ducal family of Este which reigned in Ferrara for so many Centuries, and among the State Archives he has found mentioned in a Register of the Wardrobe dated 1475 a. c. 25) a *frixo in oro da Cologna* (frieze in Gold of Cologne) and in that of 1476, dated June 5ᵗʰ (a. c. 87) an order given for a felt hat *alla Borgognona*, trimmed with a silver and silk gimp made with bobbins; besides this (a. c. 96) in the same document is noted a seat made in velvet for the great hall with the canopy trimmed

at the sides with a *frizetto* (frill) in gold and silver made in little squares
with bobbins; finally in number 112 of the same collection are inscribed the
orders for refurnishing an apartment in the palace, given by the Duchess
Eleonora, wife of Duke Hercules I. who desired it should be embellished
in honour of the expected visit to Ferrara of her sister, Beatrice of Aragon,
on her journey to marry King Mathias Corvinus of Hungary; in this manuscript one of the rooms is described as adorned mith " a frieze of gold
made with bobbins „.

In Florence in the Fifteenth Century the luxury in clothes was at least
equal to that of Venice, and Savonarola in the stirring sermons which he
preached from 1484 to 1491 against the follies and extravagances of the time
frequently reproached the nuns, especially those of the Convent of the Mu-
rate, with devoting their time to the vain fabrication of costly gold laces
with which to adorn the houses and persons of the rich, instead of conse-
crating, themselves to fasting, prayer and the glory of God in the embel-
lishment of His holy temples.

CCXC. Cases

consists of a large quantity of this lace in perfect preservation, exhibited
by Countess Agostini Venerosa della Seta, of Tuscany; it comprises the
trimming for a table-cover and contains the widest and best designs in gold
lace I have ever seen. It comes from the fingers of those very women who
provoked the great preacher's vituperation, and its glowing splendour justifies
his words.

CCCLXXXII. Cases.

After gazing on these jewels of textile art the eye turns with contempt
from the seven samples which are placed beside it, as also from

LXXXIII, CCCV. Screen

which illustrate the gold, silver and clinquant laces made in other parts of
Italy.

LXXXV. Screen.

N.° LXXXV. is also Florentine of the same period as the gold lace,
and its ground is made with bobbins of unbleached thread worked in the
same way, but it has two real *cartisane* (strips of parchment rolled with
silk) interlaced with the ground in a conventional pattern to form the
design. This kind of lace was called guipure, from *guiper* (in old French
to roll) and its name later became synonimous with all lace made in a cord
like design.

LXXXIX. Screen.

N.° LXXXIX. is an entirely different kind of work namely, of the first kind of net used in Italy as lace on garments. It is made of a very fine linen or silk mesh stiffened with wax and then embroidered in silk thread, and was the origin of *laxis*. It was in use during the Fourteenth and early part of the Fifteenth Century, as is indicated by the design and proved by an account book formerly belonging to the Cathedral of Ferrara, and now existing in the Municipal Archives of that city.

This documents contains an entry, made in 1469, of a bill presented by a certain Battista, wife of Nicolo Andrea of Ferrara, for repairing the very badly worn and damaged gramito (border) of fourteen surplices for the canons of the chapter, with detailed specifications of the work, together with the prices of thread and of the candles used for waxing it.

But the most complete and authentic list of the laces made in the Fifteenth Century is found in the lengthy document of which only the part referring particularly to lace is given here. It consists in a descriptive catalogue of the personal effects and furniture inherited by, and divided between the noble sisters Angela and Ippolita Sforza Visconti of Milan, and is dated September 12th, 1403. To those who have read that lace was invented in Flanders or in Germany in the latter part of the Sixteenth Century, and copied and developed in Italy during the Seventeenth, the following lines prove how frequently assertions are made without proper research, and that as early as the Fifteenth Century, side by side with the pillow lace made with single threads, like that found in the graves of Achmim-Panapolis, distinguished under the name of *bone-lace*, and the more elaborate and newer lace made with bobbins twirled in pairs and called as today " *fuxi* ", and *fuselli*, all the varieties of needle lace specified in the pattern books published in the following century existed, such as; *punto tagliato, punto tirato, rete a maglia quadra, Reticella punto in aria*, etc. Although, as will be seen from the Italian terms retained in translating this fragment, the abominable orthography of the epoch often strangely travestied the original term :

" One mantle of black satin trimmed round with gold tarnato (lace) ".

" One veil in spun gold ".

" Four small veils in silk; ten little veils in Neapolitan style ".

" One linen sheet of five breadths worked in *point* ".

" One piece of silver tarnato (lace) made in stars ".

" One sheet of four breadths worked in radexelo, (net lace).

" Four pieces of net lace point radexelo to put on a *mosquito net* ".

" One sheet worked with large insertions ".

" One gold veil made in the Neapolitan style with a gold cimossa (edging) ".

" One gold veil made with an applied cimossa of black silk. "

" One stomacher made in gold of *grupi*, (knotted work). „

" One *Tarneta* (edging) of gold and silk made in *ossi* (bone lace). „

" One stomacher of gold brocade, with *retini* (*net work*). „

" One stomacher of red satin trimmed with gold work a *gugia*. „

" One sheet in raw silk of six breadths worked in *Radexela*, (netpoint). „

" One small bundle of various kinds of *embroideries*. „

" Fire pairs of sheets, one worked in *radexela* (net point) „

" One sheet af four breadths in *radexele*. „

" One painted box whith certain fittings of embroidery made on veils. „

" Four pieces of redexela for a mosquito net. „

" One knotted embroidery on which were the pearls of my lady Bianca. „

" One broad radixela for a sheet. „

" Six new pieces of tiny raxela (net lace). „

" Two *tarnate* of gold. „

" One band worked *a poncto de doii fuxi* (literally in point ot two bobbins, in contradistinction to the bone lace named above).

" Half of a bundle containing certain designs for the women to work. „

" One sheet of *bombaxe* with certain fine workings; one sheet ditto worked in radicelle. „

That lace made with " pairs „ of bobbins was a novelty is indicated by its being especially thus described in order to distinguish it from the older and simpler bone-lace, and we have an illustration of it in the unpublished authentic portrait in oils of Christopher Columbus, belonging to Cavaliere de Ferrari of Genoa, of which we give a sketch, and which is the only portrait of the explorer in existence in which he is represented as wearing lace.

This quality of lace was made in Genoa and Spain, and is therefore most appropriately perpetuated on the collar of the man whose greatness brought lustre, wealth and power to the nation of his adoption, and added a glorious name to the long list of brilliant sons possessed by the classic land which gave him birth. But another historical character whom we must ever honor in speaking of Columbus has left an impress on this lace. It will be remembered that when Queen Isabella of Castile joined her husband in the Spanish crusade against the Moors of Grenada, she made a solemn vow not to change her shift until that city had submitted to the Cross. — Many weeks passed and that historical garment assumed a very doubtful unbleached hue ere Granada fell. This Great Queen, despite the political cares and grave state questions, which she never shirked, was a clever and devoted apostle of the needle, and especially excelled in drawn work and lace in which she also personally trained her daughters to work with the noble maidens under her intelligent supervision in the vast hall, near their private apartments, consecrated to the use of the ladies of the Court, so that they acquired, and when they married into England, Portugal and Burgundy carried with them the passion for the innocent and graceful Art which they had learned at their mother's knees.

All Christendom at that moment had its eyes fixed on Spain in admiration af its enterprise and victories, and so the new colour was adopted for laces and frills all over Europe in compliment to the Queen, yellow starches were invented, and this shade of buff is still designated under the litle of " *couļeur Isabel* „. This tint was especially given to the bobbin laces of Spain and Genoa called "gothic „ whether made in silk or in thread, of which, owing to their great fineness and antiquity, examples in a good state of preservation are excessively rare.

DCXXVIII., DCXXX. Cases

in buff silk, belonging to D.ʳ Silvestrini, are wonderfully fine and delicate in quality and design, and come from Spain, probably worked there by the Jews before they were expelled under the Inquisition.

CCCCXL., CCCCXLII. Cases

are two pieces, exquisite in design and execution, of bone lace made in Genoa. They have an especial historical in terest for Americans as they were brought to Perugia by a member of the Meniconi Bracceschi family of which a distinguised condottiere of the Middle Ages, Bracciaforte da Montone, was a member. This nobleman being sent by the Pope as Ambassador to the French court frequently passed through Genoa, and as the friends and family of Columbus were poor and industrious it is possible that the fingers which intertwined these linen and silk threads may have clasped the hand of the great explorer; Such thoughts cause us to touch with reverence these waifs of a bygone Age, and to realize the truth in the words of Fambri, the great prophet of the revival of lace-making in Italy, when he described the gentle maids and matrons of the Renaissance as mouldered to dust beside the heaps of ruins which once constituted the strongly fortified stone castles they inhabited, whilst the filmy ʻwork of their frail fingers lives on through centuries, ever freshly adorning generation after generation of the human race in every part of the world to which culture has penetrated.

In the milanese document of 1493 the most frequently recurring quality of lace is *reticella* (net or Greek point), and the process followed in its manufacture is described in onr Introduction. From a simple form of open work embroidery it rapidly developed into a perfect point lace not to be distinguished from " punto in aria „; it was a universal favourite side by side with point and bobbin lace all through the sixteenth century, the coarser qualities being especially adapted to body and house linen, and Burato is a modification of it. Long before the publication of books of patterns every household and convent had its sampler more or less complete, from which the stitches and designs daily reproduced were copied by the women and girls.

A. S.
M Y
OF COLVMB.

1400 to 1500 AD.

Genoa.

Portrait of C. Colombus, belonging to
Cavaliere De Ferrari.

XCVII., XCIX., CI. Screen. DXCVIII. Cases.

N.ᵒˢ XCVII., XCIX., CI., are some of these most antique samples ; N.° DXCVIII. of the Sixteenth Century is exceptionally large, and forms a complete illustration of the stitches used in this kind of lace.

Punto Tagliato lies between Trapunto and Reticella, and is simply the latter with part of the linen ground left visible, just as *Cardiglia* touches the other extreme, being made entirely whithout linen though appearing like reticella.

We have innumerable examples of all these kinds of work, each more beautiful than the other and all alike interesting, for the Italian women of that period were quick to see its beauties and its advantages, as it did not alter in the least in washing, and in the super-refined extravagance of the Renaissance it was used to adorn sheets, pillow cases, towels and table linen, bed spreads, curtains and canopies with insertions and borders ; and the passion for it went to such lengths as as to cause the bright coloured walls of the summer apartments to be entirely covered with it, which a chronicler of the period says produced a charming effect. The Sforza document speaks of sheets of four and five breadths ; this was because the old looms did not admit of weaving linen wide enough to make them all in one piece, and as seams are unsightly, pretty insertions were used to unite the widths ; and this tradition remains in Italy.

DCLVI. Cases.

And in N.° DCLVI. is exhibited a homespun sheet, such as is still in daily use among the Friuli peasants and which illustrates these observations. The simple fact that I was forced to lend a sheet to take its place during its voyage to America shows that such work is considered not luxurious but simply neat.

CCCCLXXXIV. Cases.

N.° CCCCLXXXIV. is the heading of a sheet from an old castle in the neighbourhood, and other pieces exhibited in this group have served the same purpose ; to match these sheets pillow cases with *reticella* or bobbin lace borders and openwork hems were of course necessary.

CXLII, CXXX., CXXXVIII, CCCCLXXVIII., DCLVIII., DXCII. Cases.

N.° CXLII. belongs to one of our peasants, and numbers CXXX., CXXXVIII, CCCCLXXVIII, DCLVIII, are all pillow cases in the same kind of work, executed at different epochs more or less finely according to the ability or wealth of the housewife, and shaped to fit, for centuries, the heads of successive generations of humanity from the cradle to the grave.

CCLXXXVI., CCLXXXVIII. Cases.

Form the cover and curtains a dressing table composed entirely of beautifully worked reticella paralellograms which adorned a Tuscan bridal sheet of the Fifteenth Century, they are edged with fine antique Genoese pillow lace.

CCCXXXIV., CCCCXLVIII., DCII., DCVIII., DCX., DCXII. Cases.

Belong to several beautifully executed table coths, dresser covers and towels, all forming interesting examples of reticella and punto tagliato ; each is different from the others and some are adorned with pillow-lace edges and fascinatingly complicated little tassels at the four corners.

CCCCLVI., CCCCLXII., DII., DIV. Cases.

Are also examples of Reticella and punto tagliato which have served on household and church linen, and are exhibited by the patronesses.

CCCCLXVIII. Cases.

N.º CCCCLXVIII. is particularly worthy of attention on account of its fineness of quality, perfection of execution and the curious little doge's caps and vases introduced in the design.

DCI. Cases.

N.º DCI. is also interesting as showing an entirely contrary treatment of the material, and constitutes *Punto tagliato Reale*, the designs being cut out and diversified with graceful stitches, and the ground left in plain linen as at the school in Burano, where the clever workers have recovered the secret of its fabrication.

LXXXIX., CIX., CLXXI., CCLXXXIII.-CCCLXIX., CCCLXXXIX., CCCXCI., CCCXCIX., CCCCI., CCCCIII., CCCCV., CCCCVII.,CCCCIX.,CCCCXI.,CCCCXIII.,CCCCXVII.,CCCCXIX. Screen.

Consist in eighteen samples of Punto Tagliato and Reticella exhibited on the screen, and as each one is furnished with the date of its origin and name of place of manufacture no further comment is necessary ; N.º LXXXIX. is of purely gothic design and is the oldest piece of drawn work on this list.

CCCXCVII. Screen.

N.º CCCXCVII. is a fine example of the variety of lace called *cardiglia*, which in appearance resembles Reticella but is worked as is Venetian point.

These varieties of work are so beautiful, so characteristic and so little known out of Italy that they have been chosen to form the subject of the illustration representing the fashion of using lace from 1500 to 1600. This sketch reproduces an anonymous portrait, preserved in the pinacotek of Bologna, of a delicious, jolly baby of the olden time, literally smothered in laces, lyging wide awake in a monumental crib furnished with pillow, spread, canopy and curtains of this work, and with even the corner columns swathed in bands of it; these latter were also used alone or mixed with pillow lace for swaddling the babies of the Italian Aristocracy and of wealthy Hebrews.

The latter, howeverer, in accordance with the prescriptions of the Talmud, were wrapped in bands diversified by quotations from the Law embroidered between the stripes of lace.

CCCXX. Cases.

N.° CCCXX. is one of these, worked in Burato and worn to rags by several generations of Jewish babies, while.

III. Screen.

N.° III. on the screen, and N.°˙

CCCXIV., CCCXVIII., CCCXX. Cases.

Have undergone the same process in the service of a multitude of little Christians.

DLIV, DLVI. Cases.

N.°˙ DLIV., DLVI. are two unusually long and richly worked bands of Punto Tagliato and Reticella from Bologna in a state of perfect preservation. They are edged with delicate, pointed Genoese lace, and cause us to regret that more of this artistic combination has not survived the ravages of Time.

These two pieces exactly correspond in length, width and design with those on the canopy produced in the sketch, and may have served on this very crib or on that of some other little Bolognese aristocrat of the same epoch.

The list of laces in use during the Fifteenth Century remains to be completed; we have reviewed the pretty ladies of the Court, but have left unmentioned the queen and greatest beauty of them all; she enters last and all eyes turn to her as she ascends the throne of needle work from which no changes of fashion have been able to banish her:

DCV. Wall.

We are here stand in the presence of the earliest real Venetian point, *Punto in aria*.

Since first invented this lace has ever enhanced woman's charms, and men have been so attracted by its clinging grace that they have carried it upon their breasts and sleeves in court and camp, and sometimes dyed it it crimson with their life blood, whilst inordinate love for it has played such sad havoc with family coffers that estates have been mortgaged, and whole families reduced to penury in order to satisfy the craving for its possession; many laws have therefore been promulgated against it but all in vain.

From its origin it was very expensive, and the Venetian Republic tried to eliminate a fresh excuse for extravagance by suppressing it at the outset, and so in 1476 the Senate decreed that no *Punto in Aria* whatever, executed either in flax or in silver or gold thread should be used on the curtains and bed-linen in the city or provinces; but the women were accustomed to disobey the laws, and if necessary to rebel against which were measures inspired by a desire to control their expenditure, though it were for their own good. They had tasted the sweets of victory in their great rebellion against the patriarch of Venice, Lorenzo Giustiniani, who had, in 1437, dared to forbid females, under pain of fines and excommunication, the use of costly jewelry and of every kind of superfluous adornment.

But the women of that period, like the artisans of to-day, bravely " went on strike „, refused to attend the churches, and appealed to the Pope. Their Ambassadress must have possessed not only rich and becoming garments, but also an eloquent tongue and a persuasive smile, since she induced the Pontiff to side with the women and to order the Patriarch to cancel his injunction.

And when we observe N.° DCV, belonging to Signorina Angiolini of Bologna, which is a framed example of this most antique Venetian Point, of about 1460, resembling in its design some pure spirit flower, we can understand the women, excited over these exquisite blossoms of their inventive needles, refusing to have the rare exotics destroyed by ruthless laws, and battling fearlessly to preserve these creatures of their mind and hand for their own particular adornment; they had grasped the possibilities of effect which it possessed, and had realized that the twining of its graceful tendrils in and out around the hems of their veils and coifs added a needed dedicacy to their superb costumes, and that its lily blossoms brightened by contrast the shellike tinting of their hands and necks and the rosy freshness of their cheeks.

Part IV.

The Golden Age of Lace.

From 1500 to the French Empire.

The love of lace developed into a passion during the Sixteenth Century when all that was beautiful found crowds of faithful worshippers. The first Artistic talent of Europe was inspired to compose designs for the complicated weaving with needle and bobbins: designs which were pubblished in book form and passed through numerous editions. Tradition has it that no less a painter than the great Titian in person not only counselled his nephew Veccelio in the composition of his pattern book, but himself sometimes laid aside the brush and deigned to draw designs for a favoured few. Reprints of the most celebrated of these pattern books published during the Sixteenth Century are exhibited in the collection of books, and the dedication of one of the rarest extant, addressed to the princess Margherita d'Este, Duchess of Ferrara, in 1592, is reproduced at the beginning of this volunne, for as seen from the aboe they were offered in homage to the highest ladies of the land who gladly accepted the dedication, considering it a great honor and compliment to the industry and skill of their households. For round them were gathered the daughters of many noble families entrusted to their care for instruction in the arts becoming high born woman hood; thus each great house formed a kind of training school in literature and manners a custom that was replaced by the convents of the Seventeenth and Eighteenth Centuries and the select boarding schools of to-day. In the great hall on the second floor devoted to the women and their occupations the mistress of the palace caused the young girls to execute the wondrous works of skill and patience copied from these pattern books, in which were often introduced, for the easier execution of the design, samples of the different lace stitches, as in the unique example

DCXIV. Cases.

N.° DCXIV. by Vecellio, which belonged for generations to the pious ladies who occupied a picturesque old convent in Perugia now suppressed. There was a healthy spirit of emulation among the maides of a household, each girl putting her whole soul and ability into the work alloted to her, for not only was she striving for a word of encomium more flat tering than that given to her companions, but all the women of one palace united in straining every nerve to have their work surpass that of some other great household equally celebrated for its points. This rivalry among the women went to such exaggerated lengths as to give rise to insults and bitter quarrels among the men. Princesses and Queens complied with the industrious usage of the times, and Catherine de Medici carried this Italian custom into France in the Sixteenth Century just as the constant intercourse between Italy and Spain during the Fifteenth Century had introduced it into Spain. This remarkable Italian woman — who had inherited the talent of her father Lorenzo de Medici — while directing the affairs of state found time each day to spend several hours with tha young princesses and ladies of the Court in the sunny work room of the Louvre, looking out upon the river Seine. There her danghter Margaret, the pretty, clever, giddy wife of Henry of Navarre, spent the most innocent hours of her life embroidering the squares of Reticella and net which are called after her pseudonym of Reine Margot-

CCCX. Cases., CCCXV. Screen.

N." CCCX. and CCCXV, (of this work copies in the form of tea cloths are exhibited by the school of Brazzà in the modern section).

Here her daugter-in-law, the beautiful Mary Stuart acquired love of sunshine, gaiety and laughter while defty plying the needle, and when in her emprisonment she worked the veil (still religiously preserved) which framed her pale features on the scaffold, how sadly must the sweet memories of her happy youth and gay companions in France have entangled themselves among its threads.

The mother of Henry the IV. of France and Navarre, Jeanne d'Albret, at her father's great castle in Gascony had also learned to apply herself to the needle, and when she married Antoine de Bourbon in 1556 she gathered about her the noble ladies of Navarre, and in the following years of strife she whiled amay the many anxious hours caused by the persecution of her coreligionists in making, with the assistance of her companions, yards upon yards of superb embroidered net, part of which constitutes the bed cover, curtain, and dressing table valance all edged with dainty Gothic pillow lace exhibited under

CLXVIII., CLXX. Cases.

N⁰ˢ CLXVIII. and CLXX. Net lace or *Lacis* being easy to work and not requiring great application, was a favorite fancy work among high born lace makers, as is seen from the royal account books.

CL. Cases.

N.° CL. is a beautiful piece of the earliest variety, made on the bias; it is from Genoa, the property of Countess Gambaro, and is edged with very fine Genoese lace in deep points.

DCLXII. Cases.

N.° DCLXII. is still older; it is a pillow case composed of squares of bias lacis illustrative of stories in Holy Scripture and of the virtues and vices; it has illegible lettering forming a border to each square, and the human figures are clothed in the costume of the Renaissance.

XCIV. Cases.

N.° XCIV. is a towel or credence cover, with either end formed by a very deep border of net, embroidered with unicorns drinking at a fountain;

DCXXIII. Cases.

N.° DCXXIII. is also the end of a dresser cover and repeats the same design of unicorns, although in this they are represented as suppporting the arms of the proprietor. In the Sixteenth Century the unicorns was a favourite design with which to ornament all objects used in connection with food, such as as platers, cups table linen and the like, because of the prevalence of the crime of poisoning at that period, and the belief that the horn of the unicorn destroyed all venom; so, that though this fabulous animal never existed, a regular traffic was carried on in manufactured horns by the apothecaries, and the Neapolitan use of small carved horns to conjure the evil eye is a survival of the superstition. It originated in the legend of a poisonous lake which killed all animals that drank of its waters ar well as birds that flew accros it, until, a unicorn came there to quench his thirst, and at the touch of his horn it was purified; verses allusive to this were frequently inscribed upon cups and there are many pattern books of the Sixteenth Century in the designs ot which the unicorn is introduced. XCIV. is copied from one of these, and is executed with great attention to correct drawing. These pieces, like all net lace of the same variety from Italy, are made in a straight band and edged with a " campaue „ of bobbin lace; the Germans however finished their oldest net laces with teeth edged with overcasting or with button-hole stitch, asin.

DCXXV. Cases.

N.º DCXXV. embroidered in the imperial castles, because bobbin lace was not manufactured among them until later than net lace; little tassels were sometimes added in both countries to the turretted borders.

CCCCXVI. Cases

is like CCCCXVI, which is a piece of Italian pointed net af the same period.

CCXXIV. Cases

is a border formed of a very fine quality of Isabelle coloured net, most artistically embroidered in interlaced vines among which cupids and dogs are portrayed as playing, it is edged with a fine campane and the composition is in the perfect Italian art of the Sixteenth Century; this exquisite piece of lace belongs to the Santa Lilia family which came to Naples from Spain with Charles III.

DCIX. Cases.

DCIX. is af the same period, made in silk, and effective because of its brilliant colours; it is very coarse and was evidently made to be used on furniture.

Another variety of net lace is called *Modena*; it is not generally embroidered but the pattern consists in knitting the meshes together in different shapes.

DCVII. Cases.

DCVII. is an interesting example af this work, as in it the squares of embroidered net and Modena are alternated while the border is entirely composed of Modena. This lace has always been identified with Tuscany, and the peasants of today in the mountains round Florence use bed spreads and mosquito nets made of it.

DC. Cases.

Is a curious cover composed of squares of old Burato work alternated with squares of Modena executed in cream and buff coloured thread of aloes. This was formed in a sepulchre at Ferrara belonging to the marquises of Caliagnini and is of the Fifteenth Century though it is mentioned here because placed with the other work in net.

1500 A.D. to 1600 A.D.

Portrait of a lady, the artist is unknown, in
The Royal Picture Gallery at BOLOGNA.

CVII. Screen.

A curious needle lace, of which I ignore the name, was made for a short time during the Sixteenth Century and must have been invented in Spain, as its stitch resembles more closely that composing the Hispano-Moresque head dress than any other lace; it looks something like knitting or finest net, but contains no knots, and is worked without a foundation composed of a material as is Venetian point, but differs from this in having no threads sewed down to form the outline of the design

DXCVI. Cases.

is a small table cover the border of which consists of this lace executed in a design of alternate peacocks, emblems of jealous vigilance, and doves, emblems of gentle faith. Another lace which never had great success in Italy, but was very much admired in Spain and also in France was the heavy silk Guipure of the Sixteenth Century. This was made either in bobbin lace of silk in various colours or mixed with metal, and was also made with the needle. Its characteristic consists in a narrow strip of vellum which, on account of its brittleness, was soon replaced by a coarse cord, wound smoothly in silk, or whatever other thread was to be used, and edged with tiny loops; this was fastened down round pieces of silk brocade or tinsel, see

CCCXL., CCCXLIII. Screen.

or close lace stitches forming

LXXV. Screen.

flowers, LXXV. or else caused to curve about alone, forming stems and arabesques held together by loops. These were sewed borders on heavy materials such as velvets, cloths, and brocades, but the Italians preferred to use embroidery where the lighter varieties of gold and metal laces and the delicate silk polychrome lace edgings were not appropriate. Their fondness for colour and appreciation of its value was greatly developed, as is evinced by the beautiful piece

LXXX. Cases.

of conventional design executed in pillow lace, N.° LXXX., which is unrivalled by the most scientific combination of today, Burato and reticella were also executed at this period in coloured silks mixed with thread, and added diversity of effect to the house linen.

LXXXIV. Cases.

is a table cover of burato worked in colours: it is varied with net and pillow lace, and edged with fringed pillow lace.

CCCXXVIII. Cases.

Is a band of the same work adapted as a bell-pull.

LXXXII. Cases.

Is a broad band of Cartiglia made of white thread and yellow silk in a Moorish design of discs; it comes from Spain.

CCCXXXII. Cases.

In CCCXXXII. a similar effect is produced by a fancy work which has of late become the fashion in Italy, and which consists in sewing remnants of antique white pillow lace guipure upon canvass, and filling in all the space between the designs with Sicilian stitch executed in coloured silks.

The great connection betwen Spain and Italy began with the marriage of Ferdinand and Isabella, and continued until the middle of the Sixteenth Century when Spainish families had obtained dominion over the greater part of Italy, and the Italian nuns imported into Spanish convents and the Spanish girls educated in Italian convents exchanged with their new companions the knowledge of the arts of the needle as practiced in their respective countries. With France continued intercourse began with the Peace of Bologna in 1530, although from the beginning of the Sixteenth Century Italy, full af beauty and art, had become the coveted prey of all Europe, and on its historic soil were fought out the battles for supremacy between France and Spain, which in those days meant also Austria. The nobles and princes who commanded the invading armies on both sides carried back with them the artistic spoils of its civilization, and all the laces and embroideries executed until the seventeenth Century are copies or modifications of Italian designs. Florence, Genoa and above all Venice as the most flourishing cities originated the fashions till the brilliant and extravagant Court af Louis XIV definitely established the sway of Paris as their absolute dictatress. Notwithstanding the opening of the Universities to women, which began in the Fifteenth century with the establishment of a mixed College at Mantua under the direction of Vittoria da Feltre, the Italians did not become that quality of literary women which neglects the feminine arts. At Venice, as early as 1414, Giovanna Dandolo, wife of Doge Pasqual Malipiero, whose intelligence enjoyed such renown that the first book printed in Venice was dedicated to her, founded and protected large schools in which the productions of the bobbins and the needle reached such perfection that they founded the supremacy of Venetian laces, and assured for the future their great reputation in all the courts of Europe.

The schools and ateliers opened by this benevolent women continued to spread the art after her death. The needle laces produced at this period in Venice as well as in Spain are generally known under the name of Spanish point, to distinguish them from the more elaborate designs executed in the same lace of a later period.

DCLIX. Cases.

N.° DCLIX. is very antique and is edged with deep Spanish point; it represents the transition from reticella to Punto in Aria, destined for church uses and illustrating in fine stitches the Pasqual Lamb, emblems of the Passion, the gates of Heaven, angels, birds, etc. This has been reproduced at the school of Burano.

DXV., DXII. Wall.

are photographs of some curious and antique pieces of this quality of lace consisting of elaborate and complicated figures composing entire Biblical or mythological stories.

CCCVIII. Cases.

is very old and represents tiny figures of women; it comes from a convent at Udine.

DXCIV. Cases.

is a band of „ Punto in Aria „ from an old family of Mantua.

DCVI. Cases.

is a table-cover composed of deep artistic reticella inserted in fine linen and edged with bobbin lace.

CCLXXXIII., CCLXXXV. Screen.

N.º CCLXXXIII. is a piece of the same lace placed on the screen beside CCLXXXV., which is a modern imitation of it made in Switzerland by machinery, and has been very much the fashion for dress trimming during the past two years, but can compare in no way with the original.

CCCCLVIII., CCCCLX. Cases.

Are beautiful examples of Cartiglia of the Sixteenth Century.

CCCCLVI., CCXLVIII., CCCXII. Cases.

CCCCLVI. is Punto in Aria of the same epoch, as are also N.ᵒˢ CCXLVIII. and CCCXII; the latter consisting of an artistically designed deep lace, composed of different sized conventional thistles, executed in Spain

DCXVI. Cases.

is another band of Punto di Spagna.

CXXVI. Cases.

is of interest as illustrating a special variety of Venetian Guipure made in linen thread during the Sixteenth Century; it is executed partly in needle and partly in bobbin lace; •

CCXVI. Screen.

N.º CCXVI. is a second example of the above.

CXIV. Cases.

An example of the artistic embroidery most admired in Venice during the Sixteenth Century is furnished by the table cover composed of deep red antique satin and velvet, richly embroidered in gold tendrils entwined with scattered flowers of delicately tinted silks worked with the exquisite shading and excessive fineness of execution called *needle*. In 1557 another Duchess, Zilia Dandolo, wife of Doge Lorenzo Priuli, who like the gifted Dogaressa Malipiero occupied herself in benefitting humanity, merited by her noble character and charitable deeds the honour of being personally crowned, a distinction which was not accorded to the wives of all the Doges. The costume she wore on this occasion is described as having been copied from that of one of her predecessors. Her head dress consisted of a cap of gold bordered with deep Venetian point from which a white veil trimmed with point lace hung to the ground; and the same chronicler relates that the great ladies, and the high officials' wives who attended the ceremony wore the immense collars of point lace, spangled with gold, jewels and pearls, which are seen in the portraits of the Medici family; these were supported by fine metal bars called *verghetti* which were manufacture in such abundance on account of the great demand for Venetian lace caps, collars and ruffs, that the inabitants of a whole quarter of the town were occupied in their production, and their name, which it still bears, was given to it in consequence. Others of the ladies wore lace caps and bavari or bibs for which so many designs were published during the following fifty years; others wore long veils edged with deep bands of Punto Tagliato a fiorami: the superb Venetian raised, or literally, sculptured point.

CCXLIV. Cases.

is an example of this lace in the pure design which first characterized

CLXVII. Cases.

it, and CLXVI. shows the splendour to which it developed in the Seventeenth Century; this rich and rare cape, belonging to the Countess Telffner, was evidently destined to adorn the red mantle of one of the ambassadors sent out by the Doge and Senate with special orders to dress in superb style, so as to prove to all who saw them how rich and grand was the proud Republic they represented.

CCXCVII. Screen.

is a cuff made in Venetian Punto in Aria representing animals (hares); it has the raised edge in use at the middle of the Sixteenth Century,

DCXI., DCXIII. Cases.

as has also N.º DCXI. belonging to M.ʳˢ Cuthbert Slocomb, which is finished in deep points and composed of a running design with which the dogs of the Cararrese, peacocks, scorpions and eagles are intermingled. This is an example of the Carnival lace especially manufactured for grand occasions such as marriages, births etc. and which always contained the emblems of the great families in whose honour the celebration was to take place. To this flounce belong 16 oval pats such as were used in slashed sleeves; these together form a worthy relic of old Venetian costume which receives added interest from

CLXXIV. Cases,

a piece of fine Frigio bobbin lace, exhibited by Countess Papafava dei Carraresi, for this contains also the dogs belonging to the great family of Carrara, and the quartering of peacocks used at that epoch, but this time combined with lions and foxes, so that the two pieces record different marriages in the same house, one in the Sixteenth and the other in the Seventeenth Century.

CLV. Screen.

is another interesting example of emblematic lace, consisting of deep Genoese points which must have formed the edge of some ruff or standing
collar, and represents the double headed crowned eagle of Austria and the
shield with the white cross of the arms of Savoy.

The Italian bobbin laces also made rapid progress during the Sixteenth
Century. First of all among them continued to rank the delicate conventional
gothic laces which were modified into ever varied and new patterns,

DCXX. Cases.

following, however, two systems of design, the one being round and wheel-
like, such as the Maltese and Moorish laces, see DCXX; the other pointed
like pine trees or the Oriental date palm leaf pattern which frequently composed the entire design of these latter laces.

DLXX. Cases.

N.° DLXX. is a beautiful creation, and

CCLXXXII. Cases.

is very gracefully composed in the form of a collar edged with needle lace
reticella.

DLXXIV. Cases.

belongs to the same epoch. as do also

CIII., CLXI., CLXXXV. Screen.

with deep points, and many other examples on the screen.

CXIX. Screen.

is the end of a towel with palm leaf insertion and a turretted border.

CXXI. and CXXXV. Screen.

have a graceful running design executed in the same lace.

CXL. Cases.

is a pillow-case with a deep insertion of this lace, forming beautiful, conventional flowers and leaves alternated with the same design which begins on

the opposite side, and fits into the space left between the repititions of the group of flowers; it is edged with a narrow insertion which repeats the same flowers and leaves in a different combination.

CLXV. Screen.

and several other samples of this variety of lace, Punto Tagliato, reticella and Cardiglia, which are here all marked with the place of origin and date of manufacture, were imitated with bobbins, producing a similitude of effect and wearing equally well on linen, whereas the fatigue and cost of production were vastly inferior.

CCCCLXVI. Cases.

is an example of this lace, as are

CCCLXXI., CXXIX., CXXXV., CCCLXXXI. Screen.

and many other pieces exhibited on the screen or introduced in the household linen.

CCXXXI. Screen.

is a simple insertion made in enormous quantities and used in sheets, pillow cases and coarse underwear; it was infinitelly varied in design, and coarse effective borders were produced to match it, of which

CXLV., CXXXIII., CXXXVII., CLXIX., CLXXV. Screen.

and many others, such as

DCXLVIII., DCL. Cases.

are examples. These were made in every part of Italy from the Alps to the extreme point of Sicily, In Genoa the design of this quality of lace, as well as of the others already mentioned was influenced by Spain; as seen in the guipure DCXIII. and the table-cover DCXL.,

DCXIII., DCXL. Cases.

but it also learned an entirely different stitch from Malta,

CCCXIX., CCCXXXV., CLXVII., CCI. Screen.

as is seen in the examples CLXVII, the insertion CCI., CCCXIX. and in CCCLV. which has a decidedly Moorish effect.

From the Moors the Genoese and Venetian mariners of the XVI Century also acquired another kind of artistic trimming to which they gave the name of Punto a Groppo (knotted point) now called by its Moorish name of Macramé. This complicated fringe, composed of fine knotted threads, is equal to a lace in design and execution, and when treated with long threads wound about bobbins it becomes one.

CC. Cases.

Signora Enrichetta Ruggi of Padua has composed the entire group, CC. illustrating the evolution of this kind of work from the simple knotted fringe to the most complicated lace, and Countess Avogadro of the same city contributes a rich and interesting Album

CXCIV. Cases.

of antique laces containing, at N.º 20, an authentic bit of the original *groppo*, which is very rare.

This lace is made extensively around Genoa, and is used to edge house and table linen, as are also the fringed, coarser guipure and torchon laces copied from those of the Sixteenth and Seventeenth Centuries as already mentioned, and of which N.ᵒˢ

CCCLXXIII., CXXXIX., CXCIII. Screen

are original samples.

In Venice also, and in Sicily and Naples, as in the countries and islands of the Eastern part of the Mediterranean, the bobbin laces were affected by trade with the East, and developed designs resembling those for embroidering or braiding,

CCCXXV. Screen.

The following are a few as examples of these; CCCXXV. and other samples on the screen, as well as

CCCCXC., CCCVIII. Cases

show the character of Greek lace with one or two coarse threads passing along the ribbon design which is identical with modern Russian and Hungarian Guipure;

CLXXXVI. Cases

is the same kind of design but different in treatment, having a mesh ground and thick cord following its arabesques, in the middle of which large holes are left to vary the heavy effect, and here is found the original idea which developed into Neapolitan and Milanese point.

CCCXXI., CCCXXIII. Screen.

CCCXXI. is a sample of white, and CCCXXIII. of yellow close guipure which, as well as CL are from Corfu. N.º CCCXXIII, however is composed of the renowned fibre of aloes produced on that island.

The laces from Cyprus and the Southern Islands of the Mediterranean, as well as those in Madeira, although oriental in design, see

CCLXVIII., DVIII., CCCXVI. Cases,

resemble the cloister laces of the Eighteenth Century which, though fine in effect, were not very difficult to execute and so were taught by the Nuns wherever they founded schools, see

CVI. Cases.

and others.

The oriental and Greek designs rapidly developed in the artistic atmosphere of the Renaissance into very beautiful and costly laces, the workwomen adapting their advantages while suppressing their defects, and these simple laces therefore soon developed into the highly prized points of Genoa, Naples and Milan, and into the beautiful guipures of Ragusa and Venice which have always retained an oriental character in their flowers and arabesques.

CCXXII. Cases

is a superb example of the ability of Venice in this kind of lace. It is a very deep flounce, composed entirely of tendrils, leaves and flowers, following each other in varied combinations of perfect naturalness and grace, executed in a ribbon of close stitch bordered with a fine cord, held together by purled bars and having the hearts of the flowers composed of fancy complicated stitches. It belonged to the patrician family Buoncompagni of Bologna, and is said to have been made for Pope Gregory XIII. when he was yet Cardinal Ugo Buoncompagni.

See Photographic Album.

The Italian Artist whose pictures most faithfully reproduce the embroideries, laces and splendour of costume which distinguished this century, was Lavinia Fontana of Bologna, born in 1552. She was greatly patronized by this house and received frequent orders from pope Gregory XIII.; she not only enjoyed a deservedly great reputation in her own country, (some of her paintings having been attributed to Guido Reni) but her name was known far and wide, and the king of Spain considered her work worthy of occupying a prominent place in the Escurial.

CCCCLXX., CCCCLXXXII., CCCCXLII. Screen.

Other examples of Venetian Guipure are CCCCLXX., CCCCLXXXII. and CCCCXLII, a beautiful piece of this lace belonging to a lady of Genoa, and CCCV., CCCLIX. and others on the screen.

CCCVII., CCCLXIII. Screen

are made in another variety of bobbin guipure, purely Italian in style and execution which has never been copied in other countries; it was produced in Italy alone, and there only about Venice, Ragusa and on the shores of the Riviera by the fisherfolk who destined it for the service of the church. In order to distinguish it from the numerous other varietes of Genoese guipure it is here designated by the name of Rapallo, to which village, with the neighbouring Santa Margarita, is attributed the earliest manufacture of this kind of lace. In the Register of the parish church at Santa Margarita exists an old parchment design for working this lace (which has been reproduced in the school Brazzà); it must be of very antique origin for on its back is noted a list of old fishing nets and laces presented as a votive offering to the church in 1592 by the fishermen after a successful season of coral fishing.

CCCVII. Screen., DCLII. Cases.

In N.º CCCVII., and among the samples exhibited by the Nuns of the Ursuline convent at Cividale in Friuli, DCLII. who guard the only Longobard temple still existing,

CCLXVIII. Cases.

and in CCLXVIII. 2. we have samples of this lace, of which a beautiful piece is in the possession of the chapter of St. Daniele in the same province.

The finest specimens are only to be found in the churches, but the Government does not permit real Art treasures of any kind to leave the country and we were too pressed for time to have them photographed; no more perfect example could however be desired than this rare and beautiful lace, which when it is made so very fine is called *vermicelli*, exhibited on the surplice

CXLVI. Cases.

N.º CXLVI. Here the design. is formed entirely of narrow cords, woven in the most difficult of all bobbin stitches to work continuously and with regularity, as is done here. This lace is placed at the foot and around the neck and sleeves and on the shoulders where it is mixed with reticellas of an antique surplice, the seams of which are held together by curious buttons and loops. This garment possesses a twofold historical interest. In the first place because it belongs to the son of Angelica Bafico, the clever noble-hearted woman of the people who, in the second quarter of this century, devoted her entire zeal and intelligence to the successful revival of the lace industry in Liguria, and whose name has, among lace makers, become a synonym for thrift and intelligence. Secondly, because this antique lace and the Indian Muslin of which it is composed was presented to the great Carthusian monastery in Pavia by the Emperor Napoleon the First; who knows where that great collector and redistributor of antiquities had picked it up.

In the sea-beaten villages situated on the shores of the Gulf of Genoa where these laces were made, whilst the men were engaged in fishing, or on long voyages in the great Venetian and Genoese merchant vessels, their wives and daughters who staid at home worked diligently with the bobbins or needle, producing well paid laces the price of which added to the family comfort, or formed a sum with which to start in housekeeping when the lover returned from the perils of the deep to claim the young girl whom he had courted during the previous winter; the arsenals and foundries in Spezia and about Genoa, combined with the work of that great port have modified customs in Liguria, but this simple story is repeated year by year at Burano and round Venice, thanks to the thrift of the female population and to the prosperity produced by the earnings and educational influence of the Lace schools. The romances of the lace makers have crystalized in a pretty tale about the invention of the fairy like " Rose point, *e se non è vero é ben trovato*, and worthy to be repeated. It appears that at the epoch when every second woman in Venice, rich or poor, was occupied in making point lace, a sailor lover brought home to his sweet heart some strange and lovely growths which he had picked up from the bottom of the sea while gathering coral, and thinking of her. On his return home he offered her these " frutti di mare „ — or sea-fruits — as the Italians appropriately call them, as a simple memento of his summer toils and as a proof of his faithful memory of her, and then shortly afterwards started on another much longer and more perilous voyage from which he would return with plenty of honestly earned gold with which to begin in comfort their young wedded life.

In parting he sought to console her with pictures of his glad return, and jestingly warned her not to put out the fire of her bright eyes with too much useless weeping, but to use it to direct her needle in making such a beautiful wedding veil, as would cause him to find as smart a bride as any lord's awaiting him on his return. Her loving heart treasured up this parting advice, and she determined to follow it by picturing in lace each simple gift of his, so that on her bridal day they would shew who occupied her thoughts during the months of separation. With true artistic talent and infinite patience she wove in finest thread the reproductions of the tiny shells and of the frills upon frills that composed tha delicate sea weeds, and among these she cosily placed imitations of starfish, sea anemonies and other marine gems, all held together by delicate tendrils copied from fine sea weeds. and when the happy day dawned that was to crown their faithful hearts, the simple Venetian maiden, blushing beneath her handiwork in such a veil as no crowned head had ever prided itsef on wearing, stepped forth to meet her lover and presented to the sunlight the first example of that rarest and most delicate of all laces, the inestimable " Rose Point ", of which many of the beautiful Venetian point laces

MXXXIII.-MXL. Royal laces.

from MXXXIII. to MXL., exhibited by Her Majesty the Queen of Italy are composed.

CXIV. Cases.

The small fichu N.° CXIV. and the deep cuff CLXXII.

CLXXII. Cases.

are such fine and complicated examples of this lace that they are worthy to be placed with their Royal sister to illustrate the story.

While the professional lace makers toiled with inventive zeal, they were not forgotten or neglected by the high born patronesses of all that was beautiful; a Lady Mary of the great name of Morosini, which is synonymous with the honor and glory of Venice, had no sooner married than her bright intelligence, inspired by a fervent desire to benefit her country women, made use of the experienced gained in the work room of her father's palace to start a school and large atelier which she personally superintended, and soon became one of the greatest and most indefatigable protectresses of artistic design and perfect execution in the various Venetian points. Another daughter of the same house, another Lady Mary, who married the Doge Marin Grimani, also devoted her privy purse to found a great atelier in the quarter of Santa Fosca, endowing it with a permanent teacher and directress who was guaranteed every comfort and a pension for life; this school produced the clever work women who executed those beautiful laces which tempted the wealthy of the whole of Europe, and which caused Cardinal Mazarin, and afterwards Colbert to cast such envious glances on this source of prosperity for Venice; probably its busy work rooms were those visited by the French Ambassador whom Colbert had instructed to spy out all details concerning the production of bobbin and needle lace; and probably also it was there that this same French nobleman bought the very pieces of point which he writes to Colbert he is sending him to illustrate his report, and to serve as experimental patterns for the French work-women.

The directresses of this exhibit have been unsuccessful in their endeavours to open the ancient wardrobes of this great family, and to draw from perfumed darkness some rare bit of old Venetian point which would carry to America the memory of this old atelier, and of historic and philantropic deeds in the old Republican city with which the name of Morosini is inseparably associated in the mind of every school girl; notwithstanding there are no lack of illustrations furnished by great Venetian Families, as the Countess Papadopoli has contributed a rare collection of historical laces which will be described later on and the family

CCCCXXIII., CCCCXXV. Wall.

of Falier which has counted so many doges, ambassadors and senators among its sons has had its historic laces photographed for the ladies, CCCCXXIII. shewing, interlaced among the delicate blossoms of Rose point, the doge's horn and double Fs forming the monogram of the personage for whom the lace was executed. Lucca Cathedral also sends a superb photograph

CCCCXXI. Wall.

of the Dame quality of rose point; and the princess Corsini, one of the Queen's ladies of the palace and who is also a Patroness, contributes a most interesting collection of photographs of the superb Venetian lace existing among the innumerable art treasures which form part of the heirlooms of that great Italian house; of these

CCCCXLI A. Wall

is taken from a superb piece of Reticella of the Sixteenth Century, composed of leaves and discs and edged whith deep turrets.

CCCCXLI. B. Wall

is the photograph of a magnificent deep flounce in Rose point of the Seventeenth Century, whith a monogram and princely crown surmounted by a canopy, representing the special distinction of the " baldachino „ or canopy accorded to Roman princes.

CCCCXLIII. A. Wall

Belongs to the same trimming, and constitutes the lower end of one of the lace aprons which were the fashion in the Seventeenth Century.

CCCCXLIII. B. Wall

Represents a perfectly preserved square collar in the form of a jabot, such as is worn by Colbert in his portrait, trimmed with richly worked Punto Tagliato a fogliame.

CCCCXLIII. C. Wall

is reproduced from a cuff and border of rich rose point belonging to the same family.

DXLIII. to DLXXI. Album.

DXLIII. DXLV. and the succeeding N.° DLXXI. are all photographs of Venetian embroideries and laces of this epoch, still existing in the province of Udine.

The Rezzonico Family, of which pope Clement the VII. was a member is represented not only by the superb Venetian Point lace,

MIV. Cases.

of the Eighteenth Century, belonging to her Majesty Queen Margaret, and which has been so frequently and so perfectly copied at Burano, but also by a surplice,

CXCVI. Cases.

in exquisitely embroidered muslin, with insertions of pillow lace, and bordered with chow lace of the kind made by the Salesian Nuns.

This surplice is lent by the lady patroness who now occupies the vast and solemn palace built in the childhood of that pontiff, and which of late years became the last earthly dwelling place of the glorious poet Browning, whose son she married.

CCCLXXXVI. Cases.

N.° CCCLXXXVI., near by, was also made by Nuns of the same order. Tradition says that this surplice was made for the Rezzonico Pope, Clement VII. as an offering from his native city; and the admirers of the

great poet presented it to him in recognition of his love for Italy and Venice, and above all as a memento of the mighty Pope who, in his youth,
passed musingly in and out of its great saloons and marble courts.

DIV. Cases

is another surplice and the most antique in the historic group; it dates from
the Sixteenth Century and is composed entirely of bands of finest Burato,
worked in trapunto and trimmed with insertions and borders of Genoese
point; it is the property of the old Boiognese family of Dallolio a dangther
of which has perpetuated its name and fame by her poems. Other beautiful
flounces and bits of *rose*, and the different *Venetian Ponts* which have been
left unmentioned are :

DCXXII. Cases.

a jabot of fine rose point

CCCLXXXIV. Cases.

CCCLXXXIV. a cuff of the earliest quality of the same.

CCCXLIII. Screen.

a square of elaborate rose point

CCCXLV. Screen.

a cuff of the same

CCCXXIX. Screen.

a piece of ivory point

CCCXLIX. Screen.

a square edged with Punto Tagliato a fogliame.

C., CII. Cases.

two flounces one of Punto in Aria and the other of ivory point, belonging
to tho most flourishing period of this lace, and   ,

CCLXVI. Cases.

is interesting as forming the square border, in the same lace, of one of the immense handkerchiefs which necessarily supplemented the jewelled snuff-boxes inseparable from the deep pockets of the period. Finally we linger beside

CCLVI., CCLVIII., CCLX. Cases.

a flounce consisting of the softest, most exquisite quality of Venetian Punto in Aria, composed entirely of fine leaves and delicate tendrils; this was the favourite lace of Louis XIV, and which Colbert sought but too successfully to have copied by Frenchwomen and established as a French product.

CCLX. consists of the deep cuffs or revers worn at that period; and CCLVIII. of the narrow trimming of the same lace. This superb lace originally belonged to the house of Navarre. It is not generally known how much the wise statesman coveted for the industry of his country the well-filled sacks of golden coin which were sent each year to Italy in exchange for these delicate fabrics.

From MDCXIII. under Richelieu, severe restrictions followed by absolute prohibitions such as the famous Code Michaud and the supplementary ones which continued to appear from time to time, had been promulgated in vain against every kind of lace, and have been most wittily recorded in the satire called the *Revolte des Passements*, dedicatd to Madmoiselle de la Frousse Madame de Sevigné's (*) neice. But these wise laws by which Cardinals Mazzarin and Colbert tried to limit the terrible extravagance of the French nobility had been enacted in vain, and the fashion for lace was as great, and the resistance to their decrees as obstinate as the determination to follow the example of the young *Roi soleil* and his gaudy butterfly court could inspire. For the young king was the first to defy the law, having inherited from his Italian grandmother a love for fine clothes and a special fondness for Venetian lace which set a ruinous example to those who surrounded him. His weakness was so well known that a rich Englishman, desirous of ingratiating himself with the king, travelled in his private carriage all the way to Venice, where he had a wonderful hat manufactured of the finest Venetian point all in soft, white, human hair to offer as a rare and becoming present to the youthful Monarch on his coronation, a little attention which cost the rich Briton forty eight thousand lire for the hat, without counting the expense, worry, anxiety and fatigue incident on a journey with so precious an article at that period.

Colbert's quick intelligence realized that the time had come when the rich would have their luxuries at any price, and that the only way to stop

(*) This piece is very curious, and full of information about the laces in use in the time of Louis XIV. and as it has not been given in any modern publication we have considered it worth while to reprint it entirely in the appendix, at the end of this book,

LAVORO A PONTOIN'ARIA.

the progressive impoverishment of the country was to be able to rival with home products, executed with the same means and effects, the alluring beauties from afar; for this Italian lace especially seemed to bewitch all who saw it, and to exercise a fatal attraction to reckless extravagance; he therefore studied the question thoroughly, prepared everything with minute care, and when he had found a soil suited to the coveted product, he managed, by promises of great rewards and special favour, to persuade skilled workwomen to come and teach their secrets to the less able lace makers of France. Mazarin had done the same with other trades, and Venice, who now saw her cleverest artisans slipping away from the workshops, was forced in self defence to promulgate a severe decree inflicting imprisonment, and even death, on the families of those emigrants who should continue to absent themselves, at the same time promising not only full pardon but also honours and lucrative employment if they returned; it was however now too late; the barrier was broken down; cupidity on the one side and French intelligence, high patronage and the irresistible will of the Grand Monarque, backed by the genius of Colbert on the other, had conquered, and the Queen of Commerce was destined to see her monopoly of the manufacture and trade of her laces slowly ruined by the fierce competition, business enterprise and clever statescraft of other nations. Ten years of able management permanently established the manufacture of point lace in France. The exclusive right of manufacture had been ceded for this period to a society having such directors as Pluymers, Lebie and Lebie de Beaufort in whose hotel at Paris the emporium was opened and the board sat.

The King's smile was, in those days, worth all the most attractive modern advertising. When His Majesty went after supper to the Hotel Beaufort to see the new laces, designated them by the sounding title of *Grand point de France „* and declared himself highly pleased with them, who could fail to be pleased also? and when, soon after, he opened the wonderful new pavilions at Marly, and each lady of the court who was his guest on that occasion found a complete garniture of this same lace awaiting her in her dressing room as a delicate attention from the king (a prize packet advertisement worthy of so great a personage) how could she fail to discard her Venetian point and to wear instead the new lace in honour of the most amiable of hosts? And when all the lucky women who went to Marly had French lace, how could the unlucky ones who were not invited appear at Court in Italian point as a perpetual reminder of their enforced absence?

Thus was floated a new industry in the Seventeenth Century, and it strikes me that behind its high flown compliments and graceful elegances was hidden all the business astuteness of nineteenth century work-a-day Paris.

This clever stroke is recorded by Boileau in his epitre au Roi.

" Et nos voisins frustés de ces tributs serviles

" Que payait à leur art le luxe de nos villes. „

The gains of the Society were naturally very great, but on the expir-

14

ation of the monopoly it was not renewed, as Colbert desired prosperity among the people and a more rapid diffusion of the new industry than could possibly take place under even the most extensive of monopolies. Nevertheless, the Society had started schools in Aurillac, Sedan, Duquesnoy, Arras, Loudun, etc. but these places soon lapsed again into making the bobbin-lace for which they had been previously known; it was in Alençon, in the neighbouring town of Argentan and surrounding villages that the new variety of needle lace took root, and this is easily accounted for by the fact that the tradition already existed there: Catherine de' Medici had received the county of Alençon as her dower, and on her long visits to the Castle she surrounded herself with ladies of that province whom she inspired with her love for working in reticella, embroidered net, and the laces of her time. These ladies taught all their friends, and the fashion gradually spread, so that when Colbert, in 1545, began to look round for favourable spots in which to start the new industry, the intelligent Favier Duboulay, who in his official position at Alençon had every opportunity for observing, wrote to him that all the women and children in and around Alençon and Argentan were busied in producing *velin*, which was what they called reticella on account of the parchment on which it was worked, and this term was afterwards retained by them to designate the needle point which supplanted it. He also wrote that for several years a certain Marthe Barbot, dame la Perrière, who had learned the Art in Venice, had been perfecting so many of the abler workwomen in point lace, that there were 8000 who were engaged on the finer qualities and Mme la Perrière was able to sell the products of her ateliers, for which there was great demand, at very high prices.

It would seem that here the monopoly should have immediately and greatly prospered, but the people were accustomed to work at home, and resisted the innovation in every possible way; still, forced to submission by the government officials, they produced beautiful work and, through the company and the Italian teachers furnished by it, learned what Colbert desired. This story is less romantic than that telling of Mme Gilbert, of Colbert's niece the Abbess, etc. and of Colbert's moated castle of Lonrai in which Mrs. Palliser says the manufactory was started under the direction of the wonderfully clever though mythical Madame Gilbert, who at great expense, had brought thirty lacemakers from Venice, and of which she gives an illustration in her history of lace.

This frail fabrication however crumbles before the fact that the castle of Lonrai did not come into the Colbert family until his eldest son, Jean Baptiste, married Catherine Thérèse de Martignon to whose family it had long belonged and who brought it as her dower, in 1679, fourteen years after the opening of the lace schools by the Company. The lace which the women preferred to make at Alençon was not the regular point de Venise, although this was executed when ordered, but was the lighter Burano point which came into fashion when that pretty, porcelain beauty, the Fontanges, decided to cover her skirts as well as her head and arms (she would rather have died than have hid her graceful neck) with rich though light laces, wishing to produce an airy effect suited to her style of beauty; of course the old and fat ladies of the court then adopted this style of dress also, and the more severe Venetian Punto Tagliato a fogliame and Spanish points better suited to their proportions were abandoned to the men and the priests, for the little Seventeenth Century moths, who aped the butterflies and were known as *abbés* also preferred the light laces adopted by the women round whom they eternally fluttered. *Pupazze* or *babies*, as the great lay figures dressed in the latest fashions were called in England, were sent every year from the French capital to all parts of the world. The costumes of the Italian ladies were as superb as those of the French Court, as is seen by the gold embroidery :

CXC. Cases.

made at Florence, **and by** portraits of the period. French taste was every thing; French cut " de rigueur „ and when Louis the Fourteenth visited Italy, the ladies who received and feasted him endeavoured, as we see from the paintings illustrating his three visits to Bologna in 1785-6-8, to appear more French than the ladies who accompanied him.

CCCVII., CCCIX., CCCXI. Screen.

For the costumes of this golden age of lace were, from 1530 to 1796, minutely portrayed six times a year in animated scenes peopled by celebrities, plainted in water colours on parchment and bound in sixteen large volumes wich are preserved in the State Archives of Bologna. These are the cartoons of the *Insignia* (from " Cose insigne „ or remarkable) and are the recosds of the names and arms of the Gonfaloniere of Justice and the eight " Ancients „ two for each quarter or gate of the city, who governed Bologna for two months and were then succeeded by other nine of the most prominent nobles and citizens. It was the custom to illustrate the most important events of these short administrations, and to this we are indebted for these most remarkable paintings. Now and then comes a sad note of pestilence or death, but as a rule we are treated to exact and minute reproductions of great receptions, processions, feasts, tournaments, games, spectacles and religious ceremonies in honour of some visiting prince or potentate. Here we see represented the black lace and deep point d'Angleterre, flounces which Madame de Sevigné writes about as having just come into fashion under the name of *jupes transparentes*, and as being so bewitching.

The passion for black lace was so great at the period when it first came into use, that the designs were even printed in black upon linen, and dresses were trimmed with these borders to simulate the original and expensive new variety of lace. A piece of this old-fashioned " print „ is exhibited in the *Insignia* on

CCCI. Screen.

Deep flounces and black laces are worn by the ladies, with coiffures à la Fontange (coxcombs of lace) filled in with feathers behind and exaggerated out af all resemblance to the dainty lace kerchief which the fair one, whose name they bear, tied so gracefully about her pretty head when the truant wind played havoc with her tresses at the king's hunting parties.

These same ladies have dresses cut as low as they were worn at the French court, and are edged with lace or passement. They wear long gloves and carry their muffs every where with them just as our *élégantes* did their boas three years ago. We see these muffs at the banquet given by the Gonfaloniere Francesco Ratta in 1692, which was so very grand and solemn a function that every guest appeared with her invitation in her hand to prove her right to be present, and there seems to havt been no end of jealousy, coufusion and disgust about places according to rank; the sketch illustratiug 1600-1700 was taken from this painting. The muffs, the Fontanges, and the low necked dresses accompained their mistresses also to the solemn aula of the University when they went to hear the wonderfully learned and equally yonthful and clever Laura Bassi lecture on philosophy, while they ogled the men who wore quite as big wigs, stiff coat skirts and elegant cravats and other lace furbelows and whatnots as did their cousins at the French court at Versailles.

It is to be hoped that all these dressy Bolognese were patriotic enough to wear the Burano point, from which the Alençon was copied, and had not imported all their laces with the fashions from France as they did during the Empire; for this old Burano lace is so beautiful and soft that it truly deserved a better fate.

CCLXVII., CCLXIX. Screen.

CCLXXVII., CCLXIX. on the screen and CCCCLXXVI. CCCVIII. in the cases are examples of how it was worked, being pieces left unfinished in the convents by nuns long since gone to their last home.

CCCVIII. Cases.

N.° CCCVIII. cases is especially lovely in design, with its tiny cornucopiæ full of microscopic flowers.

CCLXXI. CCLXXIII. Screen., CCCII., CCCIV. A. B. C. Cases.

N.^{os} CCLXXI. and CCLXXIII. screen and the collection CCCII. and CCCIV. A. B. C. cases, are pieces of it, many of them are in a very ragged and neglected state, but they still serve to prove the beauty of design and workmanship of old Burano lace.

CCCIV. shows the shape of the sleeve-falls made in the eighteenth Century.

CCLXVI. A. and B. Cases.

CCLXVI. A. exhibited by signora Arca of Padua

CCVIII., CCXIV. Cases.

CCVIII. is a flounce, and CCXIV. a barbe belonging to the Countess Papadopoli of Venice.

CCCCXXXVI. Cases.

CCCCXXXVI. barbes belonging to the Countess Biacceschi, are all rarely beautiful pieces of this Italian lace, and nothing from Brussels, Alençon or Argentan has ever surpassed it. That the ladies of Italy in the Eighteenth Century appreciated the French adaptation of their art is illustrated by the following lists which form a catalogue of the foreign laces which their descendants send to the Exhibition.

To begin with Alençon, as having been the first French centre of lace making:

MXLI. Royal lace.

Her Majesty Queen Margaret exhibits: MXLI., one of the trimmings which, starting from the neck and reaching to the edge of the skirt, were the fashion during the reign of Louis XV. in the Eighteenth Century.

MXLII. Royal lace.

A cap of the same period.

MXLIII. Royal lace.

A Flounce.

MXLIV. Royal lace.

" ditto "

MXLV. Royal lace.

" ditto "

MXLVI. Royal lace.

" ditto „

and MXLVII., MXLVIII., MXLIX., ML., are all small pieces of the different laces Her Majesty has lent to the school of Burano to be copied. Other
ladies who exhibit interesting pieces of Alençon are the Countess Papadopoli, who contributes the Jabot worked in tiny bees worn by Jerome Bonaparte, king of Westphalia, at the coronation of his brother the emperor Napoleon. It was presented to the Countess Angelica Aldobrandini by his son,
prince Napoleon, on her marriage with the great-grandfather of the present
Count. The reliefs in this piece of lace, as in some of those of her Majesty
are stuffed with horse hair, as was the early Venetian point lace, but it is
not pleasant to **wear as the** sharp ends come **out after** a time.

CCXII. Cases

belongs to the same lady patroness, and has a charming Louis XVI. design
of tiny bunches of flowers held by bows.

CCXVI. Cases

also belongs to the same, **but is of the reign of Louis XV.**

CCLXXII. Cases

is exibited by Signora Anais Forlani of Padua.

CXXII. Cases

is a round cuff of the same lace, exhibited by Countess Colleoni

CLX. Cases

belongs to the Countess Bonin, and was inherited from the Empress Maria
Louisa through her family; it is copied in the design 48 made at Burano.

DXX. Cases.

Two broad scarf ends.

DLXIV., DLXVI., DLXVIII. Cases,

Three trimmings of the **same.**

DLXXII. Cases.

a pretty edging of the same.

On the screen are exhibited numbers CCLXXV., CCLXXVII. and a bit of machine-made imitation, CCLXXIX, for comparison.

The Alençon lace manufacturers worked each in his own name and on his own reputation, and objected to any one of their city participating in the special privileges attendant on those days on the title and position of purveyor to the king; but at Argentan two or three ateliers enjoyed the coveted title, and most of the laces for the use of the Royal family, and especially for the Royal treasury were made there. Her Majesty Queen Margaret possesses the most beautiful existing examples of this lace, and exhibits the following pieces.

MI. Royal Laces.

Is an immense bed-cover which is used by Queens of the House of Savoy during the ceremonies and receptions following the entrance of their Royal offspring upon the stage of life; it served in the Carignano palace at Turin, at the birth of his Majesty Victor Emmanuel in the room of which Her Majesty sends a photograph.

MII. Royal Lace.

Is a deep flounce consisting of a pastoral design containing ladies swinging; it is said to have been designed by Watteau, and served, with N.° MI., in the rich decoration of the princess's apartment.

MIII. Royal laces.

Is a deep flounce, designed with illustrations of animals taken from Esop's fables.

MV. Royal lace.

was made expecially by order of Napoleon the First as a present for Cardinal Retz, and MVIII. among the narrow flounces, is the trimming that matches it. This lace is composed of large medallions containing flowers and doves on a fine tulle ground, held together by bows and garlands of ribbon on a large mesh ground. It illustrates the innovation of shading the flowers — petal one being made in close stitch, and the other in sheer stitch — which was introduced in 1807, and gave rise to a tremendous amount of criticism; but it had so lovely an effect that it established itself in lace making.

CVI. Royal laces.

is a flounce which has a design of balustrades and stairs, and vases, such as was very much the fashion in the floriate rococo decoration prevalent in the first half of the XVIII. century

CVII. Royal laces.

is a flounce on which grasses and swans are represented.

MIX., MX., MXI., MXII., MXIII., MXIV., MXV., MXVI., MXVII., MXVIII., MXIX., MXX. Royal laces.

MIX. to MXX. are all pieces of narrower lace of the same quality, many of which have served as models in the Burano Scool, MXI., MXII., MXIII., MIV. being shaped to form the Berta-like trimming worn round the shoulders, and first introduced by Madame de Maintenon; and MXIX., one of the rich frills for elbow sleeves worn at the same time.

Among other ladies who exhibit pieces of this beautiful lace

CLXIV. Cases.

M.ʳˢ Hungerford sends CLXIV., with a design of lakes and bridges in the finest possible quality of Argentan, and

CLXXX., CLXXXII. A. B.

are pretty examples consisting of 2 barbes and a trimming of one design. Marie Antoinette loved to adorn her delicate beauty with all that had a soft airy effect, and the world followed her example, for she was literally the Queen of fashion in the Eighteenth century, as she held long and serious consultations with the great milliner, Mademoiselle Berti, who was called to Versailles for the purpose as a real prime minister would be, to decide grave questions of shades and forms, and who on her return to Paris, published the autocratic decrees of fashion from which there was no appeal. This Queen, surrounded by her family, has therefore been taken as the subject for the prevailing fashion in lace during the Eighteenth Century. Her love of all that was light in effect, and of the Indian mull embroideries which resemble lace, such as

CCLVII. Screen.

called Broderie des Indes, but which were not quite light enough to satisfy her fancy, must have originated the lace composed of designs in fine linen

1600 A.D. *1700* A.D.

A Party of the guests at the rich dinner given by

Francesco Ratta, Confaloniere, the ancients or governors
of the quarters of the city.

In the Insignia degli Anziani. vols. april & july 1691 Bologna.

1700 to 1800 A.D.

Louis XVI and his family in the garden of the
Trianon.

lawn, delicately worked in lace stitch round the edge, and held together by bars as in Venetian point:

CCLXII. Cases.

N.° CCLXII. belonging to M.ʳˢ Orville Horwitz; or applied on a ground composed of all the 65 varieties of Argentan stitches as in the flounce

XCVI. Cases.

which seems the embodiment of the graceful Royal pastorals at which the youthful Queen played in the park at Trianon,

CCXCII. Cases

is a veil, most artistically embroidered in thin lawn dots on the finest Point de Paris, which is a variety of the bobbin lace made at Malines, engrafted on the coarser pillow laces made about Paris in the Seventeenth Century. This veil belonged to the Empress Marie Louise, as did the soft laces

CCXCIV., CCXCVI. Cases.

which, were worn by Napoleon, together with the three Jabots

CCC. Cases,

one of which is worked in roses, and the other two in lotus flowers, evidently in honour of the Egyptian campaign. Another piece of lace.

CCXCVIII. Cases

which belonged to the Empress Marie Louise, is an exquisite example of fine Valenciennes, and was also made when everything Egyptian was the fashion in France.

CLXXVIII. A. and B., CCLXXVIII. Cases.

are other examples of Point de Paris, belonging to different Patronesses.

CCXCVII. Screen.

Many other thread pillow laces were made in France beside the blondes of Normandy and the tambour laces of Brittany CCXCVII. embroidered on tulle — net — in chain stitch, darning, or applied mull, such as

CCCLXIV. Cases.

a veil from Spain, embroidered with the royal crown and initials, which was made for Queen Christina, wife to Ferdinand the Seventh;

CLIV., CCLXXVI. Cases.

And N.ᵒˢ

CCCXXXI. Screen.

are of the same kind of lace from Italy.

French laces in the style of Torchons were made in the mountains as at Le Puy, and the same laces were also produced in large quantities in Switzerland, in Germany and in all the other nations of Europe.

Laces in the style of Valenciennes were made on the sea-coast at Dieppe, Havre, Honfleur, etc., the other finer qualities resembling those of Belgium

CXVIII. Cases.

were made principally at Chantilly and at Mirecourt, Arras, Bailleul, and, above all, at Lille in the North.

CCCCLXXII. Cases.

is of a particularly fine quality of Lille lace, and belongs of the reign of Louis XVI during which it was very much the fashion, as were all the Flanders laces from which it originated.

In Germany the art of bobbin lace making developed in the Sixteenth Century, but it is only of late years that needle lace has been produced in any quantity by the Teutonic races. Augsburg, being in most frequent comunication with Italy and Belgium, was the centre of trade at that time; and here pattern books were published, so that this city and the surrounding country became the German centre of lace making. Barbara Ullmann was a native of this city or of the neighbouring Nuremberg, and when she married into the then wild district of the Hartz nountains, finding the miners' wives about her new home making nets of bone lace like that of Panapolis, she undertook to teach them the perfected lace she had learned as a girl. Her pupils were apt, and the industry grew rapidly under her intelligent direction, bringing money and civilization to the inhabitants of the entire province in which Annasberg, where she resided, was situated, and when she died in ripe old age, in 1575, she was mourned by thirty thousand workwomen who had learned the new trade, and 68 children and grand children accompanied her body to the grave, thus fulfilling the prophecy of a gypsy who had foretold to her that for every stitch she should teach the poor people God would send an increase to her family. The story must have grown out of the coincidence of numbers, but it is firmly believed in all Saxony and Bohemia where her name is greatly revered, and a superb statue has been raised to her memory in Annaberg. The Huguenots and Protestants who took refuge in Northern Germany, Denmark, Sweden and England spread the manufacture of pillow lace wherever they settled down, as it was the handiest means of self support, and always paid well, both in selling and in teaching its secrets to others. In England it also spread owing to the yearly distribution of special prizes to encourage perfection in his class of handy-work. In Ireland, as in all catholic countries in which lace has been introduced, Nuns taught it to their pupils.

In Scotland, Elizabeth, Duchess of Hamilton, tried in 1745, to establish it, but with small success, and its manufacture gradually died out.

Pieces of lace and samples from all these countries, as well as from South America and Ceylon are included in this exhibit, but are marked with the name of the country in which they were manufactured, as they exerted no influence on Italian lace making. With Flanders it is different; its wonderfully even and superior threads had enjoyed a great reputation in Italy as early as the Thirteenth Century, if not before, and were exclusively used for lace making in Venice. During the latter part of the Sixteenth Century it furnished most of the laces used in Spain, and was always the most celebrated producer of pillow lace, but how this art developed to the transcendental complication it reached in the finest Binche and Brussels laces, of which it takes a clever workwoman a year to produce half a yard of edging three inches wide, see

CXXIV., CCLXX. D. Cases,

I have not had time to find out, and hearsay is a poor staff to lean upon unless well coated with solid documentary evidence. In any case the manufacture of those delicate airy laces which have never been equalled by pillow laces from any other part of the world began in the XVII. century. In Holland and Belgium each town had its speciality, attractive and different from that of the others. Brussels, the capital of all, worked both in needle in the style of Burano, see

CCLXX. A. Cases.

in pillow lace resembling, the oldest Mechlin lace, see

CCXII. Cases.

and in point d'Angleterre which is a mixture of the two, originally invented for the English market, hence its name, see

CCLI. Screen.

which, with the laces surrounding it on the same leaf of the screen, illustrate all the varieties of fine Flemish laces, with the exception of

CCXLVII. Screen,

which is old Devonsire edging, copied from Trolle kant

CCLIX. Screen.

which is Cretan lace and

CCLXI. CCLXIII. Cases

of which CCLXI. is machine-made imitation of old Brussels, and CCLXIII. of old Mechlin placed with the other laces for comparison, The city of Brussels has been able, until this past year, to hold the dominant position in the lace trade despite the enormous size of Paris and London, but rumours from Belgium announce that she cannot continue to stand the competition of the rest of the world, because her work-women are paid much more than those of other nations who have learned the secrets of her art.

Queen Margaret exhibits in Flanders laces:

MXXV. Royal lace.

A superb flounce made at Brinche.

MXXI. Royal laces.

A large bed spread, strewn with flowers and butterflies in Flanders Point.

MXXII. Royal laces.

A scarf of Brussels needle Point.

MXXIII. Royal laces.

A cap of Point d'Angleterre.

MXXIV. Royal laces.

A deep flounce that matches the Flanders bed-spread, with butterflies and flowers

MXXXI., MXXVII. Royal laces.

Trimming for a costume in the style of a Bertha, and lace to match.

MXXVIII. Royal laces.

A Barbe of old rococo Flanders lace, sometimes called Brabant point.

MXXIX. Royal laces.

A pair of lappets.

MXXX. Royal laces.

An edging.
        Other ladies exhibit in Point d'Angleterre and Flanders Point:

CVIII. Cases.

A fine scarf with Apollo represented playing on the lyre and surrounded by birds. XVII Century Flanders Point.

CX. Cases.

A deep flounce with birds of Paradise and swans in Flanders point, belonging to the XVIII Century.

CXI. Cases.

A narrower flounce to match.

XCII., XC. Cases.

Trimmings of Point d'Angleterre.

CLVIII. Cases.

Ditto belonging to Baroness Treves.

CCII. Cases.

Ditto belonging to Countess Paolucci

CCVI. Cases.

A deep flounce with double heading of appliqué Point d'Angleterre specially made at Brussels for the Queen of Westphalia to wear at the coronation of the Emperor Napoleon the First, and worked with the arms of that kingdom. This piece of lace was presented by Prince Jerome Bonaparte to the Countess Maddalena Aldobrandini Papadopoli of Venice.

CCCLX. Cases.

A flounce in Point d'Angleterre.

CCCCXXXVI. Cases.

Lappets in old Brussels pillow lace.

DXVIII. Cases.

A veil in Point d'Angleterre with a design of holly leaves and berries; made in the beginning of this century.

DXX. Cases.

Two lappets in Point d'Angleterre, belonging to Marchioness Grimaldi, of Bologna.

DLVIII. Cases.

A flounce of very graceful design.

DLXXII. Cases.

A veil in Brussels Point.

DLXXIII.-DLXXX. Cases.

Two trimmings in Point d'Angleterre.

DCXXIV. Cases.

A jabot ditto.

CCXX. Cases.

A baptismal veil, adorned with Empire figures executed in Point d'Angleterre, wich belonged to Queen Carolina of Naples, sister of Napoleon and wife of Murat; inherited from her by her great-grand daughter Countess Guerini Pepoli of Bologna.

CCCXCIV., CCCXCVI., CCCCLII. Cases.

The cobweb laces CCCXCIV., CCCXCVI., CCCCLII. etc. were made at Binche. The delicate narrow flowered flounces and ruffles, dear to the heart of graceful Marie Antoinette, are from Malines.

The fine and solid Valenciennes were made at Ypres and elsewhere. From Bruges came the soft silk and thread laces in simple, graceful designs such as:

CCCLXII., CXXX. Cases.

as also the beautiful Flanders chain lace

CCXLII. Cases.

belonging to Marchesa Fianetta Doria, Directress for Genoa and one of the Queen's Ladies of Honour.

At Antwerp special laces were adopted, such as the Troll Kant,

CCCCXXXVIII. Cases.

and the Potten Kant of which examples are also exhibited, which were suited to the plaited caps of the Dutch housewives of high and low degree; and so on and on through a long list, containing the less celebrated but always pretty laces manufactured for home consumption, or for exportation in vast quantities to England, France, Italy and above all to Spain. Those in guipure with a broad bold design were made in the north and in the province of Hainault, and resemble this same quality of lace made at Genoa and Milan, see:

CIV., CXX. Cases.

The pretty *rococo* designs came from Brabant and the centre, and were so perfectly reproduced in northern Italy, where they were very much appreciated, that they cannot be distinguised from each other, see :

CCLXVIII., CCCLXVIII., CCCCLXXIV., CCCCLXXX., CCCCXCVIII. Cases.

and

CCCXXVII., CLXXVII., CCXXIII. Screen

made in Friuli.

These laces have all been described in the introduction, and the frequent reproduction of the simpler qualities, combined with the immense quantities of the finer qualities which are still treasured in Italy, are illustrations of the esteem which Flanders laces have always enjoyed there. There are Italian bobbin laces which are worthy of being placed beside the beautiful needle points above described, and the pillow laces are all artistic and have a style of their own; they originally served as models for the early Flanders laces, but are quite different from the fairy products belonging to the latter half of the Seventeenth and to the Eighteenth Century which we have been passing in review. They are suited to the rich, stately type of Italian womanhood personified in the Roman matron, draped in deep hued velvets and heavy satins; they are suited to the solemn services and rich decorations of Basilicas frescoed by Giotto, and of altars from which the pure madonnas painted by Raphael calmly gaze down on us.

The Italian designs for laces never represented pastorals. etc., and so were specially adapted for church linen and vestments as well as for personal and household decoration.

Milanese Point, like Venetian Guipure, originated in Passement, and at the end of the Sixteenth Century rapidly developed into a superb lace. The lace made in the Abruzzi resembles the Milanese lace which is made with a mesh ground, whereas the Milanese and Genoese guipures are indistinguishable; but all pieces of antique guipure having a floreate design are ascribed to Milan, and all those composed of arabesques to Genoa.

Queen Margaret exhibits two pieces of Milanese point :

MXXXI. Royal laces.

Is a deep flounce of the finest quality with vases and lambroquins, and

LAVORO A PONTO RETICELLA.

CCCLXLVI. Cases.

Is a pattina.

MXXXII. Royal laces

is a trimming of fine quality.
Other Ladies have contributed the following Milanese laces:

CCXXVI. Cases.

Is a flounce in flower design,

CCLXII. Cases.

Is a flounce, ditto.

CCLXXXIV. Cases.

Is a square Sixteenth Century collar.

CCCCVI. Cases.

a fine flounce exhibited by Countess Agostini Venerosa della Seta Directress at Pisa.

CCCCXIV. Cases.

a trimming.

DLXXXVIII. Cases.

a Flounce and several other pieces and samples, among others

CXXVII., CLVII., CCV., CCXIII., CCCLXXV., CCXXXV. Screen.

The following are Neapolitan laces of the quality known as old Abruzzi, so named from the mountainous district between Rome and Naples in which they were manufactured and in which a large production of inferior laces continues, only requiring the breath of vivifyng commerce to repristinate them in their original beauty:

CCXVIII. Cases

is a flounce with flowers issuing from bases in a conventional design of the time of Louis XIV, belongs to the Countess Papadopoli.

CCCXCVIII. Cases

is a beautiful fine piece of the same lace which was made during the Sixteenth Century in a Convent destroyed by the ill-famed Marchese Ruffo.

CCCCIV. Cases.

is a flounce of a very fine quality, exhibited under the Patronage of the
Countess Agostini della Seta.

CCCXXXVIII. Cases.

is a piece of lace bought in Spain; the design consists of the imperial Au-
strian double headed Eagle of the time of Charles the V, and of a Marquis's
coronet, as this Emperor conceded as a great distinction and mark of special
favour, the privilege of bearing the imperial arms, so often repeated in the
design books of the Sixteenth Century, to several Italian as well as Spanish
families.

CCIX., CCXIX., CCXXIX. Screen.

are examples of this lace made in Naples; and

CCXV., CCXVII., CCXXVII., CCLXXXIX. Screen.,

of the same made in the Abruzzi. Black silk laces such as CCLXXXIX.
were made at Ischia. Much Abruzzi lace was formerly made at Offida in the
Marche, as also a kind of Blonde in thread,

CCLXXIV. Cases.

and all the ordinary antique household laces, as in every province of Italy.
Besides the guipures with coarse cords, a lace resembling the Milanese
Guipure was made in Venice.

DXV. CCCVIII. Cases.

DXVIII. is a surplice trimmed with an antique piece of the trefoil design
which was universally made in Friuli in the Eighteenth Century, and CCCXLVIII.
is an exact reproduction of the same design made by a clever old Venetian
lace maker named Victoria Tranquilli, who also reproduces " Blondes „ in
perfection.

All the ordinary laces which were made elsewhere in Italy were also produced in Friuli, as well as a special quality resembling old Swedish and Danish lace, see

CLXXXVII. Screen,

and

CLII., CCCLXXX., CCCCLXIV., DCLX. Cases.

At Pelestrina and Chioggia, near Venice, there was such a large production of torchon lace that Pelestrina divides with Cantù the honour of having this quality of lace called by its name, while Chioggia is identified with a certain starred mesh,

CXXXI. Screen., CCCCX. Cases

which is used with great effect even in the finest of Belgian Pillow laces; there is much variety in these simple old laces, as well as of appropriateness of design to the uses for which they were destined; many examples of them are exhibited on the screen and in the cases. The following

CCCXXXVI. Cases,

is a table-cover composed entirely of samples of the antique Venetian laces; it belongs to M.ʳˢ Bronson who also sends a complete collection of samples of the ordinary modern laces made at Pelestrina and the other Islands round Venice.

The Ligurian or Genoese guipures have four entirely distinctive characters. The first, or Hispano-moresque and Maltese variety has been examined with the gothic laces, as also another consisting of the Vermicelli lace from Rapallo and Santa Marguerita. A third is dentical with Milanese guipure, see samples

CXXIII., CXXV., CXLI., CLI., CCI., CCCLXXVII. Screen.
CCCLXX., CCCLXXIV. CCCXC., CCCXCII. Cases.

The fourth is different from all the other varieties of lace and is called " fugio, „ (I fly) as it is very soft and airy. It is an adaptation of guipure-like ribbons of weaving, with open work variations, held together by very few bars, the arabesques being combined in such a manner as frequently to touch and so to obviate the need of extraneous supports, see

CCCXXXIII. Screen:

Contessa Pignone Gambararo of Genoa sends two beautiful flounces,

CCXLVI., CCL. Cases,

of this lace;

CCCCVIII. Cases.

is another flounce of the same, and

CCCCXCVI. Cases.

and many other examples of it are to be found in the.cases.

With the exception of the Blondes, we have now passed in review all the laces of Italy. These soft alluring, glistening, clinging tissues were ever beloved by the daughters of Andalusia, who remained faithful to them when the fickle fashions of France, which had created them in the Seventeenth Century, abandoned them in the Eighteenth, and in consequence, these laces when re-presented to the world were known by the name of the country of their adoption as Spanish Blondes.

The usual white and colored blondes with metal introduced, lack that softness of material and grace of design which, combined with durability, are the chief attractions of lace, see

CCCCXLIV., CCCCXLVI. Cases.

and DXC. cases, but some of these hybrid laces compensate by their splendour for the defects of their less artistic sisters. Of these Lady Layard exhibits a superb collection made during her sojourn in Spain:

CCCXLVI. A. B. Cases.

is a piece of antique blond, and with it is placed a modern copy of it made, as also the following copies of other laces, by Vittoria Tranquilla of Venice.

CCCL. Cases.

is a Rose Blonde, trimming, in white and silver.

CCCLII. Cases.

is a blonde scarf worked in white and silver in a design of the Rose, Shamrock and Thistle which are the emblems of great Britain and Ireland.

CCCLIV. Cases.

is a blonde scarf in white and gold

CCCLVI. Cases.

is a blonde bertha in white and silver.

CCCLVIII. Cases.

is a white and silver blonde trimming. Other ladies exhibit blondes composed entriely of white silk, which were the rage in Italy under the Empire.

DLXXXII. Cases.

is an entire Empire costume with Mantilla composed of this lace, belonging to the Countess Grabinska of Bologna.

DLXXXIV. Cases.

is another costume of the same which was worn by princess Maria Malvezzi Hercolani, Dame of the Croce Stellata and Lady in Waiting at the Vice-regal Court of Prince Eugene Beauharnais in Milan.

DXXXVI., DXC. Cases.

Are flounces, of white Blonde, worked with a honey-combed ground.
These soft silk blondes with their supple folds and great splashes of reflected light have a certain attraction, and in any case Italian hearts owe them a deep debt of gratitude, for they alone carried the traditions of lace making among the Venetian, Ligurian and Cantuese women across the sad years of overwhelming taxation and foreign aggression which for Italy composed the first half of the Nineteenth Century. These blondes of inferior quality kept the bobbins flying, and though there was no demand for point laces, the mending of those belonging to the Cardinals and Churches kept the needle at work according to the traditions of the age, and that sufficed as a found-ation for the intelligent revival which began on the Ligurian coast, about 1848, with the production of a pretty lace resembling Points de Malines and de Lille well suited to the style of costume then worn, see

CCLXXX., CCCCXII., CCCCXXII., CCCCXXXII., DXVI. Cases.

a cape, and

DXVI. Cases.

a flounce belonging to the Marchesa Cavriani.
This, when the fashion changed, was followed by the copying, about Genoa and at Cantù, of the white and black Brussels laces of which

CCLIV. Cases.

is the first piece executed at Santa Marguerita, in 1868, for the Countess Pignone Gambero; these laces required great exactness and re-developed the intelligence and ability of the work-women, so that if the demand increase in proportion to the hopes of the clever lace-makers and to the good will and necessity of the poorer classes, Italy will, in the Twentieth Century again become what she was in the Sixteenth, the guiding genius of good taste in this art and the purveyor of the most truly beautiful laces.

For though greater regularity may be found in the coarse laces of other countries than exists in those of Italy, even the most ordinary of her bobbin laces possesses, in company with her unrivalled needle laces, the quality of true artistic sentiment when the designers are allowed to follow the old traditions which gives them the prestige of originality, for they are not *modern lace*, this term, as distinguised from that of *antique lace*, being simply synonymous with mechanical perfection. The finest modern *hand-made* lace is composed of perfectly even, machine-spun silk, thread, or cotton, dyed a beautiful black, bleached to a dead white, or coloured a brilliant cream, worked, with great manual dexterity, in nicely shaded designs copied from dravings of real birds, butterflies, flowers and fruits, interspersed with meaningless scrollwork and cast iron devices which are vulgar even on café pavillions. These component parts are all worked separately, one woman making the cast-iron devices, another all the roses, another all the butterflies, etc., so as to obtain individual perfection at the sacrifice of artistic completeness, for no two human beings can execute work exactly similar. These pieces are then united with perfect nicety, carefully pressed, and a quality of work is placed upon the market which has no individuality and can be imitated by machinery, and no one but the starving lace-maker thus deprived of her means for earnning a livelihood is the loser.

Italian laces makers, as will be seen from the reproductions of old designs exhibited in the Italian Section both in the Woman's Building and in the Palace of Liberal Arts, have an indestructible sentiment of art and are capable of producing antique lace, with all its rich, inimitable forms and rich soft tones, but in strong, new thread and in unlimited quantity with the consequent lowness of price necessary to suit the present requirements of artistic homes; but alas, beside the evidences of what can be done, are placed pieces of laces which prove the lack of intelligent guidance, and the ignorance of poor, neglected workwomen who toil unceasingly, striving to follow foreign fashions which are already extinct, aping the ever changing productions of great factories in flimsy, worthless imitations copied with defective, puerile drawing, instead of reproducing the lace of their own old house-hold linen, or that before which they kneel every Sunday in church, or is brought them by their priest from time to time to be mended, and which dealers seek to buy at any price to sell again in countries were it is appreciated: Until now they have neglected their opportunities, as they themselves have been neglected; but a new era has dawned for the art life of the lower classes: in each great city and industrial centre schools for artistic and manual training have been opened, and in those for girls decorative drawing and lace making are ewerywhere taught; whereas even in small villages in the more advanced provinces industrial night schools for the instruction of the artisan and the poorest peasant alike are everywhere springing up. A sunny day is dawning for the industries of Italy, the morning glow of which will be found reflected in the objects mentioned in the following pages, the bright star which has long risen for lace-making being the Cooperative School at Burano.

1893.

Part V.

Modern Lace, its makers and its framing.

The Italian Section containing the Historical lace exhibit here described, is situated near the southwestern entrance to the woman's building in the World's Columbian Exposition at Chicago, all the buildings of which are designed in the style of the Italian Renaissance in honour of the Great Explorer, the Fourth Centenary of whose discovery of two continents this exhibition has been organized to celebrate. The Italian Directresses therefore considered it appropriate to furnish their Section, which is entirely occupied by the Lace exhibit, in the prevailing style, and their department in consequence represents an Italian *Sala* or salon of the Sixteenth Century, the cases destined for the rococo laces alone being designed to suit their contents. The artist who seconded the ladies, and has furnished so beautiful a framing for the art treasures sent across the seas, is Cavaliere Valentino Panciero Besarel of Venice, an Artist of the type of the same period with the designs he creates, as the Italian Renaissance is bred in his bones. Son of a clever wood carver who lived up to the traditions of Venetian Art although he passed all his life in the little village of Zoldo, among the first spurs of the Dolomites, those glorious Italian Alps which have ever been fruitful in artists, Panciero Besarel from his childhood determined to follow the calling of his father and his father's ancestors whilst climbing the heights of art, ever faithfully following in the footsteps of Andrea Brustolon, the greatest of Venetian wood carvers. Like many an American millionaire, like all the best artists of the Sixteenth Century, he began life by working at the hardest and most menial accessories of his profession, struggling with every nerve to obtain the pittance which would suffice to maintain him while studying at the School of Design in Venice, to change his aspirations into an art, and he succeeded. But the love of the beautiful and the good, the striving for ever after an unattainable ideal are sure to breed the noble sentiment of patriotism which is so often the forerunner of persecution and even martyrdom, and this above all in Italy, the country whose atmosphere is saturated with beauty, poetry, and art. Strangers love to linger there and ever return, trying to call the land their own, while liberty and its country is the dominant passion of the Italian heart. So when usurping Austria sought to lure the young Besarel with offers of high honours and rich emoluments to

17

Vienna he turned a deaf ear, and sent his work to the exhibition at Florence, where his faithfulness and talent were rewarded by a medal and sales to the amount of 6000 francs which procured him fresh persecution as he devoted the entire sum to assisting his unhappy countrymen in emigrating from under the foreign rule. In 1873, however, well merited success crowned his efforts, for his now established reputation obtained for him a large order from the Prince of Wales, and since that period he has received gold medals at all the expositions in which he has taken part, has been knighted, and is the recipient of honours from the Royal Houses of Austria, England, and Italy, and from the French Republic. He has always remained the same simple child of nature and of art, although his curly locks have been bleached by time and by a terrible accident which deprived him of three fingers of his right hand, which for all that did not lose its cunning. In the spacious salons of the palace on the grand Canal, which are crowded with the children of his hand and imagination, he is visited yearly by Royalty, Ambassadors, and the first of Italy, and Her Majesty Queen Margaret orders of him the artistic furniture and *bibelots* with which she loves to surround herself, and never stays in Venice without visiting his studio. The lady patronesses who know him look upon him as a friend, and therefore naturally turned to him as one who would do honour to the faith reposed in his generosity and good taste. His pretty daughter trips about the place with all the charm of an old time Venetian maiden, and her smile is as attractive as that of the delicious little cupids she sculptures; for this demure young lady, who cannot count twenty summers, has inherited her father's talent and it is to her clever hands we owe the modelling of the lace maker, who, peacefully beneath the great crucifix carved by the Cavaliere, sits dressed completely in clothes the material of which was grown, spun, woven and sewed by the industrious peasants of Friuli (*). Casa Besarel forms a charming household, and while I write the words of a cultured American, uttered as she descended the worn marble steps and entered the gondola which was floating on the lazy blue waters of the grand canal, ring in my memory, " Thank you, you have

(*) The flax used for the underwear worn by this lay figure was cultivated and spun by Maria Pazzarini, aged 20, of the village of Ceresets and cost 50 cents.

The lace was made at the school of Fagana by a girl of thirteen years named Giudita Lestani, and cost 20 cents.

The dress is composed of silk refuse from the cultivation of silk worms at Brazzh, and is used to make home-spun hunting suits and most durable garments by the peasants.

The carding, spinning, dying and weaving of the dress, and the furnishing of the necessary findings cost S! 3.50 and is all the work of Armellina Zanor, aged about 23.

The same young woman also wove the shirt and chemise for S! 1.80, the sewing of which was doné by Amalia Cervezzo of Fagagna for 35 cents; she also made the picturesque rag and cord slippers worn by the peasants in the house, the entire material and execution of which cost cents. 30.

The woollen stockings are made from the wool of sheep belonging to the Michelet family :

not only showed me the most artistic carving I have ever seen, but you have taken me back into the Venice of the middle ages; I felt, it almost sacrilege to take any thing from where it stood, for all seemed part of a picture, and so unshoplike „ ; alas the only fault of Besarel is that he is an artist and " unshoplike, „ and will leave his children richer in honours than in money, forming a great contrast with many of the modern " Merchants of Venice „ who go so far in their chase for foreign gold as to pay the gondoliers, couriers and guides who conduct wealthy strangers to their doors.

Signorina Besarel is not the only young Italian girl who has contributed her work to grace our exhibit. Signorina Costa of Rome, the daughter of one of the Lady patronesses, has spent many busy hours over the painting in Italian tempora of the Renaissance Garland of flowers which forms the frieze about the sala, whilst Signorina Celotti, of Udine, worked upon the old tapestry painting of the album to contain the example of the Brazzà Lace school for which she has a kindly affection ; and as if goodness and beauty were synonymous all three of these industrious girls are so pretty that it is only a pity their clever work cannot be rendered still more attractive by their photographs.

The graceful wrought iron gate, transparent as a curtain in black guipure, through which the visitor gains admittance to the Italian Section, as well as the Album full of beautiful designs for antique wrought iron objects, and those made in chiselled metal are the handiwork of Antonia Lora of Trissino, another typical Italian Artist whose father, a carrier between this village and Vicenza, apprenticed his son at eighteen years of age to a wood carver of that city whence he soon moved to Verona, and finally, attracted by its art traditions to Venice, where he maintained himself for twelve years by hard work whilst he studied design at the Academy and perfected himself in *niello* (one metal incrusted with another) and the lost art of casting a *cire perdue*, so that Guggenheim, Richetti, and all the merchants of antiquities found constant use for his talent.

of Fagagna, and was combed, carded, spun, dyed and knit into stockings by Angela Michelet, aged 17, who also made the garter customary in her village ; this all cost cents. 60.

The wooden shoes called Zoccoli are hand-made by the men of the family; those exhibited were made by Giuseppe Perés of Fagagna for 30 cents, the work in wood costing 10 cents and that in leather 20 cents.

The peasants buy their aprons and kerchiefs unless they make them in crochet work, and these form the great objects of luxury in their costume, costing in all, of a quality such as is exhibited, about $ 3. The lace on the apron was made by Ernesta Schirati of Fagagna, aged thirteen, and cost $ 60 cents, so that the entire sunday outfit of a well-to-do peasant made in the most durable of materials amounts to the value of about eleven dollars, but it costs them less, as much of it is made of unsaleable material prepared at home at odd moments. The lace over which the figure is represented as busied, was made and mounted on the pillow by the peasant girl Italia Canciani, aged thirteen, after ten months' instruction in the school of Brazzà, and everything connected with the figure has been produced by peasants whose families frequent this school or its branches established in the neighbouring villages.

The green silk, the soft lustre of which adds beauty to the laces within the antique carved furniture, and causes those of Her Majesty to appear like lacy white caps and foam upon the beautifully tinted naves of the Mediterranean, was spun, dyed, and woven entirely by women in the silk and damask manufactory of Signor Domenico Reisere, Figlio, founded in 1848 in Udine, who also exhibits an album containing a few samples of his rich damasks and velvets, exact reproductions of the celebrated antique Venetian silks, and which are sold as they come from the loom, to adorn our drawing rooms, without any preparatory dressing, and are therefore like those which have survived the wear of centuries, quite indistructible. During this time he also modelled the bronze basrelief erected in Venice to the memory of Sirtori, Garibaldi's Aide de Camp, and carried carried off prizes at the Universal Expositions of Vienna, London etc., as well as in the National Exposition. The beautiful gates in wrought iron of the Museum at Turin are his handiwork, as well as others in London, Odessa, Frankfort, Berlin, and even in the United States; while for an amateur of Paris he has executed a perfect copy of those of the renowned monument of the Scaligeri in Verona. His work in *niello* is equally pure in design and beautiful in execution, and whoever visits Vicenza and finds attraction in the traditions of the life of the Middle Ages cannot but feel an interest in taking the pretty road out across the laughing plains and the high bridge over the roaring Agno which leads to an old-fashioned peasant house in a quaint court-yard full of cackling hens, and with low, rough rooms out of which the family has been crowded by the products of the master's art. Antonio Lora in metal-work is like Besarel in wood carving, an artist of the Renaissance, as were the great examples whose work they seek to emulate, and both belong to a type which has survived the hurry of the nineteenth Century in classic Italy alone, and if one wishes to stand face to face with the life led by genius in the past, he need only seek Besarel among his pupils in a remote corner of his palace on the Grand Canal at Venice, or Antonio Lora in the simple smithy at Trissino, frowned upon by the bleak, ruined castles of the proud Montecchios and haughty Capulets which he told us once smiled on the loves of Romeo and Juliet. Here, like his prototype Vulcan, this master of the anvil limps about among his workmen helping them to twist the glowing iron tendrils into artistic flowers, and into exquisite forms of lanterns, gates and balconies, products of his creative genius which the great dealers in Bric-à-brac sell as treasured remains of the Renaissance for triple the sum paid grudgingly to the artist.

Above the court yard, and behind the busy forge, rises a hill crowned with superb gardens, terraces and green-houses, in the midst of which stands the beautiful castle of Trissino, which forms the summer studio of Countess Loredana di Porto, the most distinguished lady photographer in Italy, whose works are known far and wide far their wonderful artistic grouping and perfect execution, and have won for her the gold medal at the International Exhibition of Photography in London, and elsewhere.

She exhibits 42 groups MMLI. which speak for themselves, and when the best are offered, will our visitors complain of the restrictions which limited space caused us to place on this branch of woman's work?

The mother of this gifted lady, the Countess Bonin, another of the Lady Patronesses who lives on the other side of Vicenza, favours an industry which saves from want the unoccupied of all the villages of the Seven Communes, the inabitants of which are the descendants of the ferocious Cimbrians who could boast of having routed two great armies composed of the flower of Roman valour, and yielded at last to the effects of the climate, not to the attacks of their disciplined enemy.

Albums from Marostico. MMLIII., MMLIV.

MMLIII. and MMLIV. are two Albums composed of samples of plaited straw made in Marostico and in the remainder of these communes, where all the women and girls, with infinite ingenuity and ceaseless industry, twirl and plait straw instead of flax and hemp into laces which are afterwards sewed together to form hats, or are exported to foreign countries where they are much prized for their lightness and solidity.

Another Italian lady, the Marchesa Negrotti Passalacqua of Genoa shows that she has inherited the talent of her ancestresses.

CCXXXIV., CCXXXVI., CCXXXVIII. Cases.

She exhibits a large table cover CCXXXIV. and the front of a gown CCXXXVI. and CCXXXVI worked by herself alone in unbleached thread in *Punto Tagliato a fogliame* before which all must pause in admiration, and realize that the poor lace maker, if only guided by such refinement and artistic talent as she possesses must produce superior work; and for this reason we will turn to the schools, as it is in these lace makers are trained and ladies seek to improve the work produce by cultivating the young girls.

These institutions are divided into two distinct classes: those which are organized as cooperative societies, the pupils continuing to work in or for the school after their training has ceased, and enjoying an augmentation or suffering a reduction of pay as the market fluctuates; and the merely industrial schools, which train the pupils for a fixed period, selling their work to help to maintain the institution and instruct as many as possible, the pupils once having left being forced to provide personally for the sale of whatever they may produce. We will begin with those founded or directed by the lady patronesses, the most important exhibitor being Burano School, which sends over ten thousand dollars' worth of lace to Chicago.

The 400 industrious merry, laughing girls whose fingers gaily worked these beautiful needle Laces while singing the sweet boat songs of Venice are now sorrowful, and the whole school in silence, mourns, for the intelligent, the good, the beautiful, the pious Countess Andriana Marcello who for years had been its guardian angel, and whose last work for them, three short months ago, was to plan with infinite care all the details for this wonderful exhibition. The golden cord of her noble life has been snapped, and she has been prematurely called to enjoy the reward of a life spent for others. The echo of her dirge has scarcely died into silence, and the ripples caused by the passing of her funeral across the lagune — which for so many years gaily bore her to and from the school at Burano — are yet breaking upon the shores of that mourning Island.

The emotion of one who for the past six months worked daily, guided by her experience and noble rectitude, and who in turning to each branch of this exhibit finds proofs of her activity, is such that no words can express, but the visitor who gazes on the sweet loveliness contained in the simple black velvet frame, placed near her beloved laces, will realize all that Her Majesty Queen Margaret, the Committee of Directresses, the school of Burano and Italian womanhood have lost. It was Paolo Fambri who first thought of raising the poor fisher-folk out of their squalor, rendered deadly by the fearful winter of 1872, when the frozen lagoons presented a stony breast on which they beat in vain for bread. He tried having fishing nets made, but they had enough of these already, and other fishing communities made their own, and so his kindly heart caused him to revert to the talent for lace-making which lingered among the people, and seeking out old Cencia Scarparola he found the embodiment of the tradition and decided to revive the art. The Patricians of Venice seconded him with sympathy and money, and among them he chose two of the noblest as of the most beautiful, both since ladies of honour to the Queen, both patronesses of this new enterprise to carry across the Seas the work of these girls redeemed from misery by their efforts. The Princess Nana Giovanelli, with her long absences from Venice could not carry on the work; The young widowed Countess Andriana Marcello saw in it the realization of a dream of her noble husband's and threw herself heart and soul into the work. God has blessed her faithfulness, and Burano with its 6000 inhabitants is now bright, prosperous and contented, and has drowned the memory of the horrors of 1872 in the tender, protecting smile of the Countess Andriana, but she is gone for ever, and it depends upon all who love noble, untiring devotion to carry on the work which she has founded, and so perfectly organized that its only necessity is to sell, and that we, out of our abundance, should buy for our adornment rather the artistic work of these intelligently-guided work-women than machine-made or less artistic lace.

All of the designs of Burano lace are taken from the best antique models, and Her Majesty — who as Princes Margherita di Savoia accepted the

Honorary Presidency of the school — has allowed the superb Crown laces to be copied there, and entrusts them to no other hands for repairs. For this reason, and because they can brave the most rigid comparison, these laces are placed near those of her Majesty, and each one copied from a Royal lace is so marked. The beautiful bridal veil — which alone we have space to mention here — is copied from the historical Argentan flounce given by Napoleon the first to Cardinal Retz, and design N.º V, is copied from the superb Royal piece of Rezzonico lace in Venetian Point which has been reduplicated for crowned heads to present to Royal brides.

Coccolia School. MMXVII.

Another cooperative school, but younger and much smaller, was founded in 1884 by a lady patroness, Countess Maria Pasolini, at Coccolia in her vast possessions in Romagna. This property is situated near the picturesque historical town of Ravenna — of which she sends a collection of photographs — where lie the ashes of the immortal Dante, and in which for many years lingered the sweet, inspired and discontented Byron whose happiest hours were spent in adored and adoring Italy. The cultivation of the fertile plains forming the surrounding Province of Romagna, the inhabitants of which are a sturdy indipendent race, is conducted on the system called *mazzadria*, the proprietor furnishing the land and houses, the peasant the cultivation, and the two equally dividing the profits. The population increases rapidly and the superfluous members of the family must seek occupation by emigrating to some other farm or become labourers. The men have therefore organized cooperative societies which undertake important contracts in other provinces and in neighbouring nations, and these are executed with rapidity and exactness to the satisfaction of those who employ them and to the mutual benefit of all parties concerned, Countess Pasolini, who is as intelligent and active as she is charitable, has thoroughly studied the economic questions of her surroundings, and has published the result of her observations in several pamphlets which have been reprinted in the first periodicals and found so important by French economists as to deserve translation, being considered invaluable authorities for consultation on this subject. The Countess observed that the weak point of the whole system was the disoccupied life led by the women and girls belonging to the families of the labourers. There are no factories around Ravenna in which to employ them, and in this day of machine-made stuffs there is no economy to be found in home spinning and weaving unless the first material is produced on the farm, and so the Countess decided on founding a lace school for these women, permitting them to work at home as soon as they become proficient in the execution of the finer laces, which as they share the artistic temperament of the Italian race, they learn to make with great facility, and the products of their industry, copied from antique designs, are worthy of the exquisite vellum album MMXVII., and the rich satin leaves on which their noble hearted directress has placed them. The school of Coccolia deserves encouragement, and besides its album exhibits all too few pieces of its beautiful work, preferring to execute the complicated designs in filling orders to running the risk of having expensive laces left long unsold.

Brazzà School. MMXX.

A still younger school is that under my direction at Brazzà, near Udine in the province of Friuli; it was founded September 8th 1891, at a small show of peasant products and industries held at our country home by the seven communes which surround it, with the object of developing the small household industries and thereby forming means of accessory occupation and emolument for the large peasant families during the long winter when the ground is frozen or snow bound. Six girls, of which four remain among the best workers of the school, had been personally instructed by me in the rudiments of the art for only ten days, and did such justice to their intelligent natures and short training whilst working before the visitors that the vast public remained enthralled and could not be persuaded to move on, and the Jury of the exhibition decided that this handicraft was adapted to the requirements and circumstances of this part of the Province. Three schools have been opened in quick succession symbolized in the trefoil or clover leaf chosen as the trade mark for their products; a fourth small leaf is budding which promises to bring the proverbial good luck if only the children continue good and industrious, and the public be lenient to their defects. The oldest of the baby schools has scarcely doffed its swaddling clothes, though brave and sturdy, for on the anniversary of its first birthday the precocious infant, with its sisters, had a hundred pairs of hands at work at the peasant show at Fagagna in 1892, received a diploma for merit and good conduct, and many of the little hands closed over small pecuniary prizes. In fact the infant developes with such unheard of rapidity and consumes such larges quantities of pins, thread and bobbins, upon which indigestible articles it thrives, that it quite frightens its foster mother who must appeal to all the friends of honest industry to buy the products, so that a lack of plenty of fresh food, thread, pins etc. may not stunt the child in its happy growth. The girls who attend the school vary in age from seven to twenty, and when they are seen twirling the bobbins and merrily singing in chorus the musical snatches of Friuli, or seated under the great chestnut trees of the park, eating their frugal meal which they bring with them in neat baskets, or romping across the lawns, the heart involuntarily exclaims, " God bless them, and send the work to their willing hands, and to those of their children and children's children, that they may never be raised for wrong doing through dire necessity or lack of work. „ For some of these girls are orphans or

lame or otherwise deformed or miserable, and on the slender threads wound about their bobbins, hangs their whole means of honest existence.

The Brazzá schools are conducted on the principles of a sweepstakes, each one being rewarded according to her deserts, and the work is paid for by the piece, the prices fluctuating according to the amount that can be realized by its sale, the standard taken being the wholesale Paris market; new and original designs command naturally a higher price than more hackneyed ones. At the end of each year prizes are distributed to the most regular, best and cleverest workers of each separate school, and there is a grand prize for the first among all the schools; but, like in a race among young colts, the last sometimes carries off the honours, as she suddenly blooms out into an artist of the bobbin to the joy and surprise of every one, and most of all of herself. The schools of Brazzá exhibit a large album, MMXX, and a quantity of the work done by the girls, mounted into objects for household use either by the girls themselves or by their seamstress sisters — who are peasants also. — Pleading the excuse of a parent's loquacity, let me pass on to the Charitable Institutions and Industrial schools which exhibit, and first among which ranks the Institution of the SS. *Ecce Homo* at Naples, for its size and because several of the Lady Patronesses are on its board of Direction. This institution, which had lingered along as a sleepy refuge for indigent old women and crippled children, sprang into terrible activity during the fearful Cholera scourge of 1884, which swept away all the grown people of whole families and left hundreds of hungry ragged orphans wandering about the streets. Daily this institution, Christ-like in action as in name, gathered scores of the little innocents under its fondling care, and the King, the government, and the city helped in the good work so that to-day it contains 350 inmates and instructs 280 day scholars, many of whom belong to the most miserable class who come to its great industrial school rooms to learn different trades suited to women, and are strengthened in body by its nourishing soups.

Album from Naples, MMXII. A, B.

All kinds of laces are made there from the antique (see MMXII. A, B) valenciennes, Venetian Point, Cardiglia, Reticella, Torchon, Neapolitan-Abruzzi and Milan Point, *fugio,* and a wonderful new lace formed by copying the exquisite gothic designs published by padre Pissicelli in the palæographia of Montecassino.

Reproductions of Reticella. MMXVI. A, B, C.

Other beautiful examples of cardiglia and reticella in exact reproduction of the Antique are here exhibited by Signora Enrica Franchetti of 68 Via della Carità, Rome, who has been honoured by Her Majesty with orders for the finest work.

An Industrial school of which the Lady Patroness Countess Agostini Venerosi della Seta is one of the most active directresses, is that of San Ramiri at Pisa, which exhibits an Album MMI. in which the work is well executed.

Album from Pisa. MMI.

This school was instituted in the middle of the last century by the Grand Dukes of Tuscany to teach weaving to the girls of the poorest class, but this industry, as well as that of straw plaiting met with no success, and so it was turned gradually into an Industrial school in the modern sense of the word, in which hand and machine knitting and sewing, the making of artificial flowers and of needle and bobbin lace, decorative designing and embroidery, cooking, washing and the rudiments of education adapted to women of humble extraction are taught. This metamorphosis into the existing type of Italian Industrial schools was accomplised in 1879, and here, as in all of these institutions, there are always more applications for admittance than can be accepted, although there are about three hundred Pupils in constant attendance and the maximum of instruction is concentrated into three years.

Bologna. MMXIII.

Schools establised on the same system are those of the Institution of San Pelegrino at Bologna, which sends in MMXIII., two beautiful examples of its work in lace and Sicilian Trapunto.

The Educatorio of St. Paolo in Modena, of which Queen Margaret is Patroness, sends an artistic and perfectly embroidered screen

Modena. MLI.

executed for Her Majesty by the girls, who enjoy the immense advantage of artistic education under Count Gardini, and can embroider quickly and perfectly copies of any of the celebrated antique pieces of Italian work contained in the collection of textiles in the Museum.

This collection has already been twice copied by them for German industrial schools, to the great advantage and instruction not only of the girls who did the work, but of the hundreds of foreign children who could thus profit by the unique possessions of the Modenese Museum in textile art.

Sardegna MMII.

On the Western Slopes of the great mountainous island of Sardegna, which rises like an immense foot out of the Mediterrean, surrounded by a shoal of smiling islets, is perched the picturesque city of Sassari, and here, in 1832, seven poor orphans girls were taken charge of by a benevolent soul and placed under the pine trees and among the olive groves in a tiny private house that they might no longer wander homeless. This was the foundation of the Great Institution still called by the name given to them of " Figlie di Maria „ (daughters of Mary) which under the direction of the grey sisters of Saint Vincent de Paolo has gradually grown and been transformed into the centre from which education, civilization and all the virtues go out to the whole Island; for, under the administration of the able suor Agostina Gassini, no less than one thousand five hundred orphans, deaf, dumb or abandoned children, or little ones whose parents are otherwise occupied, or rich girls whose parents desire them to profit by the remarkable educational advantages offered in it by these cultured women, are daily taught and cared for in the various departments of this great beehive, which includes also night schools for men and for women and which therefore exercises an influence for good which may be imagined. We can only speak here of the deaf and dumb children who are the exhibitors of the net lace contained in the

Album from Sardegna. MMII.

Number MMII. Their merry faces are reproduced in the photographs placed with their work; and no one would ever believe they belonged to poor mutes; the reason is easily found, for the motherly hearts of these childless grey sisters have appreciated the longings of the maimed for the company of the more blessed normal children, and so here during meal and pay hours they are constantly with the orphans, and amid smiles and romps and gestures, they learn to imitate their young companions, and guided during the hours of lessons by the wisdom of the sisters, quickly learn to lisp the few uncertain words of which they possess the power of articulating; but better far than this is the effect on the character produced by this busy common life, and no words can depict the transformation from sad moroseness to gay kindliness which occurs in the poor deaf mutes who bask in the sunshine of this sweet and simple though great community.

Florentine Albums. MMV., MMVI., MMVII.

Another orphanage and refuge for abandoned children is that of Saint Silvestro, Borgo Pinto 14 Florence, which sends a large Album, MMV. and six photographs of laces which have been executed by inmates of this institution which is greatly assisted in its noble work by the proceeds from peddling its excellent lace from house to house and in the hotels of Florence. Album MMVI. contains samples of the work executed in the Institution of Santa Teresa Via dei Serragli 108, in Florence which is one of the poorest schools and is under the guidance of the Teresian nuns. MMIII. is the Album of lace samples sent by another Forentine institution in which the young idea is taught to shoot and the young fingers are trained to useful occupations: it is from the Leopoldina Industrial school, which is conducted on the same principle as that of San Ranieri at Pisa.

Cantù School of Art. MMIX. A., B.

Two immense portfolios MMIX. A., B. represent the work executed by the Pupils of a different kind of Industrial School, that in which only one kind of trade, and the designing for it, is taught. These are from the School of art applied to the manufacture of lace at the small town of Cantù, which is situated near Lake Como and forms the centre of one of the greatest lace producing regions of Italy. The lace industry was planted here in the Sixteenth Century by nuns of the Benedictine order, and until about fifty years ago was confined to the production of torchons and simple patterns. To appreciate what it was at that period and the rapid progress since made, compare work **exhibited in these** Portfolios of the School of **Design, or in these of the Cantuese producers, with**

Album from Offida. MMXIV.

the Album from Ascoli Piceno sent by the **Lady** Patroness from the Marche, Signora Tinti, which **is** composed of the most rudimentary quality of pillow lace, for to such depths the once celebrated industry of Offida has fallen, this, lace being now noticeable for its remarkable cheapness alone, or with

Piedmont. MMXIX.

consisting in a collection of simple samples of the laces worked in the Valley of Aosta, sent by one of the Lady Patronesses from Piedmont, the Countess Francesetti; those Ladies trust that in obtaining a ready sale for these simple laces, the poor workwomen will be encouraged and the antique industry be revived.

Lace at Cantù is mostly produced as an accessory to the other occupations of the inabitants. Many factories exist in this part of the country and the fields are rich and require much work at certain seasons, and so whenever a spare moment is found amid the cares of housekeeping the mother picks up her cushion and sets the bobbins flying, the children come home from school, and fetching their cushions, seat themselves beside their mother, and later, when the factories close and the sun has set on the fields, grown up daughters come home and taking the remaining cushions set merrily to work while recounting the simple adventures and gossip of the day. This kind of sociable busy life can but produce an elevating effect on the morals of a community and it has been noticed that wherever this

industry flourishes, the people enjoy the reputation of being both thrifty and
moral. About ten thousand women work at lace making in the immediate
neighbourhood of Cantù alone, beside which a great many more support their
families by this means in other parts of the Province.

The work is produced either independently and sold to merchants who
go from house to house for the purpose of buying it, or at the weekly
market, or else it is executed upon the designs and with the guidance furnished by the shopkeepers and lace merchants of Cantù. Some of these have
representatives travelling from city to city at certain seasons, selling their
products to the great shops, or established in one city or another; many others
execute work by contract for the lace emporiums, not being allowed to sell
the designs furnished to them; among others the house of Jesurum at Venice finds it worth while to have certain work for which the Cantuese enjoy
a special reputation executed there; and I seize this opportunity to thank,
in the name of the Commitee, the Cavaliere Michelangelo Jesurum, head of
this house, for the flattering interest he has evinced in our undertaking, and
the loan of some of the beautiful.

Polichrome laces. MML.

made in his Venetian School of Maria Pia, to complete his illustration of
the present condition of Italian Lace-making. This system is defective, for
the producer is very poorly paid and the middleman is in constant fear of
being crushed between the anvil and hammer, but many of these Cantuese
Merchants have, through inheritance or personal industry acquired a small
capital which enables them to stand alone, greatly to the advantage of their
work women, of their own self respect and of the public. The cleverest among
these are the following, who have produced really artistic work and already
enjoyed distinctions, medals and diplomas at various Exhibitions.

Antonia Meroni, who is head of an intelligent, artistic, kindly and clever family, and is most honorable in all her dealings and therefore a favorite
among the patronesses, sends an Album

Meroni Cantù. MMXV.

containing samples of perfectly executed lace, and a large collection for exhibition and sale, consisting of beautiful designs from the antique, as also
Duchess silk Blondes and torchon laces. Large orders for pillow lace can be
more quickly executed by the firms of Cantù and those of Liguria than in
the schools because they have more skilled hands at their command, but the
object of our organization is to distribute the work, when necessary, among
several different producers so as to satisfy a great demand in the shortest
space of time.

Colombo Cantù. MMXVIII.

Angelo and Giuseppina Colombo exhibit an album containing 127 samples, as also a quantity of lace for sale which is superior by far to the samples, and contains pretty veils, scarfs and handkerchiefs in Duchess Blonde and antique laces.

Marelli Cantù. MMVII.

Marelli Benedetta, the present head of a very old firm, exhibits also an Album of samples and a large quantity of torchon silk blonde and Guipure laces, besides distinguishing herself with some fine black Brussels lace scarfs and shawls, and by great exactness in all her designs.

Gabri Carimate presso Cantù. MMIV.

The family of Marelli, through one of its daughters, Maria Marelli, who married an Arnaboldi, also founded in 1821 at Carimate near Cantù the firm now belonging to Vittorio Gabri which employs about 650 lace makers The trade was established and flourished entirely for many years on orders received from France. This firm has always enjoyed an enviable reputation for the good quality and excellent designs of its work, especially for delightfully soft silk blondes.

Another great and productive centre of lace making is the beautiful Riviera di Levante, between the ports of Genoa and Spezia. Strangers who linger in the Maritime Alps cannot imagine the charm of this exquisite region when the Riviera di Ponente has already become hot, dusty and enervating, and this favoured region enjoys two seasons, that of the strangers in winter, and that of the Italians in summer, for the latter find it more beneficial than watering places farther away from home, as it possesses the rare combination of sea and mountain air, with a good surf greatly charged with salt and iodine. But foreigners in the summer pause alike to watch the diligent lace makers who remain peacefully at home attending to their household duties and supporting themselves and their little ones by the yards of snowy lace which roll off the cushions from under the fingers of the entire family, while their husbands on fishing smacks and ships scour the sea to bring home a patrimony for their children. Genoa is the centre of the lace trade; Sta Marguerita and Rapallo are the greatest producers of pillow lace on the coast, and Chiavari is entirely devoted to that speciality of the Riviera, the fascinating knotted lace fringes for household linen called *Macramé*.

Chiavari Macramé. MMXLI., MMXLII.

Vincenzo Badarucco MMXLI. and Nicola Bianchi exhibit quantities of exquisite and artistic towels executed in this antique work.

The lace makers of Rapallo, who exhibit under the patronage of the wife of the Mayor, Signora Castagnetta Ricci, have sent an Album composed of leaves, each dedicated to a different exhibitor.

School of the Providenza.

Rapallo. MMXXIII.

The School of the Providenza comes first in the portfolio, followed by

Nicoletta Castagnetto Tessara. MMXXIV.

whose laces are beautifully executed and have received diplomas and medals.

Luigia Campodonico. Rapallo. MMXXV.

Number MMXXV. represents the well known and long established shop of Luigia Campodonico, who exhibits both samples and laces of thread and silk, and has been honoured with medals and diplomas.

Teresa Canevaro. Rapallo. MMXXVI.

MMXXVI is the Number assigned to Teresa Canevaro who sends all the kinds which are made in the neighbourhood such, as Lille, Malines, Chantilly etc. Like many of the others she also has enjoyed distinctions, but we desire all these laces to stand or fall on their own merits, and will cease the lengthy enumeration of their qualifications.

Maria Schialtino. Quirolo. MMXXVII.

Maria Schialtino of Quirolo exhibits samples and laces of the same type with the above, as does also

Gheraldella Campodonico. Rapallo. MMXXVIII.

Every variety of Ligurian lace is made by

Rosa Lavata. MMXXXV,

but her speciality is an artistic quality of Chantilly. She exhibits a pretty design of roses of which she sold a quantity to Her Majesty the German Empress Frederick on her last visit to the Riviera.

Angelo Morelli. Rapallo. MMXXIX.

Gaetano Vassallo. MMXXXI.

Colombo Caprili. MMXLVIII.

Anna Barbieri. MMXLIX.

all exhibit the same qualities of lace, but with no samples. The following are the exhibitors from the neighbouring commune of Santa Margherita, the most celebrated of which is, of course that of

Angela Baffico. MMXXXIII.

whose intelligent enterpsise has been mentioned as the cause of the present prosperity of the lace trade in Liguria ; her heir, Lorenzo Barbagelata, sends an album as well as a quantity of lace, principally by the yard, and a fine deep flounce of Chantilly made in one piece with thousands of bobbins.

Felice Foppiano. MMXXXIX,

exhibits laces alone, and

Marianna Marigliano. MMXXXVI,

samples alone, but accompanied, as are the goods of several other exhibitors, by a Pillow with lace upon it in process of fabrication.

Maria Raffo Costà. MMXXXVII.

has a speciality in Blondes, Point de Lille and Duchess Laces.
From Sampierdarena almost at the gates of Genoa,

Ernestina Zanotti. MMXXXVIII,

sends most artistic lace of perfect execution in gold, silver and white thread ; her lace is of the highest merit and deserves to be universally copied in Liguria, for she has returned to the original famous type of work.

Genoa. MMXL.

Giuseppe Russo, of Genoa, exhibits a large collection of samples of modern laces made in Liguria, and

Doctor Vittorio Macchiarello. MMXXXIX,

10 panels illustrative of lace-making in the same provinces.

Perugia. MMXI.

is part of an album exhibited by the ladies of Perugia and contains 101 samples of modern lace which they manufacture in their leisure hours, but this is not the only exhibit of modern lace from Perugia. We have already mentioned the superb, antique volume of Veccellio full of designs and samples which belonged to a suppressed convent in that city. The nuns have, since the secularization of their convents become a busy race without losing any of their taste, and not only direct the children in the Asylums and nurse the sick in the hospitals, but gather round them the miserable and disoccupied everywhere. Some of the gentle sisterhood have descended to the lowest step of abnegation, and in their humility have undertaken the superintendence and instruction of the most debased class of woman hood — that of the convicts in the prisons, so that by their constant presence and loving, pitying care they may redeem them, if possible, and show them that they are lost by association and not by nature. To these the being taught lace-making has proved invaluable, as it not only interests their artistic temperament, but it permits long hours of personal civilizing intercourse, unsuspected by the shy, shamed outcasts, who at the same time learn a trade which furnishes them with an easy means of support for the first moments of sad liberty when want and misery often impel to fresh deeds of crime.

Album from Perugia. MMX.

Number MMX. is the Album composed of beautifully executed samples of torchon and Brussels pillow lace exhibited by the Sisters of Providence, and worked under their direction in the great woman's prison at Perugia.

Messina. MMXXI.

is the album from the female prisons at Messina, where pillow laces and Sicilian drawn-work are perfectly copied from the antique.

Tuscan Homespuns. MMXLVII.

Another field of the Sisters' activity in Tuscany is illustrated by the rich toned material which covers the walls and drapes the (*) windows of

(*) The fringe is also woman's work, being dyed and woven by Maddalena Salvadori, Calle di Pietro n. 5087, San Bartolomeo, Venice, whose specialty is the copying of antique fringes.

the Italian Section. Album MMXLVII. is formed of varied samples of this quality of picturesque homespuns, made upon hand looms by the peasant girls of Tuscany, under the direction of Suor Denis and the sisters of Charity at Migliarino, Province of Pisa, where these indefatigable women, with no capital but faith and perseverance, have struggled on and planted a small though flourishing artistic and deserving industry, the material which they use being of the best, and the combinations of effect chosen with the unerring good taste which is possessed by ladies of culture alone, no matter what humble garb may conceal their identity.

These ladies hope that the appreciation of their artistic products, which must arise when they are known, will bring them many orders which will enable them to increase the looms, employ a larger number of destitute girls, and form a small capital in cotton bought at wholesale prices which would procure for them the possibility of selling more cleaply the artistic materials, dress cottons and coarse homespuns, which are purely woman's work and essentially original, as being produced without any assistance whatever from the stronger sex.

But the gentle nuns have occupations further afield, wherever there is ignorance and misery, and they do not hesitate in their self-abnegation to seek the most distant lands in which to cultivate the industrious characteristics dormant in the laziest savage natures. They only follow the example of their sisters of the Sixteenth century who meekly followed in the destructive footsteps of the fierce and brutal conquerors of Peru and Mexico, seeking to bind up the hearts which the latter had broken, and to cure the wounds inflicted by their barbarity. They sought too, with the healing balm of Christian charity, to soothe the distracted minds of the poor aborigines committed to their charge, and to train the trembling hands to firm self-reliance through the practical arts of industrious peace. They caused the men to build houses and churches under their direction, while they taught the women to sew and make lace to adorn the altars of Him for love of whom they toiled so patiently among these desolate races, and that their work was not in vain is proved by the curious lace

DXCIX. Cases.

which has become identified with the inhabitants of Paraguay, and with the lace makers still found among the Pacific Coast Indians of North America, who have been considered worthy to form part of the great World's Fair which constitutes the apotheosis of Woman's development throughout the ages.

The Italian missionary nuns of to day follow in the paths laid out by their predecessors, humbly thanking God that the inventions of the nineteenth century render their task less arduous, and in Ceylon

DCXV. Cases.

in the Islands of the Archipelago, in far Japan, and in isolated China

DCXIX., DCXCVII. Cases,

in every land where Christianity has penetrated they train the girls in womanly occupations, so that the little heathen orphans entrusted to their instruction owe them a knowledge of lace-making which, practiced with industry, even should other means fail, would always keep them from misery and starvation. Since History began Italy has ever marched in the vanguard of progress, and when under the barbarian invasions which followed on the fall of the Roman Empire all Europe was one battle-field of strife and bloodshed engendered by envy, hatred, malice and all uncharitableness, fair Italy first awoke from her shame, and raising her head shook off the insidious barbarism of the middle ages which was trying to destroy all record of her great Latin past, and uprose with a mighty determination to redeem her reputation, and recivilize and educate mankind. The other nations of Europe stood awestruck by the products of her fertile genius. The writings of her great sons penetrated every corner of the continent and quickened the hearts and souls of intelligent men to higher aspirations. The beautiful remnants of her frail laces, stranded in every town of civilization, are but the straws left by the current to indicate where its vivifying waters have passed. But alas, the taste of these was very sweet and strong, and proved as intoxicating as wine from Sicilian vineyards, and so each nation determined to call the fountain head its own, and the clamour of strife re-echoed from the Alps to the Apennines and once more the sons of the soil were ground down beneath a usurping foreign heel.

The Powers of to-day still gaze longingly towards the sunny hills and blue skies of United Italy, and the young nation is forced to spend all that it can earn to arm itself to the teeth and defend its hearths and homes against the covetous, instead of using it upon the education of her poorest children. Oh, proud and rich Columbia, if you want Italians to remain at home and keep far from your cities and your ports, open these instead to their trade; let the oil and the fruits, and the silk and the flax, the beautiful artistic carvings in wood and in stone, the original paintings and the reproductions of the glorious works of the past, the soft laces and rich embroideries executed by the women, enter your land in their stead; they love their simple homes with a passion that is unquenchable and will bless you for the alternative. Cause your happy citizens to remember the pleasant weeks of travel they have enjoyed among the beautiful views of Italy, the foreground ever composed of wondrous monuments and works of art; cause them to think of the potent charm which has moved them in your theatres or in their own houses while listening to the superb music of Italian composers,

148

the rich voices of Italian singers; or when alone beside their hearths, winter cold and summer heat have been alike forgotten in conning the enchanting descriptions of Virgil, Pliny, Tasso, Petrarch, Manzoni and half a hundred others. Cause them to think of the teachings of Saint Augustine, of Savanarola, and of Galileo, and of the emotion experienced when first stirred by the overwhelming, awful language of great Dante, and the next time they have to do with poor benighted Italian emigrants, let them remember that the same rich soil gave birth alike to all these, and if this fail to touch their hearts, and charitable Americans should still desire to close your door on these brothers in faith and feature, whose only fault is lack of education, let them pause and remember: God did not send one of the great Italians in 1492, across the ocean to discover " an America for the Americans „ as these existed already in your first dusky sons who have been cruelly sacrificed to the exigences of progress, but to found a home full of prosperity and freedom alike for the persecuted and enterprising sons of all Europe in which they might grow and develope into a grand new nation. Cristoforo Colombo of Genoa, who sailed from Spain with a crew composed of reckless souls from all the ports of the Mediterranean coast, brought no money in his hand, no treasures in his ship; his riches were *Intelligence* and *Will*; the early settlers, fleeing from persecution were no better provided, and as the centuries have rolled on and you have grown, rich and powerful, the personal condition and the character of the Italians who seek your shores has not changed; Oh hearken, fair, mighty, glorious Columbia! God-child and namesake of the great Genoese! it is one of your own daughters who calls to you across the waters he traversed in search of you: Close not your doors against his kinsmen, lest in the throng you shut out one of his own children, heir to that genius to which you owe your very being.

Castello di Brazzà, March 11ᵗʰ 1893.

ERRATA

The gentle reader is requested to excuse the typographical errors which have crept in, as they are due to the fact the Compositors were Italians entirely unacquainted with the English language.

Page	Line	For	Read	Page	Line	For	Read
7	19	Manufacturies	Manufactories	85	21	honse	house
9	3	mast	most	»	32	maides	maidens
12	18	given	given to	86	2	flat tering	flattering
»	25	holeing	holing	»	15	dangther	daughter
14	11	elaboratly	elaborately	»	23	defly	deftly
15	9	formely	formerly	»	32	amay	away
»	25	sexagonal	hexagonal	87	18	platers	platters
16	24	holeing	holing	»	20	so, that	so that,
18	12	he	be	»	25	acceros	across
20	18	of or	of one or	»	33	asin	as in
21	18	sexagonal	hexagonal	88	15	af	of
22	20	Spitze	Spitze	»	30	formed	found
»	34	This it the	This is the	95	1	repititions	repetitions
26	22	this work in	. This work is	»	6	origin	origin
»	30	requiring	require	»	30	CCCLV	CCCXXXV.
32	17	Lawer	Lower	99	20	honsekeeping	housekeeping
37	1	lor	for	»	15	willages	villages
»	9	stour	flour	»	21	yonng	young
51	34	Palia	Palla	»	28	abont	about
68	8	fasionable	fashionable	100	7	tha	the
71	17	floreate	floreate	»	29	experienced	experience
72	20	through	though	107	23	plainted	painted
»	24	courd	could	»	26	recosds	records
»	»	fat	at	108	15	havt	have
80	15	in terest	interest	»	16	confusion	confusion
84	31	dedicacy	delicacy	»	20	yonthful	youthful
85	16	volunne	volume	125	24	revival	revival
»	»	aboe	above				

Venezia, 1893. — Tipografia Emiliana.

PART VI.

A FRAGMENT OF THE

RECUEIL DE PIÈCES

EN PROSE

LES PLUS AGRÉABLES DE CE TEMPS

COMPOSEÉS PAR DIVERS AUTHEURS

[5 VOLUMES]

À PARIS

CHEZ CHARLES DE SERCY,

AN PALAIS DANS LA SALLE DAUPHINE

À LA 'BONNE FOY CONRONNÉ.

MDCLXI

AVEC PRIVILÈGE DU ROY.

La Révolte des Passemens.

A Mademoiselle de la Crousse.

Belle et sçavante de la Crousse,
Mon humeur aujourd'huy me pousse
De vous décrire les combats,
Les regrets et les embarras,
Les retraittes et les tuéries
De Mesdames les Broderies,
Des inutiles ornemens,
Des poincts, Dentelles, passemens,
Qui par une vaine despence
Ruinaient aujourd'huy la France;
Leurs vains efforts et le dépit
Qu'elles conceurent de l'Edit,
Lequel l'an mil six cent soixante
Rendit chacune mécontente ;
De plus leurs imprécations,
Leurs belles résolutions,
Les desseins de chacune d'elles
La conversion des dentelles
Qui voulaient par dévotion
S'enfermer en religion
Lors qu'une pauvre malheureuse,
Qu'on appelle, dit-on, la *Gueuse*,
Sans en craindre le démenty
Leur fit prendre un autre party
On deslors qu'elles consentirent
Bien-tost après se repentirent
De s'etre mises au hazard
Mais il estait desia trop tard;
Et pour punir leur entreprise
Je croy qu'une telle sottise,
Méritait, comme on fit aussy
Que l'on leur fit crier mercy.

Il estait environ les cinq heures du soir, lorsque les broderies, les poincts et les Dentelles, entendirent parler des passemens. Vous pouvez vous imaginer leur surprise, après l'éclat où elles s'estoient vetés à l'Entrée, et comme elles se plaignirent de la

Fortune, de ne les avoir élevées iusq'au Trône, que pour les précipiter dans la boüe. Aussi-tost que cette fascheuse nouvelle fut divulguée par tout, et que le bruit universel luy eust donné une entière croyance, ou ne rencontrait plus dans les ruës que des broderies en carosse, qui se plaignoient les unes aux autres; que des poincts, qui dans leur affliction ne prenoient pas seulement la peine de se mettre en linge blanc, et que des Dentelles, qui d'elles mesmes, s'effoçoient de quitter la toille d'où elles devoient bientôst estre séparées. Il y avoit desia quelques jours qu'elles déploroient leur malheur, lorsque le poinct de Gènes se trouvant dans la compagnie du poinct de Raguse, du poinct de Venise, et de quelques autres, se plaignit en cette manière.

C'est aujourd'huy, noble assistance,
Qu'il faut abandonner la France,
Et nous en aller bien et beaux
Pour n'estre pas mis en lambeaux:
Ne croyez pas que ie me rie
Il faut revoir nostre patrie
A mon gré fort pauvre rangoust
Pour estre le baille-luy-goust,
D'un mari de qui l'œil sévère
Redoute toûjours l'adultere
Ou nous serons mis en prison
Dans quelque maudite maison
Et toi pauvre poinct de Venise
Tu dois craindre pour ta franchise
Et que t'en retournant sur mer
Par un malheur bien plus amer
Un corsaire, ou bien pis encore
Ne te traitte de Turc à More ;
Que peut-estre dans le sérail
Où le jour par un soupirail
Vient le long d'une sarbatane
Tu ne serve à quelque sultane
Qui peut-estre, pour ton malheur
Sera femme du grand Seigneur.
Encore si ce coup de tonnerre
Nous fut venu durant la guerre
Peut-estre ma foy qu'en ce cas
Je ne m'en tourmenterais pas
En retournant dans ma patrie
J'eusse fait quelque *menterie*
J'eusse dit quelque *faussète*
Que c'eut été la pauvreté
Et le manquement de finance
Où chacun avait veu la France
Qui m'eut fait revoit mon Païs
Et du Danube au Tanaïs
On aurait crut par ma sortie
Que i'eusse quitté la partie

Au lieu que l'on voit clairement
Que nous sortons honteusement
Encore pour vous poincts de Raguse
Vous qui n'êtes pas ma buse
Il est bon crainte d'attentat
D'en vouloir purger un Estat ;
Les gens aussi fins que vous êtes
Ne sont bons que comme vous faites
Pour ruiner tous les Estats ;
Mais pour nous autres poincts, helas
Et vous Aurillac ou Venise
Si nous plions nostre valise
Et si l'on nous presse si fort
C'est ie vous iure bien à tort.

Les autres parlerent à leur tour, à peu près aussi douloureusement que le poinct de Gênes, lorsque d'un autre costé, les broderies ayant été rendre visite aux Detenlles d'Angleterre, une vielle broderie d'or, qui aurait desia vu un autre decry et qui ne seachant plus que devenir, s'estait mise en tour de lit, et puis aurait été employée à la housse d'un cheval à l'entrée de la Reyne, s'efforça de consoler les Compagnes, en leur parlant de la sorte.

Sans faire la petite bouche
Il est vray que ce Decry me touche
Et m'attaque aussi fort les sens
Comme à vous autres jeunes gens :
Car dites-moi je vous en prie
Poincts, Dentelles ou Broderies
Qu'avous nous donc fait à la bour
Pour qu'on nous chasse haut et cour
Nous par qui la noble jeunesse
Méprisant toujours la bassesse
N'avait point d'autre passion
Que la gloire et l'ambition
Pour nous seules faisant dépense
Vivoit quasi dans l'uinscence * * * * * . . .
* * * * * * . . . . . .
Mais ces discours sont superflus
Mes compagnes n'y pensons plus
Et sans en deviner la cause
Soyons desormais autre chose
Et dans un semblable conflit
Faisons nous toutes tour de lit
C'est une agréable corvée
Pour moi, je m'en suis biens trouvée.

Là dessus me grande Dentelle d'Angleterre prenant la parole dit.

Compagnes, mes chères amies
Après toutes ces infamies
Qui doivent bien crever le coeur

A toutes Dentelles d'honneur
Cet infortune sans seconde
Me fait bien renoncer au monde
Et me fait connaistre assez bien
Que l'éclat du monde n'est rien
Ce n'est qu'un vent, qu'une fumeé
Esteinte plutost qu'allumée
Qui dans chaques occasions
Se chaques en illusions
Ses faveurs ne sont que des songes :
Hélas ! qui peut de ces mensonges
Vous rendre compte mieux que moy ?
J'habitaie la Maison du Roy
J'ai vu toutes ces momeries
Que l'on nomme galanteries
Ou Royaume des beaux Esprits
J'ai veu ceux qui gagnent le prix
Ces grands debiteurs de fleurette.
** . . . .
Souvent cabochet trés-mal faite
Débitent d'un air surprenant
Des *mensonges* à tout venant
Vous autres, belles broderies
Vous avez de ces menteries
Entendu ie pense ma foy
Peut-estre dix fois plus que moy ;
Mais encore que cela déplaise
Ie les entendois à mon aise ;
Car plut-on sans ces deplaisirs
Satisfaire mieux ses desirs
Que de passer toute sa vie
Dans des lieux qui fervient ennie
Aux esprit les plus delicats
Demeurant tantot sur les bras
Tantot sur la gorge charmante
De Philis on bien d'Amarante ?
Quel plaisir de toucher à nu
Nu beau sein tout nouveau venu
De baiser les lys d'nu visage
Non terni per l'esier de l'age
De toucher l'embonpoint d'un bras ;
Mais à tout ces plaisirs, hélas
Ie decouvre bien de meconte
Un Evit nous semble de honte
Mon coeur en est tout abatu
Mais quoi mon coeur faisant vertu
Des necéssités de la vie
Et prenant desormais l'ennui

De renoncer à ce plaisir
Que pouvions nous ici choisir
Qui nous put être convenable
Ou qui put être comparable
Pour ne plus tourner à tout vent
Comme d'entrer dans un consent ?

C'était assez bien raisonner, ce me semble pour une dentelle qui venait d'un païs où la liberté de conscience n'est pas permise et je trouve que pour le peu qu'elle avait habité en France, qu'elle n'y aurait pas fait un petit progrès. La harangue entrat si avant dans l'Esprit de ses compagnes, et les persuada si fortement, qu'elles ne songèrent plus à leur liberté, et qu'elles ne pensérent plus qu'à faire un bon usage de leur disgrace. Mais les dentelles de Flandre ne pouvant pas souffrir une si rude réforme, se contentérent d'obéir seulement à la rigueur des loix, et de se cacher à jamais aux yeux des Hommes.... Ce fut plutot un aheurtement qu'une résolution, et il n'yeut que le dessein d'être rebeller qui leur peut faire abandonner celui qu'elles avaient prise de se loger dans un poste si avantageux où elles croyaient d'être à l'abris des insultes et des insolences des Hommes. Pour les broderies elles en voulurent faire chacune à sa teste. La Lesine en fut resoudre quantité de devenir ameublemens d'autres, plus pieuses, prirent dessein de s'employer aux chasubles, et aux devants d'autels d'Eglises ; mais celles qui avait veillez parmi les divertissements, ne pouvait pas faire sitot de nécessités, vertu, resolurent de s'employer aux habits de mascarades, esperant qu'en cet equipage elles pourraient encore estre de tous les plaisirs ; de la Cour, et se trouver quelquefois aux balets, aux Comédies et à tous les divertissements du Carnéval.

La dentelle noire d'Angleterre se loua à bon marché à un Gibayeur, pour lui seroir de filets à prendre des Becapes dans les bois, à quoy elle se trouvait assez propre dans l'habit ou la mode l'avait mise depuis peu.

Tous les points en resolurent de s'en retourner dans leur païs, expecté le pouvet d'Aurillac, quifut plus de difficultés que les autres, craignant qu'aussitot qu'on le verrait de retour-on ne l'employat à parer les Formages d'Auvergne, dont la senteur lui estoit insupportable, après avoir gouté la civette, le Muse, et l'eau de fleur d'Orange, dont il estoit arrosé tous les matins dans Paris ; soit que ce fut pour corriger l'odeur de quelque gousset, ou quelque sueur trop aigre, où pour attirer les Amans, comme on ammorce les pigeons d'un Colombier.

Chacun dissimulant sa rage
Doucement plioit son bagage
Résolu d'obéir au sort
Ne se voyant pas te plus fort
Lorsqu'une petite rusée
Leur donnant un autre visée
Leur fut bien depus ce sujet
A toutes changer de projets.

Cette petite revoltée s'appellait la gueuse qui arriva d'une petite ville autour de Paris, qui s'en vint comme une enragée faire un vacarme épouvaable. Elle leur quoy qu'elle ne fut pas de si bonne maison, qu'elle avait du moins le coeur aussi bien placé qu'une autre ; et que quand elle serait toute senté de son party elle ne souffrirait pas de semblabes injustices demeurassent impunies ; qu'elle ne sçavait pas quel refuge elles avaient resolu de prendre, mais que pour elle pourrait se retirer, puis qu'on ne luy offroit pas mesme une place à l'Hopital; que si on la voulait voulaît croire, elle engageoit sa chainette ; qu'elle les remettrait toutes dans leur premier eclat, qu'ai reste **elles** ne devoient pas estre si dégoustées, que de ne vouloir pas faire alliance avec elle; qu'elle avait eu pour le moins d'aussi beaus emplois que les autres, et que si on s'etait servi d'elle pour le faste, et pour eblouir les yeux, que pour sa discrêtión on lui avait confié les plus grands secrets des Dames.

Tout ce discours remply **d'audace**
Fit regarder chaquun en **face ;**
On fut un temps sans dire mot
Chacun croyant estre un grand sot ;
Puis rompant ce morne silence
Chacun pour dire ce qu'il pense
Voulant parler à haute voix
Tous commencèrent à la fois
Ce qui causait un grand vacarme ;
Mais après de crainte d'alarme
On appaisa tout ce grand bruit
Et comme il estoit dejà nuit,
Chacun se retirant d'emblée
Et se frappant dedans la main
Toutes dirent qu'au lendemain
Elles s'assembleroient encore
Dès qu'on decouvrirait l'aurore
Se montrer dessus l'Horison
Toutes dedans quelque maison
Afin de voir plus net qu'un verre
Tous les accidents de la querre
Que la nuit il faudrait resuer
A ce qui pourrait arriver
Cependant il remercièrent
Madame Queuse, et la prièrent
Dedans ses accidents pareils
De leur fournir de ses conceils
Ainsi finit, comme ie pense,
Cette agréable conference. —

C'estoit une chose assez agréable à mon gré d'entendre des dentelles discourir de la guerre, raisonner sour toutes ses difficultez, en prevoir toutes les disgraces, et parler en leur langage sur tous les évènements d'un chose si douteuse. Le lendemain un passement qui estoit accoustumé à **ne** point dormir, pour avoir servi à la coëffe du Bonnet de nuit d'un vieux jaloux, les alla cuellir deux heures plus matin qu'on n'avait arresté et elles se trouvèrent toutes comme elles s'estoient doné le mot, au logis de Perdrigeon, croyant que ce devait être un lieu de seureté pour elles ; mais elles remontrère:t la place occupée par les rubans qu'elles trouvèrent si bouffis d'orgueil de n'être pas com**pris** dans l'Edit, qu'il en estoient insupportables : si bien que ne voulant pas avoir de commerce avec de telles gens, qu'elles ne prenait que pour des esclaves ou des fous, que l'on ne laisse jamais sans être liez, que la superfluité avoit mis en credit seulement depuis le règne de Louis XIII, et qui ne passoient auparavant que pour des noüeurs d'eguillettes, à qui on faisoit mettre bien souvent les fers aux pieds, comme à des criminels, elles s'assemblérent toutes au vase d'or, dans la rüe S: Denis, ou on les reçut à bras ouvers.

> Là chacun parlant à sa teste
> Raisonnoit ainsi qu'une beste
> Un autre se tenant debout
> Voulait mettre son nez partout;
> Tel qui proposait une affaire
> Aussi tost conclud le contraire
> L'autre faisant le rafiné
> Le fourmentait comme un daumé.
> L'autre de tout faisant mystere,
> Parle, raisonne, delibére
> Enfin pour le dire internos
> Ce n'estoit du tout qu'un cahos :
> Mais cependant foy de Dentelle
> Disoit pour témoigner son zèle
> Un grand cravate fanfaron
> Il nous faut venger cet affront:
> Revoltons nous, noble assemblée.
> J'en ai l'âme trop : bourrelée
> Et dit en jurant par la mort
> Voyons qui sera le plus fort.

Vous pouvez vous imaginer facilement combien ce discours chatoüilla l'oreille de la gueuse, qui n'aspirait qu'à la révolte et à la sedition. Quelques unes remontrérent toutes les difficultez qu'il y avait dans une semblable entreprise, veu que n'estant plus en credit, elles manqueroient de toutes les choses necessaires; mais ce doute fut bientot levé par un poinct qui asseura qu'il trouverait crédit de deux millions dans Paris, et peut être davantage, si on pouvait voir quelque iour leur entier rétablissement.

> Il n'en fallut pas davantage
> Pour leur augmenter le courage.
> Là-dessus, le poinct d'Alençon
> Ayant bien appris sa leçon,
> Poinct qui sçavait plus d'une langue
> Fit une fort belle Harangue.
> Remplie de tant de douceurs
> Qu'elle ravit, dit-on les cœurs.
> Chacun témoignait sa furie.
> Lorsque de la coutellerie
> Il leur vint par un coup du sort
> Dit-on un très puissant renfort:
> C'estaient Mesdames les Espées
> Encore presque toutes trempées
> **Du** noble sang des ennemis.

Ces Espées, après que le port d'armes fut defendu plutost que de demeurer inutiles, s'estoient resoluës de se racourcir, c'est à dire les couteaux de devenir couteaux de poche, et les estocades de se changer en Bayonnettes; et pour en venir du projet à l'exécution, elles s'en alloient toutes ensemble à la Coutellerie, lorsqu'entendant parler de la Révolte des Passements, elles changèrent bien tôt de dessein et se résolurent de leur aller offrir leur service.

Vous pouvez vous imagener si on les recent favorablement; et si on fit leur composition avantageuse. Premeriement, on leur promit, que si le party demeurait victorieux, à pas — une de toutes celles qui se seroient employées pour leur service, ne pendroît plus qu'à des bandriers en broderie; qu'on les feroient toutes damasquiser à la mode et qu'elles ne coucheroient plus que dans des foureaux parfumez : Les poincts mesme leur promirent de leur part, de les mettre en si haut crédit auprès des Dames, qu'elles passeroient desormais, aussi bien que les plumes, pour l'ornement le plus surprenant et le plus avantageux pour leur plaire.

> On dit que quelqu'une d'entr'elles
> Qu'on disait venir du Marais
> Leur apprit aussi des nouvelles
> De leurs amis les pistolets :
> Tout, aussi-tot de haute lute
> A l'instant mesme l'on députe
> Vers ces ennemis de la paix
> Ou les assura désormais
> Quelque chose que leur pût plaire
> Tout au moins de les satisfaire
> Que si pour les vouloir vanger
> Ils se vouloient tous engager
> Pour plus grande reconnaissance
> On ne les chargeroient en France
> Qu'avec des pondres de parfum
> Et quelques amis de Verdun.

Il ne fallut pas grande eloquence pour persuader les pistolets d'accepter un semblable party. La misère on ils estoient les y fit bientost resoudre; comme il ne voyoient aucune ressource d'autre part, ces propositions leur éblouissant les yeux, ils promirent de faire merveille, ce qui remit le cœur au ventre de bien des poincts et de bien de broderies, qui n'auroient autrement accepté la guerre qu'à écorche cul. Combien vit-on après cela de Dentelles qui se faisoient toutes blanches de leur epées? Pour s'exciter les unes les autres, elles se raccontoient à combien d'occasions périlleuses, elles s'éstoient rencontrées. Telle Dentelle de Flandres, disait avoir fait deux campagnes sous monsieur le prince en qualité de cravatte ; une autre se vautait d'avoir appris le mestier sous Monsieur de Turenne, une autre raccontait comme elle avait ésté bléssée au Siège de Dunquerque et que s'il n'y paroissait plus, c'estait qu'elle s'éstait fait penser sur le metier: Il se trouvoit mesme uue grande garniture, toute entière de poincts de Raguse, qui disoit avoir appris le mestier sous Monsieur de Candale, lorsqu'il commandoit en Catalogue. Enfin en entendoit racconter partout un nombre infiny de belles actions ; il n'y en avoit presque pas une, qui ne se fut rencontrée à quelque Siège, à la journée d'une bataille, et qui n'eut du moins fait deux ou trois campagnes, et telle broderie, qui n'avoit jamais éstait plus loin que du Faubourg S. **Antoine au** Louvre, raccontoit mille beaux exploits, qu'elle avait fait tanstot sous un tel **capitaine,** et tanstot sous un autre chef.

> Ainsi souvent les ridicules
> Rencontrant des esprits crédules,
> Le vautent de mille beaux faits
> Et pour que chacun les honore
> Leur testes dignes d'helebore
> Raccontait des combats qu'ils ne oirent jamais.

Ce n'est pas une chose rare dans le monde que ces sortes d'extravagances. Combien voyons-nous tous le iours de ces Braves jusqu'à degainer ? Combien de ces gens qui se font tenir à quatre, pourven qu'il y ait quelqu'un pour les séparer, et qui ne parlent que de mettre sur le carreau, de casser les jambes, d'abbattre un **bras**, pourven qu'ils ayent perdu l'ennemy de veirë ? Nos passemens en firent bien de mesme lorsq'ils virent le renfort des épées et des pistolets. Jamais **on** ne vit de plus grand Rodomons. Une dentelle d'Angleterre s'ecria la-dessus.

> Qu'avons nous donc à redouter
> Puis que la cour reste sans armes ?
> Ie croy qu'il ne faut pas douter
> Qu'elle ne fasse un beau vacarme ;
> Mais sans que sa fureur nous donne aucune alarme
> Il la faudra laisser pester.

Cette dentelle s'imaginoit qu'elle n'avoit plus à craindre que quelque Halebarde ou quelque Pertuisanne, dont les coups passeroient d'outre en outre sans l'offencer. Le poinct de Gennes pui avoit le corps un peu plus gros, dit qu'il ne s'en mettoit guère en peine, et qu'il feroit faire de caisses à l'épreuve de la pique et du baston à deux bouts. La broderie estant faite en chemise de mail, se mit à siffler quand elles entendit parler de toutes ces difficultez ; si bien qu'on ne vit jamais de gens si braves, parqu'elles s'imaginoient n'avoir plus rien à redouter. La-dessus il leur vint encore une autre avis, que pour quelque desordre on vouloit defendre les mascarades, ce qui n'encouragea pas peu de broderies, tant à cause qu'elles voyoient leur beau dessein renversé que parqu'elles s'imaginoient que cela renforçait leur party, et qu'elles s'en pourroient servir despions dans leur armée, sans qu'on put les jamais reconnaître.

> Enfin tous estoit resolu
> Et chacun d'eux hur-lu-Crelu
> Voutoient demeurer sans oreilles
> Si tous ne faisoient des merveilles ;
> Et sans presqu'avoir contester
> Ils signèrent tous le traitté
> Qui fut depuis mis en lumierè
> A peu près de cette manière.
> Aujourd'hui, solemnellement
> Nous pirons, foy de Passement,
> Foy de poincts et de Broderie

De guipure, d'Orfevrie
De gueuse de toute façon
Que nous voulons mettre à rançon
La cour du roy, notre bon sire
Et que ce qui sera le pire
Nous voulons bannir hauctement
Le Conseil et le Parlement
Pour, d'une honteuse manière
Avoir voulu faire litière
Tant des plus nobles ornements
Que de nous autres passements
Qu'il faut que le Diable s'en pende
Où qu'on le condamne à l'amende
Que pour semblables trahisons
Pour telles, et autres raisons
Voulant toujours aller grand-erre
Nous voulons déclarer la guerre
Et dire partout hauctement
Que sans un retablissement
Qui fut d'eternelle durée
La guerre sera declarée
A tous les ennemis du repos
Et que nous casserons les os
A ceux qui voudront enterprendre
Tant seulement de les defendre.
Ce que nous signons tout entier
Ce dix-huitième janvie
Tant les nouvelles broderies
Comme celles des friperies
Tant les gueuses, les agréments
Comme les autres passemens.

Le traité ayant été signé, on ne songea plus qu'à choisir un poste avantageux pour les trouppes, mais il s'ement quantité de difficultez sur le sujet. Les uns soutenaient par vives raisons qu'il fallait sortir de Paris, parce que tant que l'on habitait avec ses ennemis il estoit impossible de se garantir de leurs embusches, que si l'on faisoit ce pas en arrière, ce n'estoit que pour mieux santer ; et qu'il vallait bien mieux voir venir l'ennemy à soy, que de l'avoir de quelque costé que l'on se tourne. Mais une dentelle qui avait autrefois servy à..........soustint qu'elle sçavait par experience que de quitter Paris, c'estoit abandonner la party, et qu'il valait bien mieux s'emparer du terrain et le disputer que de l'abandonner sans éspérance de la prendre puis après d'emblée : que de plus elle sçavait bien qu'ils ne manqueroient pas de partisans, qui leur donneroient tous les iours de nouvelles forces et de nouvelles lumières des affaires ; aulieu qu'estant hors de Paris, on n'en pouvait sçavoir que par les espions ; et que le Regiment de Garde estant tout les jours à l'affut pour les découvrir ils ne perdroient autant qu'ils ne feroient sortir de leur armée.

Il s'ement encore une seconde difficulté pour sçavoir si on feroit la guerre ouvertement, si on mettroit dabord le siège devant quelque place, et si on rangeroit tout d'un coup l'armée en bataille ; où bien si on si menageroit davantage, si on ne se contenteroit pas de repousser les insultes et si on ne se metteroit pas plutôst en éstat de faire une retraite honorable, que de s'engager tout d'un coup dans des combats, dont le seul appareil serait capable de les épouvanter. On fut encore partager sur cet article : les uns soutenaient que c'estoit trop hazarder, que de donner bataille tout d'un coup ; qu'il estoit difficile que des trouppes, qui n'avoient habité que parmy les femmes, fussent sitost aguérries ; et que si elles venoient à la perdre, elles seroient perduës sans ressource et ne se ralieroient iamais. Les autres soutenoient que les premiers efforts estoient touiours les plus violents ; que tel qui fournissait bien une carrière, n'estoit pas quelquefois à l'épreuve d'une seconde, et que des cœurs mal aguérris se ratentissoient assez tost ; que la moindre pluys, et le moindre mauvais temps, les rendroient toutes males et sans vigueur ; que ne combattant pas à force ouverte on les dissiperoit toutes petit à petit ; que deux millions n'estoient pas suffisants pour faire subsister si long-temps une armée si nombreuse, et que quand leur finances servoient épuisées, elles ne voyoient pas à qui elles pourroient avoir recours. Comme elles en estoient sur toutes ces difficultez, une d'entre elles, dont je n'ai pu sçavoir le nom, les vint avertir qu'elle avait practiqué sous la main une affaire d'une haute importance et que moyennant une somme assez considérable, elle s'estoit rendue maitresse de la foire S. Germain, mais qu'il lui estoit défendu d'en ouvrir les portes publiquement iusques au troisième février, et que cependant il faudrait faire marcher toutes leurs trouppes et garnir la place de toutes sortes de munitions. Ce dernier advis les emporta tout d'un coup ; on se resolut que l'on demeurerait dans Paris et que l'on tiendroit toujours l'armée en bataille de peur de surprise: que l'on feroit tous les ious des sorties considérables, et que par ce moyen on pourroit se ménager sans rien craindre.

La dessus on donna les ordres nécessaires à toutes les trouppes et on ordonna qu'elles fileroient petit à petit et que sans faire en bruit, elles se rendroient dans la place; ce qui fut executé ponctuellement iusqu'au troisième de février auquel iour, le généralissime Lux, avec la superfluité et le vain orgueil, *qui ne l'abandonne iamais*, firent faire la revue et les rangèrent en bataille comme vous verrez par la suite.

> Mais pendant que ce jour viendra
> Abandonnons un peu la prose
> Et discourant sur autre chose
> Parlons de ce que vous plaira.
>
> Par les Dieu qui lance les flammes
> Dites moy pourquoy vos attraits,
> Ne seront-ils fait tout exprès
> Que pour faire enrager nos âmes.
>
> Vous, pour qui cent cœurs chaque iour
> Souffrent mille cruelles gehennes,
> Vous, qui causez toutes leurs peines,
> Pourquoy n'aurez vous point d'Amour ?
>
> Quoy, ny le rang, ny le mérite
> Le renom, l'esprit, ny le cœur
> A vostre inhumain rigueur
> Ne feront point prendre la fuite ?

Vous voyez où je veux aller
Et comme vous êtes très fine
Ie vois que vous me faites signe
Sur ce fait de ne plus parler.

Tout beau muse trop libertine
Avez-vous l'esprit de travers ?
Meslez vous de faire des vers,
Vous êtes un peu trop badine.

L'ordre ayant esté donné de la manière que vous avez entendu, le Colonel Sotte—despense qui avait prit le soin de la marche, fit arriver les trouppes dans la place par quatre costez differens afin de donner moins de soupçon de leur enterprise.

Lors, comme i'ai veu dans l'histoire
On vit arriver à la foire
Sous de differens estendarts
Des Dentelles de toutes parts,
Mais selon l'ordre expedié
On marchoit enseigne pliée
Et pour faire encore moins de bruit
On n'alloit presque que de nuit
De peur qu'on ne demanda qu'est-ce
On n'oza pas battre la caisse,
Et chacun alloit doucement
Tant le poinct que le passement
Qui pourrait nombrer chaque sorte
De ceux qui vinrent par la porte
Qui prend nom de Luxembourg,
Combien par celles du Fauxbourg
Et par les autres moins fameuses.
Combien il arriva de gueuses,
Combien il en vint sourdement,
Combien d'autres plus hautement,
Pour vous en descrire l'histoire ;
Toute l'encre d'une écritoire
N'y pourrait pas suffir encore.
Il en vint dont le pesant d'or,
N'aurait pas payé leurs dents creuses,
Tant elles estoient prêcieuses ;
Il en vint que le plus souvent
On disait venir du Levant,
Il en vint des bords de l'Ibère,
Il en vint d'arriver nagueres
Des pays settentrionaux,
Enfin il en vint des tonneaux
Tant de méchante, tant de bonne
Que le seul nombre m'en estonne.

Quand elles furent toutes arrivées dans la foire S. Germain, ce fut un désordre et une confusion épouvantable, chacun voulait avoir le premier rang, et comme l'ordre et les dignitez n'avoient pas encore été décidées, n'ayant iamais été mises sur le tapis, ils se seroient tous égorgés les uns les autres, et les pistolets que faisoient desia feu, et qui sçavaient un peu mieux la guerre, alloient faire main basse, si le généralissime Lux, accompagné de sa suite, ne fut venu mettre l'ordre parmy les trouppes de nouvelle impression, qui s'immaginoient que pour être braves, il ne fallait que faire du bruit et iurer deux ou trois morguïennes pour être asssi bon soldats que les Allemands. Aussitôt qu'ils furent arrivez, ils firent tracer deux ligues pour mettre l'armée en bataille, comme ils avaient desia proietté. On distribua les quartiers à chaque trouppe, et on chercha le poste le plus avantageux, et le moins apparent que l'on put, pour l'artillerie qui estoit composée de trois cens paires de cannons à passement, tous chargés de quartiers de rondache, et de chainettes de Ruban figuré, ce qui devoit faire un fracas effroyable, et emporter les regimens tous entiers. Deux cens cravattes volontaires tenoient la campagne et ne cherchoient pas tout qu'à faire le coup de pistolet. En suite on donna l'aisle droitte à commander au Colonel Raguze, composée de six escadrons, chacun de cens cinquante ballots de dentelle d'Angleterre, dentelles façon d'Angleterre et de moresse. L'aisle gauche estoit composée d'autant d'escadrons de Neiges et tous estoient commandés par le Capitaine Orgoglio. De corps de bataille estoit de huit bataillons tous bordez de deux rangs de piquots en haye et soustenons par deux autres rangs de pistolets.

Les premiers estoit composé de cinq à six cent quaisses toutes l'éspée au costé de dentelles d'or et commandées par le capitaine Brocar d'or et portaient pour enseigne un amour habillé en broderie avec de grands canons aux jambes et des rubans jusqu'au bout de ses souliers, en sorte, qu'avec sa petite taille, il ne ressemblait pas mal à un pigeon patu avec cette inscription au haut du drapeau : Ingannator ti donné, voulant temoigner que les beaux habits et les riches ornements estoient pour l'ordinaire ce qui surprennait le plus les femmes. Le second estoit composés de 400 ballots de Dentelle de Flandre et de dentelles du Havre et estoit commandé par le colonel Poinct de Gènes ayant pour enseigne la reyne de Suède avec cette inscription : "Famosa per omnes terres." Le troisième soutenait cinq cens livres de dentelle de soye noire, commandé par le colonel Brocar d'argent et portait dans son drapeau un diable fort beste, fort poudré et fort affeté à qui bien des gens faisoient accueil, et un autre tout un, à qui on donnait des coups de baston avec cette devise : Fa ti vestire, voulant dire qu'au siècle où nous vivons pour estre reçeu favorablement il faut estre magnifique et qu'à moins d'estre leste, il ne faut pas prétendre d'estre considéré dans les Compagnies.

Le quatrième estoit composé de trois cens grands coffres de broderies d'or et d'argent, sous la conduite du Colonel Somptuosité ; leur Drapeau estoit d'une étoffe précieuse, enrichie de broderies fort relevées avec ces trois ou quatre mots : Et pour le poil, et pour la plume, voulant marquer par là que la broderie estoit necessaire pour la guerre, qu'elles servaient à faire reconnaître les principaux chefs, et qu'elle estoit aussi de grand usage durant la paix, pour se donner quelque entrée parmy le monde.

Le cinquième éstoit de huit cens ballots de Gueuses commandez par le capitaine Parcimonia et portait une enseigne assez sale, et presque toutes en lambeaux où on lisaient à peine ces mots espagnols : No siempre relumbra el coraçon, qui signifiait en notre langue, que le cœur ne se remontrait pas plus dans les personnes éclatantes, que dans celles qui ne faisoient pas un si grand éclat.

Le sixième comprenoit quatre cens quaisses de poincts de Gênes, poincts d'Aurillac, poincts d'Alençon, poincts de Raguse, et quelques autres, qui marchaient sous la conduite d'un estranger, nommé poinct d'Espagne ; leur enseigne estoit de toille de Hollande, toute parsemée, d'aiguilles, et d'espées sans nombre, avec ces mots : De lago alla spada duro passagio ; ce qui voulait peut-être signifier que pour eux qui avoient esté faits à l'aiguille et qui n'habitoient que parmi les femmes, il estoit difficile de s'accoustumer aux fatigues de la guerre.

Le septième contenoit douze cens gros pacquets de boutons à queüe, tant de canetille que de soye commandé par le capitaine Agrément ; et dans leur Enseigne on voyoit la figure d'un Homme l'épée à la main, qui remettoit dans un sac quantité d'argent dont une grande partie estoit encore compté sur un table, avec cette inscription : Si non auro saltem, gladio quaerenda libertas.

Le huitième estoit composé de cinq cens quaisses de dentelles escruës, que le lieutenant du colonel Brocar d'or commandait, et l'on voyait ces mots écrits : Gia di vanita hor di marte è sempre serva, se plaignant de ce qu'elles estoient toûiours esclaves, ou de Mars pendant la guerre, ou de la vanité durant la paix.

Quand toutes ces trouppes furent passées, et qu'elles eurent toutes pris leurs postes sur la première ligne, le généralissime donna les ordres pour faire avancer le reste qui devoit composer la seconde ; mais une petite dentelle d'un pouce, qui avoit quelque correspondence à la cour, vint avertir un grand passement de Flandres avec lequel elle avoit encore quelque intrigue, pour lui avoir autrefois servy de pied, que l'on les venoit attaquer avec toūs les canons de l'artillerie, et que s'ils n'abandonnoient ce poste, deux volées seules estoient capables de les foudroyer.

Ce bruit à quoy elles ne s'attendoient pas, passant aussitost de quaisse en quaisse et de ballots en ballots, ietta une épouvante si grande parmy le soldat passement, qu'il fut impossible de le retenir et que quelques efforts que purent faire les principaux chefs, ils ne furent pas capables de les arreter : tous se débandèrent avec une telle confusion, qu'à moins de rien ou n'en vit plus parvistre aucun sur les rangs :

> Chacun pour éviter l'assant
> Le seroit ietté d'un plein saut
> Dans une plus noire caverne
> Que ne sont celles de l'Averne.
> Chacun pour sortir se pressoit
> Une dentelle un poinct poussait,
> Puis pour eviter la tuërie
> Ou voyait une broderie,
> Le voulant pousser par un coing,
> Recevoir plus d'un coup de poing.
> Un ballot poussait une quaisse
> Et tant pour sortir on s'empresse
> Que maints passemens sur leurs dos
> Sentirent maints coups de piquots.
> Alors mesdames les Espées
> Voyant qu'elles estoient dupées,
> Ayant les esprits mécontents
> De s'estre iointes à tels gens,
> Retournèrent tout en furie

Tout droit à la constellerie ;
Et pour messieurs les pistolets
Poussant mille et mille regrets,
Dans le dépit qui les accable
Le donnèrent, dit-on, au diable
Qu'ils s'en vengeroient un petit:
Pour cela chez Monsieur Petit
Ils firent soudain la retraitte
Où depuis ils tinrent diete
Pour plus aisément convenir
De ce qu'ils pourroient devenir.

Le party des Rebelles ayant donc esté dissipé de la sorte, toutes ces trouppes épouvantées se retirèrent avec precipitation du mieux qu'elles purent dans les lieux ou elles crurent avoir plus de protection, pour y avoir esté autrefois assez bien receuës, et elles y demeurèrent quelque temps cachées. Cependant pour les punir de leur révolte, on proposa de faire rendre en arrest solennel, par lequel on auroit declaré que tous les poinct serviroient d'oresnavant à faire de la mesche qui ne seroit employée que pour les mousquets de la compagnie des Mousquetaires du roy; que toutes les dentelles serviroient à faire du papier sur lequel on devoit érire leur condamnation, pour en envoyer la copie par toute la France ; que toutes les dentelles de soye, dentelles écreuës, gueuses et autres sortes de passemens, seroient employez pour faire des cordes, et qu'aussi elles seroient envoyées aux Galères à perpetuité pour servir chaisnes aux galériens, la bouté du roy ayant en quelque pitié du poids et de la dureté de celles qu'il leur avait ven traisner à Marseille ; que pour toutes les broderies d'or et d'argent, que parce que par un faux advis, on s'imagina qu'elles avoient excité cette sedition, on ordonna qu'elles seroient bruslées toutes vives. Pour les Espées, on leur devoit laisser à la Constellerie jugeant bien que ce seroit une assez grande punition pour elles ; mais pour les pistolets, à cause du grand service qu'ils avoient rendus durant l'espace de plus de vingt années, on feroit leur composition meilleure et on leur offreroit un vaisseau pour les porter en Portugal, eû on les assureroit de leur faire trouver employ.

Ce sanglant arrest qu'on estoit sur le poinct de publier contre ces rebelles les obligea de se tenir encore plus cachez que jamais ; il y eut pourtant quelques broderies et quelques poincts qui plus hardis que les autres, se hazardérent de sortir les soirs en habits deguisez, et s'estant une fois rencontrez avec Mesdames les Plumes dans une celebre mascarade qui se fit sur la fin du carneval, dont le dessein estoit de représenter le triomphe de l'amour, ils renouvellèrent l'etroite amitié qu'ils avoient toujours en ensemble, pour s'estre trouvé dans les mesmes occasions, ayant tous été employez toute leur vie pour plaire aux Dames.

Quelques uns d'entre eux tombant adroittement sur le suiet de leur disgrace, sembloient ne se plaindre pas tant d'estre banny pour iamais de la societé des hommes, comme de ne pouvoir plus travailler avec les plumes à de si glorieuses conquestes, quoy que par une fausse humilité ils avoüassent qu'ils ne pouvoient pas prétendre d'y avoir iamais travaillé avec autant le succez.

Ainsi les poincts, les broderies
Gaignerent comme ont fait souvent
Par ces adroittes flateries

Les plumes qui vont à tout vent;
Ces ornemens des ieunes testes
Leur promettet déjà mille et mille côquestes,
Le voyant ainsi caresser
Protestent desormais de quitter les ruelles,
Si on ne les veut exancer.

Par ces beaux discours les plumes s'engageoient déjà à l'etourdry dans le party de ces miserables et ie ne doute pas que ces gens qui sont tout à la légère ne les eussent seroy comme ils leurs avoient déjà promis, si l'amour qui faisoit luy mesme son personnage dans cette célèbre mascarade, voyant que toutes ces prattiques luy pourroient apporter grands dommages pour le rétablissement de ses affaires car se voyant déjà privé du secours des dentelles et de passemens qui lui avoient rendus de si grands services, il apprehendoit extrémement de se voir encor abandonné des plumes, qui estoient pour lors les seules forces qui lui restoient et dont il tiroit le plus d'avantage, prevoyant bien que ne pouvant s'en passer absolument, il seroit contraint d'arracher plustôt celles de ses aisles pour les pester aux galants qu'il employoit pour son service, estant absolument impossible qu'il pusse reüssir dans leurs entreprises, sans leur aide; et que lui-mesme après cela n'en ayant plus, ne pouvant plus voler si haut, seroit obligé de ramper sur terre, et de se reduire comme autrefois parmi les bergers, ne pouvant paroistre à la Cour, n'y s'elever à de plus hautes conquestes.

Ces considerations le portérent à rompre la partie qui s'estoit liée, et pour le faire de meilleure grace, il s'avisa d'offrir lui-mesme aux Passemens d'employer le crédit qu'il avait à la Cour, pour leur rétablissement, les priant de se reposer sur luy du soin, et de la conduite de cette affaire, que la reconnaissance des services qu'ils luy avaient rendus iusque icy, l'obligeoit à l'entreprendre, et qu'il ne doutoit pas d'y pouvoir reüssir pourven qu'ils ne précipattesent rien, et qu'ils se gardassent d'irriter de nouveau la Cour par leur déobeisance.

Lors considerant meurement
L'effet de son engagement
Et que s'il vouloit defendre ,
Au lieu de leur faire faux bon;
Le petit Dieu, plein de finestre .
Resolu de les servir mieux
S'adressa d'un air plein d'adresse
Au plus gallant des demy-Dieux.

Ce n'estoit pas d'auiourd'huy qu'il avoit de surettes pratiques avec que lui; ils avoient touious tant d'affaires ensemble qu'ils sembloient ne se pouvoir passer l'un de l'autre; mais l'occasion luy estoit d'autant plus favorable, qu'il venoit tout de nouveau de le faire ouvertement déclarer de son party, en sorte qu'il avoit tout lieu d'esperer un succès favorable à sa requeste.

En effet, il ne se trompa pas; notre demi-Dieu fut ravi de lui rendre ce petit service, pour le payer de tant d'obligations qu'il lui avoit, en sorte que par son crédit il obtint de la Cour, l'élargissement de quelques uns de ces misérables, que l'on avoit pris prisonniers, pour en faire l'exemple des autres, avec l'entière liberté pour tout le reste, dont ils iouissent maintenant en faveur de l'Amour.

Mais après que ce Dieu viét de nous faire voir
	Le crédit qu'il a dans la France
Pensez-vous qu'il soit lèps de faire resistâce ?
	La plus prude comme je pense
Pouroit bien, sans songir, ceder à son pouvoir ;
	Et quoy qu'en votre humeur altière
	Vous le preniez pour un Cysoñ
	Vous avez beau faire la fière
Il sçaura bien un iour vous mettre à la raisô.

PART VIIa.

BOOKS COLLECTED BY ORDER OF MR. COLUMBUS R. CUMMINGS, OF CHICAGO.

677. **L'Ecole de Dentelles a Burano Venezia, Imprimierie.** Kirchmayr & Scotti, 1882.
678. **I Merletti ad Ago o a Punto in Aria di Burano.** Richiamo Storico di Pasqualigo Conte Dr. Giuseppe, Treste, Tipografia, Pastori, 1887.
679. **Cenni sull' Industria dei Merletti.** Michel Angelo Jesurum, Venezia, Tipografia del Commercio.
680. **La Storia della Conquista di Due Medaglie d'Oro.** Merletti di Venezia, nel 1878, da Fambri, Firenze, Tipografia, Lemonnier, 1879.
681. **I Merletti nel Circondario di Chiavari.** G. B. Brignardello, Firenze, Tipografia G. Barbeca, 1873.
682. **Scavi di Claterna nel Comune di Ozzano dell' Emilia.** Roma, Tipografia della R. Accademia dei Lincei, 1892.
683. **Designs for Point Lace.** W. Barnard, 119 Edgeware Road, London.
684. **Hand-book of Point Lace.** W. Barnard, 119 Edgeware Road, London.
685. **La Paleografia Artistica nei Codici Cassinesi.** Applicata a Lavori Industriali, Merletti, dalla Tav. 1, alla Tav. 20, Litografia, Monte Cassino, 1888.
686. **Descrizione di Alcuni Minutissimi Intagli a Mano.** Properzia di Rossi.
687. **Spitzen Munsterbuch Museum fur Kunst und Industrie.** Wilhelm Hoffmans.
688. **Histoire du Point d'Alencon depuis son origine jusqua nos jours.** Mme. G. Despieures.
689. **La Vita dei Veneziani nel, 1300.** Le Vesti, B. Cecchetti.
690. **Tessuti e Merletti Esposizione, 1887.** Ercules.
691. **Rapport sur les Dentelles, les Blondes, les Tulles par Felix Aubry.** Esposition de Londres.
692. **Il Fiore delle Donne Italiane dall' Av. to Franciosi.**
693. **Lecons Pratiques pour Executer la Dentelle aux fuseaux, de la Bonne Managere.**
694. **Donne Illustri Italiane, Proposte ad Esempio, dedicata a S. M. la Regina Margherita,** Eugenio Comba.
695. **Histoire de la Dentelle par Mme. de X—, Paris, 1843.**
696. **Note per le Giovanette Studiose.**
697. **Alcune Donne Illustri Italiane di Giuseppe Spallicci.**
698. **La Dogaressa di Venezia, Pompeo Molmenti.**
699. **Costumi del Tre Cento.**
700. **Guide to Old and New Lace in Italy by the Countess Cora di Brazza.**

COLLECTION D'OUVRAGES ANCIENS SUR LA DENTELLE DE VENISE. FERD. ONGANIA, EDIT.

701. **Vecellio.** – Recueil des nobles et vertueuses dames, en quatre livres dans lesquelles on voit en 119 dessins toutes les especes de parements, de points ouvrages d'ornements, de fleurons, etc.; fac-simile de l'edition originale de 1600, etc. Venise, 1876....80 fr.
702. **Franco J.** Nouvelle invention de divers ornements tels que le point en l'air, 24 dessins de dentelles, etc.; fac-simile de l'edition originale de 1596. Venise, 1877........20 fr.
703. **Lucrece Romaine.** Ornements nobles pour toutes les elegantes dames, ouvrage contenant des cols, dentelles d'une tres grande beaute, 20 planches in-4°; fac-simile de l'edition originale de 1620. Venise, 1876................30 fr.
704. **Pagan Math.** – Le bon exemple du desir louable qu' ont les dames d'une grande adresse a preparer les points ouvrages en feuillage, 31 planches gravees; fac-simile de l'edition originale de 1550. Venise, 1878................30 fr.
705. **Zoppino (Nicholas d' Aristotile dit).** – Recueil de belles broderies anciennes et modernes dans lequel une rare adresse soit d'homme soit de femme pourra s'exercer dignement avec l'aiguille, etc.; 52 planches gravees; fac-simile de l'edition originale de 1537. Venise, 1877................30 fr.

706. **Vavassore And.** (dit **Guadagnin**).—Œuvre nouvelle universelle intitulee: Recueil de broderies ou les respectables dames et jeunes filles trouveront des ouvrages varies pour faire les cols de leurs camisoles, etc.; fac-simile de l'edition originale de 1546. Venise, 1878 ....30 fr.

707. **Ostaus Jean.**—Tres belle maniere de tenir ses jeunes filles occupees, comme le faisait la chaste Lucrece Romaine avec ses femmes, alors qu'elle fut surprise, travaillant avec elles, par Tarquin accompagne de son mari; fac-simile de l'edition originale de 1567. Venise, 1878 ....30 fr.

708. **Pagan Mat.**—Ouvrage nouveau, redige par Dominique da Seva, dit le Franciosino, ou l'on enseigne a toutes les gracieuses demoiselles a travailler en toute sorte de points, etc.; fac-simile de l'edition originale de 1546. Venise, 1878....................40 fr.

709. **Paganino Alex. (Burato).**—Livre premier des broderies au moyen duquel on apprend de differentes façons la maniere de broder, chose qui n'a encore jamais ete faite ni montree, maniere que le lecteur apprend en tournant la page; fac-simile de l'edition originale de 1527. Venise, 1878..40 fr.

710. **Serena.**—Louvel ouvrage de broderies dans lequel ou trouve diverses sortes de points en natte et de points a fil, etc. Venise, Dominique de Franceschi; fac-simile de l'edition originale de 1564. Venise, 1878 ....30 fr.

VIENT DE PARAITRE: I. bis VECELLIO C.

717. **Corona Delle Nobili et Virtvuose Donne Libro Qvinto.**—Nel quale fi contengono molti, and varii Diffegni di diuerfe forti, and specialmente che feruono per Bauari ch'in Venetia fi coftumano, and in molte altre parti del mondo. Opera molto vtile, and neceffaria per quelle virtuofiffime Donne che fi dilettano di lauorare con Aco, punti in Aria, punti Tagliati, and a Reticelli, cosi fopra Cambradi. e Renfi, come fopra altre Tele. Venezia, appresso Cesare Vecellio, 1596......................Prix fr. 20

 •

PARASOLE C.

718. **Teatro Delle Nobili et Virtvose Donne.** Doue si rappresentano Varij Dissegni di Lauori nouamente Inuentati, et disegnati da Elisabetta Catanea Parafole Romana. Roma, 1616..Prix fr. 40

719b. **Urbano** See yellow leaf.

720. **Corona delle Virtuose Donne.** Libro quinto, Vecellio, Venezia, 1590.

721. **Prima Parte de'Fiori e Disegno di Varie Sorti di Ricance Moderni come Merle, Bavari, Manichetti etc. in Venezia.** Appresso Francesco dei Franceschi, Senese all' Insegna della Face.

722. **Catalogue Ongania.**

723. **J. Beal, dentelles et broderies 145 planches.**

724. **J. Beal.** Nouvelle edition dentelles anciennes, Paris chez Calaves 68. Que de Lafayette. Foglie 26.

725. **E. Kumsch.** Spitzen und Weiss Stickerei des XVI, XVIII. Jahrn. K. Kunst gewerbe Museum zu Dresden. Foglie 50.

726. **Prof. B. Hoffman, director der K. Industrieschule Stilisirte Planzenformen in Industriella Verwendung.** Serie I. Spitzen 12, blatt.

727. **Photographs of Cluny Museum, published by A. Calaves, 68 Rue Lafayette, Paris, 35 foglie.**

728. **R. Forrer.** Die Graeber und Textilunde von Achmin, Panapolis. Strassburg, 1891. Druck von Emil Birkhauser, Basel.

729. **R. Forrer.** Romische und Byzantinische Seiden Textile aus den Graeber Felde von Achmin Panopolis, Strassburg, i-e, 1891. Druck Emil Birkhauser, Basel.

730. **Prehistorische Varia aus dem Unterhaltungsblatt fur Freunde der Alterthums kunde Antiqua.** Herausgegeben von R. Forrer und H. Messikommer, Zurich 1889.

731. **Reproduction of Ancient Lace Plates of the end of the last century, very rare, called:** Nova Espositore di Recami e Disegni alla Molto•Illustre Signora Ippolita Manfredi appresso Giacomo Antonio Somascho.

732. Quental Ornament und Stickmusterbuch von Peter Quental, 1527-1529. 80 Tafeln, Leipzig von A. M. Golze.

733. Joh Sibmacher's Neues stick, Spitzen Musterbuch von Jahre, 1604. Herausgegeben von Dr. Georgeus, Berlin, Ernest Wasmuth. 60 Tafeln.

734. Livre d'Heures, editeur Alfred Mame et Fils, Tours, Dessins, Henri Carot, Illustre d'apres les Dentelles de toutes les Epoques et toutes les styles. Foglie 360, e Introduction au sujet de la Dentelle.

735. Guarich's Reprints of Rare Books. III.—Pagan Mathio, La Gloria et l'Honore de Punto Tagliato e Punto in Aere. Venezia, Mathio Pagan, 1558. London Bernard Guarlich 15. Piccadilly, 1884.

736. Idem.

737. Parasole Isabella, Catania. Studio delle Virtuose Donne, Rome, Antonio Facchetti, 1597.

738. Teresa Guattrocolo Giaglio, Guida ai Lavori Donneschi. Libreria G. B. Petrini, Torino 15. Via Garibaldi, 1890.

739. Alfredo Melani. Svaghi Artistici Femminili, Editore N. Hoepli, 1892.

740. Livre de Dentelles No. 1. Chez Amand Durand sous la Direction de Emmanuel Bocher. 69 Rue du Cardinal Lemoine, 1883. Foglie 20.

741. Idem, No. 2. Foglie, 20.

742. Idem, No. 3. Foglie, 10.

743. Idem, No. 4. Foglie, 21.

744. Idem, No. 5. Foglie, 20.

PART VIIb.

List of the names of the ladies forming the subscribers and Committee for the Italian Lace Exhibit in the Woman's Building at the World's Columbian Exposition in Chicago, United States, America, during the summer of 1893.

Initiators constituted into a Board of Administration.

The Countess Cora A. di Brazza Savorgnan, nata Slocomb, elected president and representative of the Committee in America.

Her Excellency the Marchioness Paula Pes di Villamarina, Grand Mistress of Ceremonies to Her Majesty the Queen.

The Countess Teresa Agostini Venerosa della Seta (replacing her mother, Countess Andriana Marcello, deceased, Lady in Waiting to Her Majesty).

Princess Elizabeth Brancaccio di Trigiano, nata Field, Lady of the Palace to Her Majesty.

Countess Maria Pasolini, nata Ponti.

General Secretary and Italian Correspondent, Signorina Dorina Bearzi assistant, Signorina Victoria Fanna.

Address CLAVIANO, Provincia **di Udine, Italy.**

I. *ANCIENT VENETIA.

DIVIDED INTO TWO PARTS—VENETIA AND FRIULI.

1st.   Venetia—Capital Venice.

	LIRES.
Directress.—Countess Andriana Marcello, deceased, Lady in Waiting to Her Majesty for the School of Burano	800
Patronesses.—Duchess Biancha Bianchi di Casalanza, Mogliano....	100
Signora Teresa Paccagnello, nata Pigazzi, Mogliano	100
Countess Maria Bonin, nata Nievo, Vicenza	100
Countess Carolina Colleoni, nata Ginstiniani Bandini, Vicenza	100
Princess Giovanelli, nata Chigi, Lady of the Palace to Her Majesty, Lonigo	100
Countess Loredana di Porto, nata Bonin, Vicenza	100
Countess della Torre, Vicenza	100
Countess Maria degli Azzoni Avagadro, Padua	100
Signora Stefania Ombone, Padua	100
Countess Papafava dei Carraresi, nata Menicon Bracceschi, Padua	100
Signora Anaïs Forlani, Padua	100
Countess Brandolin, nata d'Adda, Lady of the Palace to Her Majesty, Venice	100
Mrs. Arthur Bronson, Venice	100
Mrs. Robert Browning, Venice	100
Countess Eleanor Papadopoli, nata Hellenbach, Lady of the Palace to Her Majesty, Venice	100
Countess Miniscalchi Errizo, nata Ponti, Verona	100
Total, Venetia....	2,400

2d. Friuli—Capital Udine.

	Liras.
Directress, Province.—Countess Cora di Brazza Savorgnan, nata Slocomb—for the Lace School of Brazza	800
Collected	285
Patronesses,—Mrs. G. Pendleton Bowler	100
Mrs. Cuthbert Slocomb	100
Signorina Jenny Cecconi } of Mount Ceccon Signorina Elvira Cecconi }	200
Directress, City of Udine.—Contessina Vittoria Cecconi Beltrame	210
Signora Camilla Pecile	160
Signora Elio Morpurgo	150
Countess Vera di Brazza, Marchesa Simonetti	100

*The ancient divisions of Italy are ranked in this list according to the sums of money collected within the provinces which composed them.

Contessina Giulia di Concina	100
Signora Emilia Girardelli Muratti of Trieste	100
Total, Friuli	2,394
Total, Venetia	2,403
I. Total, Ancient Venetia	4,708

II. ROMAN PROVINCES.

CAPITAL ROME.

	Liras.
Directresses.—1. Her Excellency Marchesa Paula Pes di Villamarina, the Grand Mistress of Ceremonies to Her Majesty	100
2. Princess Elizabetta Brancaccio di Trigiano, nata Field, Lady of the Palace to Her Majesty	400
Italian Patronesses.—Signora Antoinette Costa	120
Countess Barbiellini Amidei, nata Lewis	100
Countess Caprara	100
Marchesa Gravina	100
Countess Giannotti, nata Kinney	100
Countess Santa Fiora, nata Santa Croce, Lady of the Palace to Her Majesty	100
Marchesa di San Severino	100
Countess Ada Telfner, nata Hungerford	100
Marchesa Vanni Pasqua	100
Princess di Venosa, Lady of the Palace to Her Majesty	100
Duchess Lante, nata Davis, Viterbo	100
Total	1,420
Foreign Patronesses residing in Rome.—Mrs. Orville Horwitz, of Baltimore	300
Mrs. Stanley Hazeltine, of Philadelphia	100
Mrs. Hungerford, of California	100
Mrs. Nathan Sargent, American Legation	100
Foreign patronesses, Total	600
Italian patronesses, Total	1,420
II. Total, Roman provinces	2,020

III. TUSCANY.

Lires.

Directress of Province.—Countess Teresa Agostini Venerosa della Seta, nata Mar-
cello—Pisa 420
Patronesses.—Countess Larderel, Leghorn.. 120
  Signora Maria Mimbelli, Leghorn.. 100
  Other ladies of Leghorn... 110
  Countess Bernardi, Lucca.. 180
  Signora Costanza Huffer, Lucca.. 100
  Other ladies of Lucca... 40

      Total.. 1,076

Capital Florence.

Lires.

Directress.—Marchesa Anna Torregiani, nata Fry.................................... 210
Patronesses.—Princess Anna Corsini, nata Barberini, Lady of the Palace to Her
  Majesty.. 100
  Marchesa Gentile Farinola, Lady of the Palace to Her Majesty.................... 100
  Mrs. Fahnestock, of New York.. 100
  Countess Josephine della Gherardesca, nata Fischer............................. 100
  Marchesa di Montagliari... 100
  Marchesa Lily Spinola, nata Page.. 100
  Marchesa Giulia Torregiani, Lady of the Palace to Her Majesty.................. 100

      Total, Florence... 910
      Other Cities.. 1,079

    III. Total, Tuscany.. 1,989

IV. SICILY.

Lires.

Directress for Messina.—Countess Marullo, Lady of the Palace to Her Majesty,
  assisted by a Committee of Ladies in Messina................................... 958
Patronesses for Palermo.—Princess Sofia Trabia di Butero, nata Galeotto, Lady of
  the Palace to Her Majesty... 225
  Princess Baucina, Lady of the Palace to Her Majesty............................ 100
  Princess Sofia Belmonte Montroy, Lady of the Palace to Her Majesty............. 100
  Signora Tomaso Crudeli.. 100
  Signora Florio.. 100
  Countess Mazzarino, Lady of the Palace to Her Majesty.......................... 100
  Princess Maria di Sant Elia, nata Menebrea, Lady in Waiting to Her Majesty... 100
  Signora Tina Whitaker... 100

      Total, Palermo.. 925
      Total, Messina.. 958

    IV. Total, Sicily... 1,883

V. LOMBARDY.

Lires.

Directress.—Marchesa Maria Trotti, Lady in Waiting to Her Majesty................ 150
Patronesses for Milan.—Signora Cramer, nata Pourtales........................... 160
  Marchesa Maura di Cassini, nata Ponti... 100
  Marchesa Isimbardi.. 100
  Signora Remingia Ponti.. 100
  Signora Virginia Ponti.. 100
  Countess Erminia Sala, nata Trotti, Lady of the Palace to Her Majesty.......... 100
  Princess Ida Visconti di Modroni.. 100

      Total, Milan.. 910

Patronesses for Other Cities.

	Lires.
Countess Suardi nata Ponti, Bergamo	200
The Administrative Committee of the Industrial School at Cantu	100
Signora Ester Isingrini, nata Ponti, Monza	100
Countess Gwendolina della Somaglia, nata Doria, Lady of the Palace to Her Majesty, Monza	100
Signora Charles Leonino, Varese	100
Total, Other Cities	600
Total, Milan	910
V. Total, Lombardy	**1,510**

VI. ROMAGNA.

	Lires.
Directress.—Countess Maria Pasolini, nata Ponti; for the school of Coccolia, by Ravenna	800 00
Collected	120 00
Patronesses.—Marchesa Virginia di Mazzocorato, Bologna	167 50
Duchess Massari, Ferrara	100 00
VI. Total, Romagna	1,187 50

VII. LIGURIA.

	Lires.
Directress.—Marchesa Fiammetta Doria, Lady of the Palace to Her Majesty, Genoa,	700
Patronesses.—Princess Camilla Centurione Scotti, Genoa	100
Total, Genoa	800

Other Cities.

	Lires.
Duchess Canevero di Zoagli, Chiavari	200
Signora Castagnetto Ricci, Rapallo	100
Total, Other Cities	300
Total, Genoa	800
VII. Total, Liguria	1,100

VIII. NAPLES.

	Lires.
Directress.—Donna Maria Spinelli dei principi di Scalia	100
Patronesses. Baroness Baracco, Lady of the Palace to Her Majesty	100
Princess Colonna Stigliano, nata Mackay	100
Signora Sofia di Luca, nata Kennedy	100
Princess di Moliterno, Lady of the Palace to Her Majesty	100
Princess Pignatelli Strongoli, Lady in Waiting to Her Majesty	100
Marchesa Santasilia	100
Duchess Tommacelle della Torre, nata Haight	100
Baroness Testi	100
VIII. Total, Naples	900

IX. PIEDMONT.

	Lires.
Patronesses.—The Ladies of Her Majesty	150
Baroness Blanc	100
Countess Natalie Francesetti, nata della Rocca	100
Countess Incisa di San Stefano, nata Sambuz	100
IX. **Total,** Piedmont	450

X. EMILIA.

LIRES.

Patronesses.—Marchesa Rita Schedoni, nata Princess Manoukbey, Modena......... 135
    Countess Gaddi, nata Pepoli, Lady of the Palace to Her Majesty, Forlim popoli.. 125

    Total, Emilia.. 260

XI. UMBRIA.

LIRES.

Patronesses.—Marchesa Chigi Zondadara, Sienna............................ 100
    Countess Meniconi Bracceschi, nata Brazza-Savorgnan, Perugia......... 100

    XI. Total, Umbria....................................... 200

XII. ABRUZZI.

LIRES.

Patroness.— Marchesa Cappelli, nata Hirsch, Aquila...........................**Total** 100

XIII. MARCHE.

LIRES.

Patroness.—Signora Antoinetta Tinti, Ascoli-Picena.......................Total 100

XIV. SARDEGNA.

LIRES.

Signorina Giordano Apostoli, Sassari............................ ....Total 100

Patronesses Residing in Foreign Countries.

LIRES.

Signora A. Ravagli for the Italian Colony in Cincinnati, United States of America... 295 25
The Consul for the Italian Colony in Chicago, United States of America......... .. 129 60
Countess di Cesnola, New York, United States of America...................... 125 00
Baroness Fava, Legation at Washington, United States of America............... . 100 00
Signora Bruni Grimaldi, Denver, United States of America. 100 00
Countess Galli, nata Roberts, Paris, France..................................... 103 50
Marchesa Maria d' Adda Salvaterra, nata Hooker, Paris, France.................... 100 00

    Total.. 953 35
Contributions received from the Royal Ministry of Commerce and Agriculture 1,000 00

RECAPITULATION.

I	Venetia..	4,708 00
II	Roman Provinces......	2,020 00
III	Tuscany......	1,989 00
IV	Sicily............	1,883 00
V	Lombardy...........	1,510 00
VI	Romagna......	1,187 00
VII	Liguria............	1,100 00
VIII	Naples	900 00
IX	Piedmont.	450 00
X	Emilia......	260 00
XI	Umbria......	200 00
XII	Abruzzi	100 00
XIII	Marche......	100 00
XIV	Sardegna.....	100 00
	Patronesses residing in Foreign Countries........	953 35
	Contribution from the Royal Ministry of Agriculture and Commerce........	1,000 00

    Total..18,460 35
    Donation from the Countess di Brazza to assist in defraying the expenses of the Lace Exhibit—all the proceeds of the author as royalty on the sale of this book.